THE ASHIPPUN TRAP

A novel of Baseball

and the Milwaukee Braves Final Season

DOUG WELCH

BLACK ROSE
writing™

The final approval for this literary material is granted by the author.

First printing

Most of the characters appearing in this work are fictitious. Any resemblance to real persons, living or dead, has been authorized.

ISBN: 978-1-61296-306-8

PUBLISHED BY BLACK ROSE WRITING

www.blackrosewriting.com

Printed in the United States of America

The Ashippun Trap is printed in Calibri

To Jean and Lauren, of course. . .

And to Gene Oliver (March 22, 1935- March 3, 2007)

Special thanks to former Rock River League Commissioner Carl Schwarze; and Dana Schardt and the Gene Oliver family.

Cover art by Peggy Taylor, Artworks, Milton, Wisconsin.

Cover design by Susan Angell.

Back cover photo courtesy of the Gazette, Janesville, WI

THE ASHIPPUN TRAP

CHAPTER 1

I guess the first time I ever played ball was the first time I seen it. Something I'll never forget. Was like I knew baseball my whole life. Just didn't know where I learnt it.

Was a camp rat for a cavalry outfit up in the Dakotas. Wadn't more than fourteen at the time. Had run off from home. Unit was mostly a bunch of quick-triggered young'uns not much older than me lookin' for something to shoot. Acting like they was sad they missed the big war and what happened later further out on the Plains. Seems the army always finds a way to accommodate them kind of desires. They'd get their fill of killing 'fore it was done with.

Older guys in the unit, they was the one's who'd fought in the Civil War, twenty-five years before. Army lifers, they was. One of the older ones they said had been behind that stone wall at the end of that open field at Gettysburg when the seceshs made the charge. As much as the younger guys tried to get him to talk about that, he never would. What he would talk about is this feller from Michigan he was a campmate with during that long siege of Petersburg. Said that fella could hit and catch any ball like no one he'd ever seen. Baseball was big in them camps during the war. Thousands of soldiers, most never played before and probably didn't ever again after the war. They all needed something to do.

Abner Doubleday my ass. To hear them older guys tell it, the game was thought up in them camps and there wadn't no Doubleday or Spaulding to be found nowhere.

Up in that Dakota camp they was soldiers what would take a good piece of Hickory that was suppose to be for a wagon spoke and they'd go to whittlin'. They weren't like them fancy bats fellas like Cobb or Hornsby got to swing. No sir, but they was a work of art themselves. I watched them games for several days after I hooked on with the camp, runnin' water, helping with the horses, cookin' grub.

Took me a few days watchin' to figure out what it was I was lookin' at.

I'd study the batters, the ones who could hit anyways. When I was off by myself when the unit was drillin' or patrolin' I'd grab a hold of one of them Hickories and I'd stand there and imitate what the batters did. One day the grub sergeant tells me to get out there and play. Boy, I couldn't get there fast enough. My turn to bat and the pitcher's standin' out there with the ball that ain't nothing more than strings of ditch hemp wound tight as can be. He rares back and heaves the ball and I keeps my eye on it like everyone said you'se suppose to. I swung the Hickory and hit the ball and I'll never forget it like it was stopped up there in the air as it sailed over the left fielder's head. Seems like I watched it for the longest time 'fore I lit out.

It's been more'n fifty years now and I'll never forget that feeling in my hands and arms of making contact and watchin' that ball fly over that fella's head. From then on I couldn't play enough.

***

The gray rain picked up and was coming straight down as Parlee, under his cap, squinted toward home plate from his right field stance about medium-deep in Ashippun's Fireman's Park. A babyface no more than nineteen, a kid who filled out his Lebanon uniform like some gym classer five years younger, cut through one of Clay's sliders, missing the ball in the dank twilight by a foot.

"Damn, these teams that don't even try to compete are a waste of time," Parlee cursed to himself. He wondered aloud why any team would ever send to the plate against a pitcher like Clay, a kid who looked as if he wasn't able to play high school ball let alone fill out his uniform.

This little shit aint got a clue, he thought to himself. Parlee knew the only thing that could happen from encounters like these is the kid will get so frustrated he'll quit the game. Parlee knew full well because, years ago, he had almost been there at least a dozen times himself.

He shouldn't be here and I shouldn't be here because we don't need outfielders for guys like this, the words staying in his thoughts.

Parlee stopped himself from thinking about the over-matched Lebanon kid and tried his best to keep the dim, yellowy lights of the Ashippun field just over the bill of his cap so he could get a good read on the ball in case this kid got lucky on a swing and made contact. He didn't want to be there. That's something Parlee could not say very often as long as he was standing somewhere on a baseball diamond – any baseball diamond – including this Ashippun Trap on a rainy Thursday night.

It'd been raining since the third inning. Water was dripping off the brim of his hat, mixing with the diamond dust left on the bill from Neosho three nights before, Clyman the day before that, and the Ashippun clay he picked up in the second inning on a head-first slide into third.

His skinned knees still stung from the slide and he tried to shake the itch of his rasp berried right throwing hand. He forced himself to look beyond the murky, dirt-filled droplets that were beading off his hat and dropping inches from his eyes, occasionally blowing onto a cheek where the bitter grit of baseball would find its way to his tongue – a tongue sore now from the tobacco chaw of playing three games this week.

"Shit," he said as he glanced again at the near-empty wooden grandstand behind home plate. A few faithful huddled near the concession stand off the right field line, close to the beer and the radio that was tuned into the final, lame-duck season of the Milwaukee Braves.

The gate wouldn't be shit tonight, Parlee knew. Probably not even enough to pay for the gas and beer needed to get up to Plymouth tomorrow for the Flames' weekend tournament where the purse was real. Gas and beer. That's about all Parlee played for these days, gas and beer. Tonight wasn't going to buy much of either. But if things went well this weekend in Plymouth, the payoff by itself would just about make a summer of the Rock River League circuit worthwhile.

First, Parlee and his guys had to get the hell out of Ashippun and on the road to Plymouth. They already had to burn Clay here on the night before the tournament began and Parlee had wanted a fresh-arm Clay to make sure they could deliver the promised championship this weekend.

That was the bad part of the Ashippun Trap deal – nights like these when a rescheduled league game got rained on once again and a Thursday meant some of the normal crowd stayed home in front of the television. Gunsmoke and Burke's Law was on Thursdays and was a much more attractive alternative to the dark, moist wooden grandstand of Ashippun Fireman's Park on a wet night -- even if Clay was pitching.

The locals loved Clay. He'd strikeout ten or twelve flailing guys a game and the rabid Ashippun faithful were confident their boisterous bravado and profane slurs slung at the visiting team would be backed by one of Clay's dominating performances. The locals lived so vicariously through guys like Clay it made Parlee laugh.

"Ashippun Assholes" is what guys on other teams in the Rock River League called the Platers' fans. Parlee delighted in the banter the Assholes provided, often distracting the visitors from the on-field task at hand. Just the same, he knew the name fit.

Clay was supposed to be ready to throw Friday night in Plymouth. Having his ace on the mound to dominate the first game and still have enough for Sunday's championship was Parlee's plan. But that all blew up when the rain washed out Wednesday's game and the Turk rescheduled for this drizzly Thursday and then insisted Clay pitch in order to boost the gate. The young fans, especially the girls, loved to come and watch Clay throw -- not so much to see his high-voltage arm at work, but with the hope of having his electric smile flash their way after the game.

Parlee knew there wouldn't be much to smile at after this game as even the sound of Clay snapping a return throw from the catcher echoed off the trees in the stillness of the empty park.

This was the third season Parlee found himself stuck in the Ashippun Trap. The Turk gave him half the gate each night if he'd agree to secure three other guys all season that would bring another

Rock River League title to this small, unincorporated crossroads where what happened on the diamond each summer was about the only source of civic pride for the locals.

Civic pride didn't mean anything to the Turk. He simply wanted to keep the locals coming to Fireman's Park where he could over-charge them for the beer he got on the cheap from his brother who worked in the Milwaukee Gettelman plant. He'd gouge them for the hotdogs he ground himself from the hogs slaughtered at his other brother's place over near Johnson Creek. The Turk would make his faithful fans over pay for the assorted t-shirts and hats he'd have his estranged but indentured daughters ostensibly produce for their 4-H projects. You had to look close before buying a t-shirt that was probably misspelled. The few shirts that weren't misspelled were used for the grammatically-challenged daughter's fair exhibits and school projects. The remaining stock, numbering in the hundreds of shirts each summer, was sold by the Turk to the unsuspecting Ashippun fans at seven-fifty a pop. "Ashippun Loins Club" was Parlee's favorite. He particularly loved it when the girls misspelled the name of a sponsor. The other night, Russ Thieme, the president of the Ashippun Lion's, and seemingly unaware of the Turk family's dyslexic spelling issues, was proudly displaying the shirt across his barrel chest while gouging for Gettleman from behind the concession stand counter.

The Turk knew how to work all of the angles, including ways to dupe sponsors into working his concession stand for nothing. In Russ Thieme's case it cost the Turk however much beer Thieme could put down during the course of a three-hour game.

The Turk's most lucrative angle was getting ball players good enough to draw people to the diamond and keep the money flowing through the concession stand. That's why Parlee was part of the deal. It wasn't because at thirty-two Parlee was a particularly good ball player. It was because Parlee could always get the right guys to play for him.

Clay was part of the deal. And he was the real deal. He'd served a short stint in D ball in Janesville right out of high school three years ago. But he Cubs moved their minor league team out of Janesville and didn't take Clay with them – a decision that baffled Parlee and anyone who'd watched Clay pitch and play. Clay was still playing for a chance to get back into pro ball – a chance Parlee could see was dwindling with each month a guy like Clay wallowed in a league like the Rock. Parlee didn't tell Clay that. He could still bring it from the mound and quickly became one of the best hitters in the league, making him the cornerstone of Parlee's plans for a lucrative baseball summer.

Clay still wasn't as good a hitter as Colton, who kicked around in D ball for five or six years. He was a couple of years older than Parlee but could still square up the hard slider any pitcher in the Rock or any other league could throw. He was over on the bench tonight because he hated night games. He'd play at night only when he had to. A pitch to the temple from a hard-throwing lefty had detached retina in his left eye. Colton was left wearing glasses with lenses thick as a car's headlight. It was a look unbefitting of a player the caliber of Colton and made it difficult for him to see at night. It's the reason Colton was let go from pro ball and it was a secret only Parlee and a few others knew.

Deke, over there at third was also part of the deal. Deke drank as hard as he hit the ball. With wrists as strong as angled tire irons, Deke had as natural a baseball swing as anyone in the Rock has seen and would routinely pop the cap off a beer bottle without an opener. The girls loved Clay, but the women loved Deke. Both ball and the booze cost Deke two wives and any dream he may have had to play pro ball. But he didn't care, as long as there was a game, any game, to be played.

"Christ, don't even bother showin' your forkball to this gum popper," Parlee muttered to himself as Clay leaned in for the sign. Clay shook off his catcher twice before settling into his windup. The catcher that night was a kid none of Parlee's guys liked playing with. They were eight games into the league season and Parlee had long forgotten the kid's name. Parlee was well past giving a shit about his name. All Parlee knew is that this kid never called a good game. He was one of those guys who always wanted to be the show, Parlee knew. He'd get too cute calling breaking balls and junk when very few hitters in the league could do much more than listen to a good fastball. When Parlee and Colton and the other older guys on the team tried to teach him something about the catching skills he was certain he'd already perfected, the kid would scoff, "What the hell do you know? You're thirty years old and still playing in the Rock River League."

"Thirty-two," Parlee had corrected him and never spoke another word to the self-anointed catching phenomena the rest of the season. That was okay with Parlee. Each year he'd become less patient and more annoyed with having to share the diamond with young, cocky guys who took for granted their talent to the point where they didn't respect the game. The worst of it, Parlee thought, was that guys like the prick behind the dish were totally unaware of the fact they didn't respect the game.

After the two shake-offs, Clay delivered a letter-high fastball that dissected the plate. When the Lebanon kid began his swing, the ball was already in the catcher's mitt. By the time he finished, the kid looked like an unmade bed. His helmet on the ground, spinning as it kicked off his back heel toward the Ashippun dugout. The dark, water-stained hat remained on the kid's head, askew, covering one eye, its "L" pointed toward the sky like the formation of a small flock of geese. He'd nearly swung right out the loose-fitting wool uniform.

"Let's get the hell out of here," Parlee yelled, wanting only Clay and Deke to hear. The three made their way to the dugout, slogging in the wet grass, their spikes soaked through to their socks. The rest of the team lined up to shake hands with the Lebanon players.

On the way in, Deke kicked the loose Lebanon helmet into the dugout, where it clattered down the concrete steps and under the bench.

"Won't be much to collect tonight," moaned Colton, already stripped to the waste in the dark confines of the below-ground dugout, a bunker-like structure fit on a night like this only for the salamanders that sought its damp refuge during hot afternoons. "Think it will even cover our gas to Plymouth?"

"I dunno," Parlee said. "I haven't seen the Turk in three innings. I hope he ain't duckin' us again."

"Goddamn it!" Parlee shrieked as he peeled his pant leg over his left knee, a bloody, puss-ridden serum oozed from the scab that was reopened on the third inning slide. Half the scab hung on Parlee's pant leg, the other half tried desperately to cling to living tissue on the knee, a moist, pink string connected the two.

"You think I'm duckin you?" a voice behind Parlee growled.

"Hey Turk, What's ya got for us tonight?" Parlee chirped. "Pretty slim pickin's it looks like."

"No shit, you guys play like a bunch of dogs," said the Turk, a fat stub of a cigar no longer than two inches protruded from the corner of his mouth. "No one's comin' out to watch you guys."

"What the hell?" Parlee countered. "Twelve-to-one in seven innings aint good enough for you? The way we play doesn't have anything to do with tonight's crowd. I told you last night it'd be a mistake to reschedule this game for tonight. Too many people starting to stay home to watch TV."

The Turk knew Parlee was right. In the last few years, people were getting more and more comfortable in front of their TVs, especially during the week.

"You insisted that Clay pitch and still no one showed because of the weather."

Parlee felt the anger boil up inside him over Turk's constant meddling. Parlee, Clay, Colton and Deke could split a five hundred dollar purse this weekend if things worked their way. Tommy Schmidt, up in Plymouth, promised Parlee the tournament's first-place prize money if he'd bring enough good ball players to put on Flames uniforms and win it. Schmidty ran a mediocre Plymouth Flames team in the Lakes League but could fill Plymouth's park at least once a summer for the Flames' annual tournament. Schmidty would hit up local businesses to front the prize money for the tournament and five hundred bucks was about as large a take as Parlee had ever seen for a weekend tourney. Parlee knew Schmidty didn't care where the prize money went. Schmidty, Parlee's La Crosse college chum, had things figured in the same manner as the Turk — only he wasn't such a dick about it. As long as the Flames were in the tournament, Schmidty knew the Plymouth locals would turn out in droves, no matter who filled out the Flames uniforms. Schmidty would make a killing on admission, the concession stand and with fifty-fifty raffles as long as the park was filled to see the Flames play. Parlee fully expected to be playing in front of almost seven hundred people each game — maybe even as many as a thousand for Sunday's championship game.

But if the Flames dropped early in the tourney, Schmidty knew he'd be lucky to have two hundred people in the stands for the championship and consolation games on Sunday. That's why Schmidty could afford to offer Parlee the prize money each year. Last year's winnings went a long way toward making the season a financial jackpot for Parlee, Colton and Deke.

For Parlee and his guys, it was win or get nothing and the big cash prize was drawing better teams to Plymouth each year. And now, because Clay pitched tonight, he couldn't open the tournament Friday and then come back for the championship game Sunday. Parlee knew Schmidty wouldn't be happy about that. Through most of the game, Parlee stood in his wet shoes in the outfield wondering how he was going to ease Schmidty's mind once they rolled into Plymouth.

"What's this shit about me duckin' you?" the Turk growled as he handed Parlee an envelope that felt like it couldn't have more than twenty dollars in singles and assorted change.

"Sorry about that Turk," Parlee offered. "I guess I didn't mean to say it, but I meant what I said. Where'd you disappear to Sunday? There must have been six hundred people here Sunday afternoon and then when I came to collect at the end of the game you were nowhere around."

"Theime told you I had to get over to Watertown for a funeral," the Turk said. "I settled up with you Wednesday."

Parlee dropped it. Right then he didn't want to bring up the fact that the take for Sunday's game seemed light. When Parlee got to the bar after Wednesday's rain out to count the mish-mash collection of bills, fifty-cent pieces and other change the Turk had stuffed into an old sock and handed to Parlee as if it were some sort of Spanish bolo, it came nowhere near to matching Parlee's expectations. He'd bet himself the Turk had been pilfering some of the take between Sunday and Wednesday.

Parlee had become pretty good at estimating crowd sizes at Ashippun's Fireman's Park from his panoramic right field view. On last Sunday's hot, sunny afternoon he'd guessed there had to have been at least six hundred people in the park. The wooden grandstand and its immediate area rife with picnic tables and benches sat about two hundred. Down each line from dugout to outfield fence people sat four and five deep on their aluminum-framed folding lawn chairs or on blankets. The small, concession pavilion had a constant flow of customers and grill smoke billowed from behind the shelter all afternoon.

According to Parlee's educated estimate, at fifty cents a head, Turk took in over three hundred dollars just on admission. The take for Parlee's guys should have been half that — by far the best payday this year. But no matter how Parlee counted Sunday's offering, he couldn't come up with more than one hundred thirty-five dollars and twenty five cents.

Parlee doled out forty bucks each to Clay, Colton and Deke and avoided an all-out mid-season mutiny by not mentioning the discrepancy. That left just fifteen bucks for himself as Parlee, after two smooth seasons in Ashippun, was getting his first real look at why other guys who'd been around the league for a long time called Turk's gig here the Ashippun Trap.

Parlee had been around the league long enough to realize there wasn't a guy running a team in the Rock who could be trusted. They were the P.T. Barnums of their communities, whether it was the tiny burgs that weren't even aspiring villages in Ashippun, Neosho, Clyman and Lebanon or the small cities of a couple thousand people in Juneau, Mayville and Horicon. Instead of a circus tent under which Barnum over-charged for popcorn, cotton candy or a gander at the bearded fat lady, the Rock teams used the community's park, many of which were maintained by the local volunteer fire department. In Ashippun the Turk made a trifle donation of a case of Korbel brandy to the local fire department each year in time for the department's Christmas party in exchange for having the run of the park all summer. Like circus barkers, Turk and his league brethren combed their communities each week with posters, gossip and menial bribes in the form of hotdog coupons or free beer chips to get people to the park for the next game. There wasn't a guy running a team in the league who wasn't working some sort of angle for attendance and titles – two things that always seemed to go hand-in-hand.

Parlee had a knack for delivering the titles and was working on his fourth straight Rock championship. No matter where he played – in Ashippun or the years prior to that in Neosho – he was always able to work the team for a substantial piece of the concessions or gate.

He'd make enough not to have to work during the summers between his teaching job in Jefferson. But now the Ashippun Trap was interfering with his plans to make bigger scores at tournaments in Plymouth and other places. With the Turk stepping in to dictate pitching even on a night where there was no money to be made, Parlee felt himself falling deeper into the trap. It was a feeling of the beginnings of resentment for all things Ashippun.

"You remember Clay, Colt, Deke and I won't be at Sunday's game up in Juneau?" Parlee reminded the Turk for at least the third time.

"Yeah, yeah, I know, you guys go and win your little tournament," the Turk said, falling short of calling Parlee a "Benedict Pontius Pilate" as he had Wednesday after he'd been drinking most of the day away. "What'd they do? Offer Deke free beer all weekend and that's all it took?"

"Hey!" Deke piped in from the end of the dugout. "I resemble that remark."

Deke was sitting on the bench, pounding his spikes together to free them of the game's muck. A small mound of mud and clay, mixed with small stones and grass rose between Deke's feet, now bare and hunkered into a pair of sandals.

"I told you I don't want this team to take on too many loses and then be a couple of games back at the end of the season," Turk said. "You cost me a title with this kind of bullshit and they'll be hell to pay."

"Us goin' up to Plymouth for the weekend ain't going to prevent you from having to settle up in Hell one day," Parlee laughed. "Jesus, if this team can't handle Juneau without us, there will be hell to pay but in a different way. Shit, Lebanon beat them last week. I'll talk to Pete and tell him what he should do with the lineup."

Parlee didn't feel much sympathy for the Turk — not that he ever did. He'd made a point to tell Turk about their Plymouth plans before the season started so he could reschedule the Juneau game if he wanted. If he had, Parlee felt like he could grab other players like Pete to take along and not leave the team short on Sunday.

"I still don't like it," the Turk said. "What the hell does the rest of the team think when you guys show up whenever you like?"

"Not so loud, here they come," Parlee said as the remainder of the team headed toward the dugout. "You'll hurt their feelings," he whispered.

And then, "You let me worry about what they think. You worry about getting people out here on nights like this."

"Hey Turk, can we get some beer for the road?"

"How many hits you have tonight, Deke?"

"Three," Deke said. "That's gotta be worth a couple of sixes. Clay struck out, what? Nine? Ten? That's gotta be worth a couple more."

"Eleven," Clay said. "We only played seven innings, remember."

The Turk was greedy and selfish but always held a soft spot for Deke's free-wheeling ways. Whenever Parlee wanted something for the team from the Turk, he sent Deke to do the asking.

"Jesus Christ, between you guys and Theime it's a wonder I can even keep the lights on," the Turk groused. "Get your ass over to the stand and tell Russ to fix you up."

"When are you replacing some of those burned out lights, anyway?" said Colton nodding to a bank down the first base line where every second or third bulb was dark.

"Soon as you start playing night games," Turk said as he walked up the dugout steps and out of sight.

"Hey Colt grab whatever bats you think we'll need this weekend," Parlee said as he slipped out of his rain-heavy pants, a pair of dry sweats lay on the bench beside him. "We should be okay with helmets. We'll just use theirs. But grab the pine tar and rag."

The rest of the team was starting to crowd the unlighted dugout, the only glow coming from the sporadically lit field lights, now being partially blocked by the silhouettes of shadows in jerseys.

"They got one that'll fit my noggin?" Deke asked.

Deke had the biggest, most angular head Parlee, or anyone else on the team had ever seen on a human being. His hats never fit.

"Go ahead and grab the big bucket helmet we got if you think you need it. I don't think anyone else here uses it for anything other than to boil potatoes," Parlee said.

Deke kicked the Lebanon helmet from beneath the bench and held it up for all to see in the field lights.

"I'll trade this one for it," he said.

"Hey Pete, up here!" Parlee climbed the dugout steps to the field just off the on-deck circle.

Chucky Peterson was a full ten years younger than Parlee and was one of the few young guys on the team who got it. This was his second year with the Platers and he spent last year soaking in all the baseball knowledge he could from guys like Colton and Parlee. He paid attention to each game and hung onto every word the older guys on the team had to say.

As last year ground on, Pete became the best outfielder the Platers had, a fact Parlee begrudgingly acknowledged on this season's opening day when he told Pete to go to centerfield while he pissed on his own ego and trotted out to right.

Pete was especially anxious to become one of Parlee's guys and start making the hell-bent road trips to places like Plymouth. Pete suspected Parlee's guys were getting paid somehow but that wasn't why he wanted to go along. He'd listen to their dugout stories from each tournament with a mixture of excitement and envy. Pete just wanted to play. Parlee knew he had to start bringing Pete into the mix soon or he'd lose him. He'd yet to figure out when that should be. This weekend he didn't want to have to split the winnings more ways than need be and Pete would be Ashippun's best player Sunday up in Juneau.

"Hey Parlee you sure you don't need anyone else this weekend?" Once again, Pete was faster than Parlee, quick to bring up what Parlee wanted to avoid at that moment.

"I'm hopin' we'll be good," Parlee said. "Besides, who's going to run things in Juneau if you go with?"

"I know but Juneau's pitching ain't going to be for shit and I don't feel myself getting any better facing guys like what we'll see up there or that side-armer tonight," Pete pleaded. "Parlee, I want a challenge."

"Bat left-handed," joked Parlee, immediately wishing he hadn't.

"Look," Parlee said. "You lead off, play that Cremer kid at third and maybe hit him second to bunt if we need to. You'll be on base so we'll need to get you over. Always play with the lead if you can. Move Kopplein up to third, he's hittin' it pretty good. Use your gut on the rest of the lineup, maybe Marlow fourth."

"What about Wehlert?"

"Who?"

"Wehlert, our catcher. He always thinks he should be hitting fourth."

"He would," Parlee said. "Shit, we got Colt and Deke and he thinks he should be hitting fourth. Then hit him fourth, it's Juneau, who gives a shit?

"Start Carny, he should be able to go the whole way but if he gets in trouble, bring in Sabol, he's been bugging me for innings. You okay with that?"

"Hey Parlee!" Clay from beyond the dugout. "You got your keys?"

Pete looked down, shuffling his wet spikes from side to side, his new-model Maury Wills glove still on his hand.

"I'll be right there," Parlee looked back at Pete. "Hey, Pete your time's coming. You're good enough. We'll get ya some tournament games. You gotta do me just one more favor and get a win Sunday or the Turk's gonna have my ass. Come on over and I'll buy ya a beer."

"Yeah, sure thing Parlee," a small smile curled back to the corner of Pete's mouth.

Parlee knew his time was running out. He slapped Pete on the shoulder, skipped down the dugout steps to the darkness where he grabbed his duffle bag now heavy and humid from his spikes and wet pants. Back up the steps he went and out to the parking lot without a word to the rest of the team. Parlee didn't want to remind anyone else he'd be gone Sunday.

The parking lot at Ashippun's Fireman's Park is disguised as a grove of trees, the trees spaced far enough apart for folks to wedge their cars, trucks and the occasional row crop tractor between. On Sundays when a big crowd came, most people could park in an empty field across the driveway down the left field line. But it was quite a hike for those who got there late and had to park on the far reaches of the field. Most of the regulars walked to the game from the center or outskirts of the little burg that was relocated here from Old Ashippun some eighty years before in order to be near the new railroad tracks where they could cross what some said was an old Indian trail that has turned into State Highway 67—a north-south two-lane corridor that stretched from the other side of Elkhorn to the south all the way up to Sheboygan County.

Parlee navigated toward to the grove, his way dimming the further he strode from the field lights. The last thing Parlee wanted to do was go to Plymouth with a sprained ankle so he slowed his pace to avoid stepping into any hole he couldn't see coming until he got to the gravelly runway that led into the grove. Once on more solid footing, he began jogging through the grove to his left where he came upon his black 1959 Chevrolet Impala.

Colton and Clay were each leaning on one of the Impala's two black bowtie tail fins. Colton sucked a Lucky Strike as he leaned in front of the left tail light, Clay the right. Between them a pile of wet uniform pants and jerseys and one batting helmet the size of a milk pail.

"Where's Deke?"

"Over working Theime for some beer" Colton said.

"Let's get over there and grab Deke before he gets too far in."

"I bet he's got four down by now," Clay said.

Parlee took his keys in one hand and used his other to feel the back of the trunk for the key hole. He slid the key into the lock, turned it to the right and lifted the enormous, bowed trunk lid of the Impala. A light from under the lid went on. It was a feature new that model year and it lit the deep recesses of the Impala's cavernous trunk. The spare tire looked small in there. It was fastened at an upward angle toward the front of the trunk.

The three began placing their duffle bags and bats to each side of the trunk. The middle was saved for the mound of wet uniforms they piled inside, below the spare. They heaped the pounds of wet wool in the cavern and Parlee was glad he could trap the fermenting stench of their dankness by closing the lid.

"I used to travel with old Tom Bower the year I played for Jefferson," Parlee said. "He drove a '56 Chevy station wagon. It was great for hauling stuff but it was all right there with ya. We had a game about this wet and a lot colder over in Albion and we piled all our wet shit in the back. About half way home after the heater kicked in good we couldn't stand the smell. By the time we got back to the bar in Jefferson, they damn near didn't serve us because we all smelled like that pile."

"You pop that lid back open and you're gonna get the same thing," Colton said as he tossed the butt of his Lucky to the ground.

"Yeah, but we won't have to live with it all the way up to Plymouth."

Parlee loved the Impala. It was a bestial auto that could seat three across, front and back, without anyone touching elbows. The middle guy had to deal with the driveshaft hump but there was plenty of leg room otherwise. It was the first car Parlee owned that had an automatic transmission – something the used car salesman called "treble-glide." Parlee's black beast had a 348 big-block V8 under the hood and could cruise easily at seventy to eighty when the time was right. Most the time, though, Parlee barely made the Impala go more than forty-five as he navigated the back roads of Southern Wisconsin, teammates piled in, beer in ball anxious hands, headed to or from the next game. Earlier in the season Clay asked Parlee why he never pushed the Impala over forty miles an hour on the way home from games.

"When you're breaking the law," said Parlee, nodding toward the beer in Clay's hand, "don't break the law."

Colton and Clay set out on foot across the grove toward the dimly-lit laughter of the concession stand.

Parlee wheeled the Impala over to the stand, careful not to run over the dying Dogwood sapling he'd planted in April. Parlee parked on the park's lone patch of good grass, too close to the concession stand for Thieme's taste.

"We won't be long Russ," Parlee said as he closed the door of the Impala and ducked in under the pavilion's shelter, which was merely a thirty-foot roof extension off the cinder block concession stand held up by six four-by-fours and lit by four bare forty-watt light bulbs. There was room enough for a half-dozen picnic tables on the pea gravel footing.

Deke was at the counter downing a can of Gettelman while Thiemie bagged up what looked to be three six packs for the road.

About fifteen or so of the loyal Platers' fans, mostly older, opinionated grumpy men, were huddled near the counter. Parlee was certain they were accessing the Platers' sloppy play that evening and were lamenting their certainty that the overall quality of league play "just ain't what it once was".

A high school history teacher, Parlee appreciated hearing some of the tales the old timers insisted on telling and retelling about the league and its players in days past. But he'd lose patience for the constant assertions from guys who never played the game that somehow no one's doing it right anymore. "To hear them talk," Parlee told Colton one night, "you'd swear there wasn't a sacrifice bunt in all the 1940s and '50s that wasn't perfectly executed."

Parlee could hear Merle Harmon's radio voice wrapping up the

Braves' broadcast.

"Hey Deke! Gotta hit it. Find out if the Braves won tonight."

One of the old men, Walt Jaeger, standing near Deke turned and sneered at Parlee.

"Not another dime of my money goes to that bunch of carpetbaggers."

"Yeah but did they win?" Parlee left it at that, wondering if the old, ignorant Mr. Walt Jaeger had any idea of the origins of the term "carpetbaggers."

Deke was guzzling the last of his beer while he gathered up the bag of roadies. He added one more line to a story he'd been telling to the grumps and all of them, Walt Jaeger included, threw back their heads in laughter.

"You sure have a way with those old pricks," Parlee told Deke as he neared. "Where'd the other two get off to?"

Deke belched and nodded toward Clay in the corner talking to the only female in the pavilion. She was about twenty and Parlee had seen her at most the home games with several of her friends who chased the younger guys on the team. The evening dampness didn't do her sunny Sunday afternoon good looks many favors. A baggy, zippered sweatshirt covered most of a t-shirt that read "Ashippun Platers, 1964 Champians".

Colton was behind the counter in the stand's spartan kitchen filling empty hotdog buns with wieners. Colton was tall enough he had to duck his head around the several strands of brown, sticky fly paper that spiraled downward from the kitchen's low ceiling. He put the hotdogs in an empty napkin box and grabbed the glass bottle of ketchup off the counter. He tossed a knife and a half-full mustard jar with no lid into the box and headed around to the front of the counter.

"Where you going with that ketchup?" Russ Thiemie protested.

"It's got a cousin in Plymouth he needs to see." Colton said as he made a bee-line toward the rear driver's side door of the Impala. "We'll give him a ride back."

"Always the smartass," Thiemie grumbled.

"Clay, gotta go," Parlee said as he opened the front door, Deke and Colton already in there, drinking and eating.

"Let me get this straight, " said Parlee, still leaning on the open car door with his right arm on the top of the Impala as Clay swung into the rider's side back seat. "I got the car, Colt's got the dogs and Deke's got the beer. What do you suppose Clay's got?"

"The clap," Colton said between bites of hotdogs.

"Hey Parlee, thought you were buying me a beer," Pete came out from under the pavilion to the Impala.

"Oh shit," Parlee said under his breath. Then louder, "Hell yeah!"

He reached into the sack Deke had placed in the middle of the front seat and grabbed a Gettleman.

"Here ya go Pete," Parlee tossed the beer and Pete caught it with one hand. The disappointed look he'd worn outside the dugout still hung on his youthful face. "Depending on what time we get done Sunday, we'll come back by Juneau and see if you guys are still playing."

Parlee knew he'd just told another lie as he slid behind the wheel, closed the door and fired up the Impala.

Deke leaned over from the rider's seat and ducked his head low enough to where he could see Pete's face.

"Bat that fuckin' Wehlert ninth," Deke shouted loud enough to be heard by everyone in the pavilion, which now contained the entire Ashippun team, including its catcher.

The Impala bounced across the grass of the park toward the driveway and away from the concession stand. It had stopped raining, just as Russ Thieme said it would when the game was finished. In the time since the rain stopped, the wood lot behind the diamond the Impala passed to its left had been filled with fireflies. It was as if children had taken the jars full of lightening bugs they'd collected the night before and smashed them against the trees, liberating the twinkling insects. They winked farewell to Parlee as he wheeled out the driveway down the left field line of the diamond. The foggy mist gathered around the field lights replaced the moths and dancing night insects the tall lights attracted on drier evenings.

"You thinking we'll stop by Juneau Sunday if we get done early?" Deke asked as Parlee stopped the Impala at the end of the park's driveway. Across the county road stood the white-painted block building that houses the Ashippun Plating Company, the team's main sponsor and source of its name sake. The small, one story factory with loading docks added on at odd angles is also the source of the constant flow of chemicals and solvents dumped into Davy Creek, which runs behind the rail road tracks on the backside of the building.

"Shit I hope not," Parlee said. "I suppose we could, see if they're in trouble. I'd just soon head down to County Stadium on the way home instead. Cardinals are in town. See if I can catch up with Oliver after the game. You wanna come?"

"Hell, yeah, I could see doin' that."

"Count me out," Colton said from the back. "I had a hell of a time getting Friday off. Can't go in late on Monday."

"We'll see what happens." Parlee said. "Hopefully we'll still be playing late afternoon Sunday and we'll have all we can do just to get straight home."

Parlee turned right on a county road that went toward the heart of Ashippun – a heart that beats ever so faintly since the pallet making factory that kept the trains running in and out of town instead of just through, closed up a couple of years earlier.

The Impala came to the intersection of State Highway 67. A sign pointing to the right read "Oconomowoc 11 Miles." Parlee wheeled to the left to go north on 67 toward the Rock River League haven of Neosho.

CHAPTER 2

Settled onto Highway 67, Parlee was in a place he liked nearly as much as the outfield, the batter's box or dugout. Being in the Impala driving from one game to the next with teammates and an ample supply of beer was a calling for Parlee. Not unlike his high school class room, Parlee would hold court, facilitating a discussion dissecting the last game and the season to that point as well as what was coming up. Occasionally, but not often, the conversation might even drift to the players' private lives off the ball diamond.

The Lebanon game left less to digest than the eight hotdogs Colton had commissioned from the concession stand. By the time the Impala slowed to go through Neosho, its inhabitants were finished with both the hotdogs and the non-competitive kids from Lebanon.

"We've got to field better than we did tonight but we're seven and two halfway through the league schedule," Parlee said. "We're still there but the Turk's getting a little nervous. We just gotta make sure to knock off Horicon this time through."

No one in the impala had a differing opinion and the Horicon reality hung there like the full moon that just then began peeking out from behind fast-moving wisps of clouds that were making their way east.

Parlee glanced back at Clay to see he was holding a ball between the index and middle fingers of his pitching hand. After last season, Clay said he was looking for a new pitch, and Parlee told him to start working on a forkball.

"I already throw a fork," Clay said. "Kind of."

"Not like this," Parlee said. "You need to take some time to condition your fingers to spread apart to throw it right."

Parlee said it'd take months to do but convinced Clay that in order to throw the pitch right he had to use the off-season to get his fingers used to the spread needed to really throw a forkball. He told Clay to take a baseball and keep it jammed between the two fingers every waking moment possible.

"You might want to take it out at the supper table," Parlee joked.

Parlee told Clay that if he did that, his hand would feel natural with a split-finger grip like that and he would be able to control the pitch and then could to throw it anytime, any count.

Much to Parlee's surprise last spring, Clay said he had done just that. He told Parlee he walked around most of the winter with a baseball jammed up between the fingers of his right hand. Equally surprising to Parlee was the fact that the technique seemed to have worked.

It was obvious from the early season results that Clay had gone from being the best pitcher in the Rock last year to the league's most dominate this season. His new-found forkball was the reason.

Clay already had a sizzling fastball and a pretty good curve and change. But now he could throw a pitch off the same fastball motion with near equal velocity that would drop a good six inches just as it got to the plate. Clay dabbled with a forkball before that he couldn't throw for strikes. Now that holding the ball that way seemed more natural to Clay, he could throw the fork for a strike seemingly anytime he wanted. To the batter Clay's motion made the forkball look like another hot fastball they needed to time up. Parlee couldn't guess how many frustrated Rock hitters had corkscrewed themselves into the ground swinging over the top of Clay's fork so far this season.

"You use your fork much tonight Clay?"

"Maybe about a half dozen times when I wanted to work on it," Clay said. "I don't usually like to show it to teams like that."

"It ain't fair," Colton said.

It wasn't fair. The strikeouts were mounting for Clay. He'd fan at least twelve a game and, lately, more. Against a good Neosho team Sunday, Clay struck out seventeen. The Ashippun Assholes let every Neosho strikeout victim know it, cajoling each batter all the way back to the dugout.

"I don't think I ever heard so much left-right since the service," Deke said.

New this year to the Asshole's repertoire was the annoying habit of "left-righting" each strikeout victim back to the visiting dugout. In a marching cadence timed to the pace of the batter returning to the dugout, the entire Ashippun crowd would shout "Left! Right! Left! Right!" until the batter reached the top of the dugout steps. Then "Step! Step! Step!" and, after a brief pause for the big finish "Sit Down ya Bum!"

"It's funny the first hundred times you hear it," Parlee said.

"I still love it," said Clay as he tapped Deke for another beer. "Did you see in eighth when I struck out Lauersdorf and he went all the way to the far end of the dugout like he was daring them to keep it up?"

"That sure as hell was the wrong thing to do," Colton said.

"Yeah, by the time I struck out the next guy they were still left-righting Lauersdorf and they had to start all over again."

"They should left-right Wehlert," Deke said.

The four raised their beers to the baseball gods plotting strategies in some distant Valhalla dugout as the Impala continued north of Neosho.

"Who taught you how to throw the fork like that, anyway? Clay asked.

"Some old guy named Applejack I met when I was a kid," Parlee said.

"Applejack?"

"Applejack," and Parlee settled in with another beer.

Applejack spent his final days spinning stories at the Vanoy old folk home outside of Whitewater. None of the residents or small nursing staff at Vanoy ever believed a word Applejack said. He had fantastic stories about the Spanish American War, The Great War or chasing Poncho Villa with a cavalry brigade in Mexico. Some days Havana and Juarez were rolled into one, depending on Applejack's degree of recollection at the moment. Other times the listeners could take their pick and Applejack would tell them what he thought they wanted to hear. He had tales of travel, of fortunes gained and lost, women lost and gained but mostly lost, and of presidents and captains of industry met and bested at cards, dice or dominos.

Applejack had a pitted, silver penknife he'd hold up to a nurse giving him his morning cache of pills. "See this here? This used to belong to Teddy Roosevelt," tobacco juice dripping down a gray-stubbled chin.

Few could recollect his real name. Everyone at Vanoy called him Applejack because that was his chosen brand of chewing tobacco that made the leafy juice-saliva mix he'd spit into a sawdust-lined coffee can. The can never left the shadow of the chair Applejack sat just inside the entrance of the home, awaiting the relatives and visitors of the eight or so other Vanoy residents.

"That why you chew the Applejack?" Clay asked as the Impala tracked north on Highway 67, skirting the east side of Hustisford, a familiar Rock River League outpost.

"There's no such thing as coincidences," Parlee said. He could see that the lights were still on at the Hustisford Fireman's Park in the center of town. Husty played Mayville that night in a battle for a leg up on third place.

Deke looked from the glow of the lights toward the deep, stirring waters beneath the Hustisford Dam that swelled the Sinssippi lake west of town. As he opened another beer, he took himself back to the late night last season when he, a six pack and the Husty shortstop's fiancée found their way into those troubled waters.

"Hey, let's see if they're still selling beer over at the park," Deke said.

"We gotta keep heading north," Parlee told him. "It's going to be later than shit when we get there as it is. Besides, we're all stinking like a bunch of wet, rode-hard horses."

"You do know Farrington married her last off-season don't ya?" Colton said.

"That don't mean she took a vow against swimming."

For five weeks when Parlee was twelve, he'd have to go to Vanoy's every Sunday with his folks to see Gramps. His father's dad had fallen into an increasingly intense state of forgetfulness in recent months. Gramps, alone since his wife had passed seven years earlier, would drive out to the country outside of Milton in his '39 Packard coupe to take in the Sunday dinner Parlee's mom would prepare. But news came back to Parlee's dad one day that Gramps couldn't find his way back to his small, cedar-sided home on a short, four-house block of Garfield Avenue in Janesville. Before dinner that late morning with the radio tubes warming for the afternoon Cubs broadcast, Gramps took out the appointment book he always carried, opened it and read the words he'd been scribbling since he sat down in the living room. "Bethard, and Wolfe, and Parlan, and Hamm."

Bob Bethard lived two doors down from Gramps at the south end of the Garfield block. He and Gramps were friends since Gramps moved to Janesville from Rockwell City, Iowa to become Secretary of the Tri-County YMCA just before the First World War. It was Mr. Bethard who called Parlee's dad when Gramps didn't make it home that day. Harry Wolfe had the house next door and, in his late seventies was the old man on the block by a couple of years. He'd been retired from the City of Janesville accounting department for about twelve years. He was the only person Gramps knew who retired in the midst of the Great Depression. Amid the neighborhood whispers that Harry Wolfe made that retirement possible through a precise, persistent and patient extortion scheme of city taxpayer's money, he spent his time tending a small gold fish pond in his backyard garden. When the Wolfe's weren't home, Parlee used to try to hit those gold fish with small rocks he'd chuck over the white picket fence that separated the two back yards. Phil Hamm, Gramps' other next-door neighbor, was the new guy in the neighborhood. He'd only lived at the north corner of the block for fifteen years or so.

"Bethard, and Wolfe and Parlan and Hamm."

Gramps opened his appointment book and read it twice more before dinner was served that day. Parlee, first thinking it a joke, noticed the concerned look in his father's eyes.

A few weeks later, after Bob Bethard had called Parlee's dad twice more about his growing concern for Gramps, Parlee's folks went looking for a place that could take in Gramps while a room and accommodations could be made for him at Parlee's home during the coming winter. Parlee's mom knew of the Vanoy home the other side of Whitewater because she had an aunt who had spent her final four years there.

The Vanoy home was a large, linier farm house built in the early 1900s with a subdivided upstairs where the residents slept and kept what meager belongings they still possessed on rickety night stands or in closets fashioned from window dormers. The huge kitchen that once fed threshing crews and the eight Vanoy kids who grew up there was perfect for the daily needs of residents and staff. A small, understaffed team of nurses, cooks and maids was on hand around the clock. Most of the women were merely dressed as nurses with no real training beyond a knack and desire for caring for the rotating roster of residents, most of whom lived all their lives within a ten-mile circle of the Vanoys.

Parlee hated going there. It smelled of medicine and attic – musk covered disinfectant. Ghostly, ancient figures roamed the halls and rooms and lurked in shadowed corners in rocking chairs or on downstair day beds. Parlee thought it all made the large home seem very small and confined.

That's where Parlee first met Applejack, but not on a day bed or in a rocking chair.

On Parlee's second Sunday visit, he began getting restless up on Gramps' bed while his parents talked about selling the Garfield Avenue home as if Gramps and Parlee weren't even in the room.

"Why don't you go outside and have a look around," his dad finally told him.

Parlee stopped circling the small throw rug with his shoe around and around the creaky, worn but polished hardwood floor to oblige his dad's offer. He remembered on their way up the driveway he'd spotted several out-buildings that could offer adventuresome exploration.

"Don't go in the barn or sheds," his mom called as he scooted down the hall, his pace suddenly slowing.

Outside, Parlee grabbed his mitt from the car and exchanged the baseball in its webbing with a hard rubber ball that was under the front seat. He surveyed the outbuildings, looking for the best surface to bounce the ball for a round of solitary catch. He decided on the big barn, once used for milking, its roof a perfect pitch to throw at and bounce back fly balls.

He heaved several throws onto the roof, gliding under each of the high pop-ups to let the ball nestle into the palm of his glove. He purposely took a late jump on some in order to make running catches. The young Parlee then settled into an imaginary pitching sequence. He found a stick to use as a pitching rubber and eyed up the proper sixty-foot distance in front of the barn's side door. On the door was a pattern of four boards he used as a strike zone.

He then went to work on the dangerous lineup of the St. Louis Cardinal Gashouse Gang.

"You ever notice how when you ask someone what they think the best era of baseball was, no matter how old they are their answer will always coincide with when they were a kid?" Parlee asked and stated as he steered the Impala through Iron Ridge. He had turned Clay's simple question about the forkball grip into another of his long yarns. But it was a question Parlee had long pondered. "How come the Golden Era isn't this era when we can watch guys like Aaron, Mathews, Mays, Koufax, Mantle, that Clemente with the Pirates and Frank Robinson in Cincinnati?"

Parlee knew Walt Jaeger and his tribe back at the concession stand would never admit to this being baseball's Golden Era. No one in the Impala had an opinion on that, either, so Parlee moved on.

"For me it was always the Cardinals in the 1930s," Parlee said. "Never saw them play but my dad followed them in the papers and we had some relatives out in Iowa and that's all they could talk about. They got to be bigger than life to me, Dizzy Dean, Joe Medwick, Leo Durocher and those guys. That was long before the Braves showed up here."

"The Yankees of the '40s with DiMaggio and that bunch," Deke belched as he grabbed the church key to make two triangular holes on the top of another can of beer. Clay, the youngest in the car, couldn't believe there'd ever been a better team than the Braves that won the Series eight years ago.

"I gotta piss."

Parlee knew he was losing the room.

The young Parlee leaned in for an imaginary sign. Ducky Medwick had doubled with two outs in the seventh so now Parlee had to work out of the stretch against Pepper Martin. On a 2-2 count, Parlee delivered and hit his board with an off-speed palm ball he floated toward the barn. Parlee's mind saw Martin swing through the pitch, way ahead of the ball and Parlee pumped his fist, having preserved a slim one-run lead.

"You like the baseball son?" Parlee shook himself away from the mound at Sportsman Park back to the stick outside the Vanoy barn. The voice came from an old, grizzled-looking man sitting in the open door of the haymow, a lone mezzanine seat on the first base side of home plate.

Parlee gazed up to his left, surprised he had an audience of one who was sitting sideways on hay that was yellow and hard from being exposed to months leading to years of wind, rain, snow and sleet in the opening of the mow. The man spat a gooey ribbon of tobacco juice fifteen feet down to the ground. The stream nearly connected the ground with the man's mouth. A half-finished bottle of wine was in his hand.

"How long you been sittin' up there mister?" Parlee asked.

"I dunno, I seen ya stomping around like you'd just thrown a pitch that got hit off the fence," the man said. "I suspect you struck that last feller out."

"Are you supposed to be up there?" Parlee went on the offensive to deflect his embarrassment.

"I aint supposed to drink this down there," said the man, pointing the bottle toward the house. "So that tells me I'm supposed to be up here.

"You fancy yourself a pitcher son?" The man disappeared into the shadows of the haymow before Parlee could answer. He stood to his tiptoes, moving his head this way and that, trying to catch another glimpse of this ancient apparition.

With a limping shuffle old men get from carrying the weight of the world or their own personal demons he came out into the sunlight from the south end of the barn, hay stuck to his denim bib overalls. He wore no shirt under the straps that connected the back of the trousers with the front bib.

"Who are you?" Parlee asked, hoping the question would stop the man before he got too close.

"'Round here they call me Applejack," and he kept coming like a manager on his way to the mound after deciding to lift his starting pitcher two batters too late. "Gimme that ball."

An unsure young Parlee handed Applejack the ball the way a pitcher, convinced he could get the next hitter, would reluctantly give it up to his manager.

"You ever seen a drop-ball thrown?"

"I guess."

"I'll show ya how Dizzy Dean threw his drop-ball."

"How do you know how Dizzy Dean threw it?"

"Cuz I taught him."

"Holy shit Parlee, you tell some stories, but now you're saying this old drunk fart you kicked up in a barn taught Dizzy Dean how to throw a forkball?" said Deke, shaking it off as the four stood outside the Impala pissing into the ditch of a side road onto which Parlee had turned. Moonlit shadows of four fluid swords.

"I dunno," Parlee said. "Clay asked me who taught me to hold the ball like that all the time and this Applejack's the guy. That's just what he told me about Dizzy Dean."

"You think he really knew Dizzy Dean?" Clay asked.

"Shit, I don't know," Parlee said as he leaned back against the rear quarter panel of the Impala. "No one there believed a word he said. He'd tell some beauties. I tried to do the math on all the places he'd said he'd been against how old I think he was when I met him and it doesn't always add up."

Parlee started remembering some of Applejack's stories that he'd repeated himself as gospel.

"This is the same guy who told me that story about when he was bumming out west one winter sometime in the '20s. He'd hunkered down in a stock car with a bunch of sheep on a train winding through the mountains up in northern Wyoming. He rolled up a cigarette and when he lit it, the match caught the tinder bedding on the box car floor. Said he got up and the more he kicked at it, the bigger the fire got. With them flames consuming the car he said he had all he could do to get around and over the sheep to get the car's side door open so he could jump clear and into a snow bank on the side of the rail."

"I remember you telling that story to the whole damn beer tent after our game up in Brownsville last year," Colton said. "A bunch of drunk ball players hanging on every word. Tell about how he was laying there in the snow bank watching the train wind up through the mountain with the one car burning up and all of a sudden these sheep that had caught fire started jumping out of the car."

"I remember that," Deke said. "Brownsville's diamond is a goddamn goat ranch, still got barbed wire on the outfield fence. But they sure know how to throw a beer tent."

Colton had fished a Lucky Strike from his front pocket without taking the pack from his shirt. He sat himself up on the tailfin of the Impala, struck a match to the grit and imagined the match catching the bedding in that train car. Parlee looked out over the lush cornfield that sprawled for acres below the roadbed. Waist-high stalks as far as he could see shimmering like rippling water in the full moonlight.

"I don't know if I believe that," Parlee said. "Shit, I had enough beer in me that night I might have made up that part.

"He did say the god damnest thing about it was that as he lay there watching that train go up the grade and around the bend with the moon about like this one here," Parlee waved the back of his hand up towards the moon. "And the flames of the car lighting up the snow and the black Jack Pines, he'd thought he'd seen the hand of God himself painting that scene like it was the prettiest Christmas card he'd ever imagined.

"That part I believe."

Without a word, the four began chucking empty beer cans from the inside of the car and into the ditch. It was going on midnight when they jumped back into the giant Impala and Parlee wheeled around and back to 67 to head north.

CHAPTER 3

Older I got, the more I couldn't abide playin' with the young'uns. They just act like they's doin' things what never been done before. And they make dang sure ever one in earshot knows 'bout it, too. The older guys I played with always said the young'uns don't respect the game. I always thought differently 'bout that. I always thought it was themselves they wadn't respecting enough.

'Course I was no different when I was that age and thought I was better'n ever one else. I was with that cavalry unit down in Georgia 'round ought- two. Few years after that Cuba ordeal. One particular day when we was playin' I was flappin' my jaws pretty good 'bout what I'd done. Some catch I made or some other nonsense that didn't make no bit of difference to no one but me. I come up later in the afternoon and this old quartermaster who was pitchin' musta had enough, cuz he reached back and flung one right at my head. I turned but the ball hit me on the way by and broke my damn jaw. You can still see a scar here where the stitches of the ball burned into me. Put me in the infirmary eatin' from a straw for three weeks. I'll never forget the way that old boy was snickering at me when they helped me off'n the field.

This game has peculiar ways of preserving itself. I never said another such word after spending that time in the infirmary. Now I ain't never tolt no pitcher to hit no one. I sure as hell didn't like bein' laid up that time and this game ain't no reason to hurt no one over. But I played behind a lot of pitchers who didn't think twice about hittin' some guy cuz he talked too much or he played a certain way or wadn't wearing his hat right. And when that batter would get up and dust his self off after bein' knocked down and you could see that fear in his eye, I'd be standing out in the field snickering just like that mean ole quartermaster.

You just watch when you start playin' this game when you're older, you'll see. Baseball will always do right by its self, make sure it gets played the right way. It makes sure players respect it and they selves.

But that don't mean I ever found a way to tolerate the young'uns.

***

The young Parlee grabbed the real baseball from the car and he and Applejack sat around back of the barn on the hitch tongue of a dilapidated grain drill that was once pulled by horses. A summer's worth of weed and grass growth embraced the implement's stationary wooden wheels.

Applejack would alternately spit a syrupy stream, take a pull of the deep purple port wine and fit the baseball between the index and middle fingers of Parlee's right hand.

"Ya gotta get it way up in there, dead center betwixt the two fingers" Applejack said. "It's almost gotta be touchin' the webbing at the base of the fingers."

Applejack took Parlee's hand and jammed the ball as far as he could up between his fingers.

"You got some pretty small fingers there son," Applejack sat back and took another pull off the purple port. He reloaded his cheek with a chaw of tobacco he gathered from a leather drawstring pouch. He held it up for young Parlee to see.

"I wadn't much older than you when I got this from an old Indian outside of Wounded Knee just before that uprising," Applejack said. "Tolt me it was made from the bladder of a buffalo his own father'd lanced back when there was buffalo to lance and Indians to lance 'em. The way I watched them soldiers gun down them Indians a few days later, its little wonder they's any of 'em left at all."

Parlee held and carefully felt the pliable pouch that seemed as if it could expand to sizes that could fit any need. He imagined carrying three baseballs in the small sack. Applejack took the baseball and slid it between the fingers of his own left hand.

"The real secret, and this is what I told the Dean boy, is that you gotta keep that ball jammed up between your fingers every minute of the day," Applejack said. "You only take it out for supper out of respect for your ma. You do that every day for about three months, carry it around like that, and your fingers will stretch out so much that having that ball in there will seem as natural as if your hand were born that way. It's the only way you can control that pitch when you really need to throw it.

"Dizzy did that for about three months when he wasn't much older than you," Applejack leaned back and appraised Parlee. "He might have been about sixteen then, I'd guess. Once he did that, he could wind up with that ball betwixt his fingers like that and throw it just like he was throwin' his fast ball. Only just 'fore it got to the plate that ball would drop just like it had rolled off a table.

"About a year later he'd joined the Army, must have been lying about his age, and I seen him pitch for a service team in Texas," Applejack paused to scratch his bare, wooly chest under the bibs. "He struck out fourteen Airmen that day. A couple of fellas from the Cardinals were there in suits and signed him right up.

"Old Diz he pointed at me and said 'right there's the fella you want to sign up, he's the one what taught me.'"

The old man stared at the tobacco pouch he held in his hands on the lap of his bibs. "Said I gave him the Devil's Right Hand."

Applejack took another swig of the port, nearing the end, a smoky mixture with floaters circling the inside of the bottle.

"This aint nothing like the mescal we'd get into down in Mexico chasing Villa," Applejack said. "You had to drink that while you were holding on to something 'else you'd fall right over."

Even the young Parlee could see it was the purple port that gave Applejack the look grown men get when they need to cry.

"I never got a chance to play in the big city leagues like the Diz in any of them big stadiums," he said, the words getting heavy in Applejack's mouth. "I played all I could in the army. No matter where I was stationed or camped there was always a game going on. Even in the cold up in Dakota. Some guys played cards. I played baseball.

When I was out of the service and older, I barnstormed in the '20s with Ruth and some of them colored teams.

"Never got paid much to play," his eyes squinting into the bottom of the bottle. "Didn't need to. I just played 'cuz of the game."

Parlee saw he was reaching for it but whatever Applejack had to say just kept slipping farther away.

"Baseball was like that good lookin' gal you take to the dance," Applejack eventually sputtered. They were what words he could get out past the wine. "If you don't dance hard or fast enough with her she'll go find someone who will. Just like that gal, baseball is always done with you long before you're done with her."

Applejack finished the port and tossed the bottle into the tall grass and weeds where it clacked against one he'd thrown there another time.

"This game don't quit you, you quit the game. This game ain't never quit on nobody. And no matter what you're playin' for it's the playin' that's bigger than all of it.

"Time was when I could. . ." Applejack's head was getting cluttered as it fell down on his chest. "Play as long . . . play as long as you can, boy, just 'cuz of the game."

Then he lost the thread and his words just rolled off down to the tall grass and empty bottles.

Parlee walked the old man back toward the house and led him inside to one of the downstair daybeds when no one was looking. Then he went up. When Parlee and his folks came downstairs, Applejack was snoring on the daybed, one foot flat on the floor. One of the maids gingerly wiped away the brown tobacco chaw that had worked from his mouth and onto the bed's sheet.

Parlee looked for Applejack every time they went to visit Gramps. He'd wanted to ferret out more of Applejack's fantastic stories even though he knew there wasn't much truth being told.

On the fourth Sunday, Applejack was nowhere to be found. One of the nurses told Parlee's dad that Applejack had been increasingly difficult to handle by the staff, especially at night after he'd have yet another bottle snuck in for him and he'd spent the day in the haymow. Applejack, she said, wouldn't be back.

When Parlee's folks headed upstairs, the nurse stopped him.

"Applejack left this and told me to give it to you," the nurse said.

She handed Parlee Applejack's leather tobacco pouch. He could feel a couple of random leafs left inside.

"It's yours," she said. "Just make sure you're old enough when you start using it."

The next week Parlee told his parents he didn't want to go back to Vanoy that day. Parlee's dad said that'd be okay, just this once, and he dropped Parlee off at his buddy, Sam Pillard's house where they explored the woods behind Sam's place after they grew tired of playing catch and pitching to each other.

Sam's mom had just fed the boys for the second time that day, all the while wondering aloud why Parlee's parents were late getting back. As the afternoon sun faded to twilight, Parlee's folks came up the driveway in the family's 1936 Plymouth. Parlee's dad was driving but didn't get out of the car. Instead, Parlee's mom met him just outside the Pillard's kitchen door to tell him his grandfather had died. Just before Parlee's parents arrived at Vanoy, Gramps had gone into one of the small, upstairs bathrooms of the home and had a heart attack. He had collapsed against the door and the Vanoy staff couldn't get in to help him. By the time a Whitewater fireman had shimmied into the small window of the bathroom on the second floor, Gramps was gone.

"You sure you don't want me to drive?" Parlee's mom asked as she got into the front, rider's side seat and Parlee climbed in back.

Parlee's dad shook his head that he was okay. But just a couple of miles down the road, the hands of Parlee's dad began shaking on the steering wheel and he pulled over to the road's shoulder. He got out, stood in front of the car and began to weep. Parlee's mom got out and hugged his father. Parlee didn't know what to do with all that sadness. It was the only time he'd seen his father cry.

"It's the damnest thing," Parlee said as the Impala hit a long stretch of straight road of the Wisconsin countryside, the lines of 67 running together and under the Impala's front wheel without protest. "Seven years later when I was in college up in La Crosse, living in the dorm, I got woke up by the RA saying there was a phone call for me. It was January and we'd had all just got back that week from Christmas break.

"I go out in the hall to the phone and its mom, saying dad had just died. He'd had a heart attack and died in his big chair listening to 78s of Tex Ritter. I had to wake up my roommate to borrow his car to get home. He might have been the only guy in the dorm with a car and it was this piece of shit Nash. Heater didn't work. Only way it'd get over fifty mile an hour is if you'd push it off a cliff. I'm coming home on Highway 14. It was before they built the Interstate. I'm doin' alright, hadn't really thought about it yet, I guess with all the scrambling around, figuring out how I'm gonna get home and my classes and shit.

"But just as I got through Viroqua, I thought about that day when dad pulled over and began to cry. Then it just came over me and I had to pull over and do the same thing.

"Ya know, I'd give my left nut to know what dad was thinking about that made him pull over that day."

Parlee thought about all that for a moment and fought back a tear that surprised him before he turned to look over at Deke. Deke was out, his head propped against the window. A dab of drool made its way from the corner of his mouth down his chin. The Impala heaved and bucked as Parlee steered it over a set of angular railroad tracks that connected Juneau with the Village of Theresa. Parlee could see from the dash board lights that the beer Deke put on the floor hump between him and Parlee had fallen over and emptied itself onto the carpeting on the rider's side floor.

"You gave away one of your nuts?" Clay said groggily from the back seat.

"What the hell you talking about?" said Colton, who'd also just been startled awake.

"Hell if I know," Clay said. "I just woke up to Parlee saying he gave away one of his nuts."

Parlee smiled to himself, rolled the window down a ways and pitched his empty beer can across the highway and into the ditch before he might drive this traveling circus right off the road.

He didn't want another beer, he only wanted that last one again.

CHAPTER 4

At two o'clock Friday morning, the Impala rolled into Plymouth like original sin. Colton and Deke were out, asleep since Mayville when they'd stopped again to piss and Clay moved up to the front seat. Colton and Deke, worn out from their work week, snored in the back seat of the Impala. Clay was wide awake, anxious for the tournament after a couple of beers had put him down for a short on-road nap. From the front seat he listened to Parlee fight the hypnotic yellow highway lines between Mayville and Plymouth with the tale of how he came to be friends with Braves' catcher and first baseman Gene Oliver. This year and all of last, Clay had listened to Parlee's dugout stories of his trips to County Stadium where he caroused with big league ball players. In Clay's mind they were the stories that put Parlee above every player on the team.

As they rolled north of Mayville, Clay asked how Parlee came to know Oliver. So Parlee told him a story of how baseball connected Parlee with a major leaguer through a chance meeting on an Iowa farm nearly twenty years ago.

Parlee first met Gene Oliver outside of Mount Pleasant, Iowa, when Parlee was thirteen. The first summer after Gramps passed, Parlee and his family travelled parts of Illinois and Iowa connecting with kin. It was also the first summer after the war ended and Parlee's dad didn't have to squirrel away gas stamps. Gramps hadn't had any immediate family left that anyone knew of, but his wife, Garnett, had two brothers in Iowa.

The two Downing brothers were as different as they were alike. Lowell was a banker in Muscatine. When Parlee's family came to town, they stopped at the bank, a busy place on a Friday afternoon in the heart of a bustling downtown. Parlee had never seen so much marble in one place as was in that bank's lobby. Lowell directed them to one of the largest homes on the east side of town and said he'd be there directly, right after two more appointments.

Parlee went to sleep that night in a home that reminded him of Christmas. He'd never seen a home stair case that could be decorated and shown off. Extending upward from the middle of a large room that served as an entryway to the three-story home and its dining area, the staircase was the room's centerpiece, its banister sporting red, white and blue bunting on that July day. When he woke up he found Lowell to be far removed from the image Parlee had first seen in the bank lobby and later on when he came home in his three-piece suit. That morning, Lowell was out tending to what was likely the biggest garden in Muscatine.

During their stay Parlee's family dined on snap beans, carrots, turnips, tomatoes, peas and other fresh vegetables grown in Lowell's garden and served around the hearty beef, chicken and pork portions that Lowell routinely fed his family. There was an endless supply of delicious preserves -- raspberry, blackberry, rhubarb and crabapple -- that his wife, Verna had put up in Mason jars. She'd bring out shortcake with strawberries the size of plums.

After serving with distinction in Europe, Lowell's sons were away at college in locations that seemed exotic to Parlee at the time -- Berkeley, California and Providence, Rhode Island.

If tending to dirt was a hobby for Lowell Downing that filled his pantry shelves with treats and various meal garnishes, it was a submerged way of life for his brother Dwight, who wore that way of life on his dirty sleeves.

Parlee's dad followed Lowell's directions to Dwight's simple, one hundred, sixty-acre farm that finally appeared on the horizon leading from an endless maze of gravel roads off Highway 61 from Muscatine toward Mount Pleasant. Dwight's plight to put food on the table was much more than the hobby of his city brother. It was a full-time vocation of fifteen-hour days, seven days a week. He milked a small herd of cows and tended to beef cattle and hogs. He fed the livestock on the corn, oats and hay he raised, all the while trying to keep his two high school-aged sons, Dennis and Donnie, from straying too far from the farm come milking time. The war couldn't have ended soon enough for Dwight, who was at one time convinced he'd lose one or both of his sons to Europe or the South Pacific.

Parlee couldn't tell the end of the gravel road from the beginning of the driveway that took the '36 Plymouth to a tear-drop turnaround surrounded by a farm house on one side and a series of outbuildings and a larger milking barn on the other. The barn on that day was being restocked with bales of hay, freshly cut from a small field at the end of a narrow lane with fences on each side – fences that were overgrown with small Elm trees, buckthorn and black raspberry bushes.

Parlee wasn't out of the car yet when his father volunteered him for servitude in the haymow for the rest of the afternoon. Parlee's muscles ached and he was dog tired after helping the Downing boys and a kid named Gene mow the remaining five wagon loads of hay that day.

But Dennis and Donnie saw the last bale mowed not as a chance to rest but as an opportunity to throw some catch and get a couple of at-bats before milking time. Parlee made a welcome fourth to the baseball sideshow the Downing boys manufactured between farm chores.

Dennis told Parlee to fetch his glove as Donnie ordered Gene to pick up the bat resting next to a makeshift plate in front of the solid wall of one of the farm's outbuildings.

"Have a look at this kid's swing," Dennis told Parlee as he took an outfield stance with his glove now ready. "This kid's only elevan and he hits better than anyone on our high school team."

Donnie delivered a pitch toward the plate and the gangly Gene Oliver handled the bat with the confidence of a maestro with his baton. He swung and turned his hips and extended his arms as he connected bat to ball and sent one over Parlee's head on the fly. Parlee turned, tracked the ball at full speed, and nearly pulled it in on a dead run with his back to the plate.

"See what I mean" Dennis laughed as Parlee continued chasing the ball as it skimmed down the gravel driveway like a flat stone skipping across a calm lake.

"You damn near caught up to it," Dennis said after a breathless

Parlee came back with the ball.

Baseball was about the only thing that kept the Downing boys in school. Dwight wouldn't mind if either Dennis or Donnie quit school so they could be on the farm full time. But Dwight gave his blessing to his sons to play on the high school team even during the busy spring planting season.

Gene was the boy of Dwight's wife's first cousin. Jule Downing grew up in Rock Island, one of the Quad Cities of Illinois and Iowa along the Mississippi. Jule's cousin would send Gene out to the Downing farm for the summer. Dennis and Donnie knew right away they had a special ball player on their hands for the summer. On Sundays they'd bring him along to pickup games that often sprung out of family picnics in the Ottumwa band shelter. But mostly Dennis and Donnie drilled the young Oliver kid endlessly in between and during milking, baling and other farm chores.

"Watch this," Dennis told Parlee as Donnie made Gene put down the bat and pick up the catcher's mitt and mask. "We can't throw one by that little shit."

Donnie wound up and deliberately threw three straight balls into the hard dirt about two feet in front of a home plate made from a worn milk pail lid. Gene blocked or caught each one, deftly moving his feet and shifting his weight in order to keep his shoulders square to the incoming ball.

Dennis took Parlee into the barn to get the cows ready for their evening milking. The four of them took turns throwing and batting outside while helping Dwight and Parlee's dad with the hand milking. Once the herd of eighteen cows was milked and turned out, the four kids played a game of work-up until the sun set on the Iowa farm.

The three days spent at the Downing farm was like a baseball boot camp to Parlee. Every moment between farm work and chores was used by the Downing boys, Gene and Parlee to play make-shift games of five hundred, work-up, pickle in the middle or just plain old pitch and catch.

During lunch and supper, Dennis, Donnie and Dwight embellished stories of the St. Louis Cardinal Gashouse Gang, romanticizing the

Cardinals' exploits over mounds of fresh home-grown roast beef, mashed potatoes, sweet corn and raspberry preserves sent over by Lowell and Verna. Parlee listened to Dwight's stories about how Diz would try to run the team from the mound over manager Frankie Fritch's objections, and of Joe Medwick routinely picking fights with opponents and teammates, alike. Parlee had heard some of the stories on earlier visits to the Downings with Gramps. The ones that had stuck with him the most were about the '34 season when Diz won thirty games, Medwick hit at a .379 clip and how the Cards won the Series in seven games over the Tigers.

Through it all, Parlee and Gene, being just two years apart in age, became fast friends.

Even long after Parlee's family returned home, Parlee kept in contact with Gene. For a school English project, Parlee needed a pen pal and while most of the kids in his high school freshman class picked out an area serviceman still stationed at some lonely outpost around the world, Parlee chose to write a seventh grader in Moline, Illinois named Gene Oliver.

"Best baseball player I ever met," Parlee proudly told the class when his teacher asked him to describe his pen pal.

CHAPTER 5

"So you met Oliver when you were a kid and kept in touch with him all these years?" Clay asked.

"Close enough," Parlee said as he eased the Impala into Plymouth, dropping its speed to the new limit of twenty-five. "I think the place we're staying is along here somewhere. Suppose to be right on 67, this side of town."

Parlee saw a darkened sign that read "Trail's End Motor Lodge." The oval sign on a single pole was supposed to be lit by a floodlight pointing from the ground. But the light missed its mark, beaming strait up into the sky. The shadowy sign had a picture of a lone Indian slumped on a horse. A lance weighing heavy in his hand went the length of the horse, pointing toward the ground. Parlee recognized the image from the famous "End of the Trail" sculpture that sits in a park over in Waupun, fifty miles to the west.

It was a motor lodge that had individual cabins instead of the modern, one story motels that sprawled its entire lot. The cabins had two units apiece – small duplexes, Schmidty said -- each had its own black and white TV, window air conditioner, toilet and sink.

The units bordered a U-shaped driveway looping around a larger building that housed the office, laundry and showers. Parlee pulled up straight off the highway to the front of the office, not a light flickered from within.

"Doesn't look like anyone's in," Clay said.

"Schmidty set us up here," Parlee said. "His wife's brother owns the place. They were supposed to leave us keys."

Parlee kept the car running and opened the door to get out.

"Where?" Clay asked.

The Impala's headlights shone on the office window door. To its right was a large picture window with scripted lettering.

"Heap Cheap Rooms!" shouted the letters loud enough to be read from the road. The letters were underlined with a feathered lance. Under that in smaller block lettering, "Free TV and air conditioning." In the top right corner of the window sign was a drawing of a family, two children, a man and woman, dressed in buckskin and feathered headdresses lined up single file from shortest on up, each marching into a tepee, suitcase in hand.

The sign left Parlee wondering if Oliver has it this good when big leaguers go to San Fran, Philly or Chicago. Parlee tried to see into the office through the picture window. At the far end of the office the Impala's headlights showed a counter, behind it a tack board with room keys hanging from small hooks. Closer to the window was a table that had about a dozen tourist brochures. "Visit Fort Dells!" and "Ship Off to the Manitowoc Maritime Museum."

Outside, to the left of the door was hung a black rectangular mailbox. Parlee popped the lid, reached in and brought out two keys. He read them by the Impala's headlights. 8A and 8B.

"Keys to our happiness and everlasting salvation," Parlee told Clay as he got back in the Impala and slammed the door. Colton and Deke stirred in the back. There were sixteen units at Trail's End and Parlee steered the Impala around the drive until they came to No. 8.

Parlee pointed the headlights on the cabin. 8A to the left, 8B to the right.

"Welcome to paradise, boys!"

Parlee turned off the motor but let the headlights stay on the rooms. He flipped 8B to Clay, got out and tried his key in 8A. The key turned the deadbolt above the knob and Parlee pushed open a door that felt no heavier than the doors used inside any cut rate office building.

Clay's key was a bit more stubborn as he jostled the door.

"Don't push too hard on that or you'll break it in," Parlee said.

The door to 8A swung open and the Impala's headlights lit not much of a room. There wasn't even enough of anything to hide in the shadows made by the headlights. Parlee hit the wall light switch that turned on a small lamp on the nightstand between the beds. There was just enough room to swing open the door without hitting the first of two single beds. The far wall was about three feet from the second bed, leaving just enough room to slide through to the single-toilet bathroom. A sink was in the far corner of the room, below a corner shelf that held a TV up toward the low ceiling. In the wall to the left was a window with polyester curtains that had the drawings of famous Indian chiefs – Red Cloud, Crazy Horse, Sitting Bull.

"Jesus Christ," Parlee muttered as Deke stumbled through the door and dove face first into the nearest of the two beds. "It's bad enough we slaughtered their people and took their land. But did we have to put their heads on heap cheap-ass motel curtains?"

"What the hell are you talking about?" Deke said as he struggled to sit up in the bed.

"Shit, we don't even have an air conditioner," Parlee said loud enough for Colton and Clay to hear in the other room. "What a gyp!"

"We got one," Colton hollered back. "It's got a cord dangling to the floor but no place to plug it in."

"You got curtains with a history lesson?" Deke shouted.

Parlee went back out to the Impala to hit the headlights and get his bag.

"Bring in what's left of the beer," Deke said.

Parlee gathered up the beer bag, knocking an empty can out onto the parking lot's asphalt. It clanked two or three times, interrupting the middle-of-the-night stillness before Parlee heard it slowly roll to a stop somewhere under the Impala. Parlee took the beer into the room and went back out to the Impala and popped the trunk.

He tried to ignore most of what was in the trunk and its percolating odor and pulled out four duffel bags. Parlee walked two of the bags to 8B, came back and grabbed his and Deke's.

He came into 8A to find Deke teetering on his tiptoes turning the channel dial of the TV. Every channel had snow except for Green Bay's Channel 2, which displayed a fuzzy test pattern.

"You're not going to find much at two-thirty in the morning."

Deke switched off the TV and slid between the beds to grab the beer he'd opened and set on the night stand.

Parlee opened a beer he knew he wouldn't finish as Colton appeared in the doorway and grabbed two more beers that were sure to go to waste in 8B as well.

Parlee had stayed at similar motor lodges countless times and figured it'd be best to take a shower now while there was no line across the drive and, this time of night, probably enough hot water to last at least ten minutes. Mostly he wanted to get his knee wound cleaned out before it could fester into an infection like the one that laid him up for two weeks a couple of seasons ago.

He could picture the shower room -- a cool concrete, slippery floor with a couple of wall sinks under scratched but polished stainless steel mirrors. Two or three stand-up Kohler urinals and a couple of partitioned shitters. On one end would be two six-foot high cinder block partitions with rows of hooks connected by a curtain rod and polyester curtain sheathing a small room that has four shower heads tapped in the walls, two on each side. The place dimly lit by buzzing, flickering yellow neon lights that attracted the night moths. Mosquitoes in the air, crickets on the floor. Maybe a salamander or two.

Parlee dug through his bag to find a towel, shaving kit and clean t-shirt.

"I'm takin' a shower," he told Deke. "Don't wait up."

"Don't get hurt."

Parlee went out. He pushed open the door to 8B to find Colton sipping a beer as he got ready to crash. Clay was propped up in his bed, staring at the Channel 2 test pattern.

"Takin' a shower," Parlee said to the room. "We can sleep in. We don't have to be over to the park 'til the afternoon. Take some cuts, see what Schmidty's got us for players."

"What's game time again?" Colton asked.

"Six. Should be a good crowd. We're playing those guys out of Sparta."

Clay had switched off the TV and turned in. Colton was doing the same. He took one more swig of Gettleman.

"Sounds good. Hit the light will ya?"

Parlee turned off the light, shut the door and headed across the drive to the shower. There were two entrances. Each door was shielded by an L-shaped cinder block wall that came out of the main building. The left entrance had a wood carved sign that read "Chief Sweat Lodge," the other "Squaw Sweat Lodge."

"Jesus Christ all over again," Parlee muttered as he veered left.

He came out of the sweat lodge about forty five minutes later, a smidge of toilet paper clinging to a shaving cut on the left side of his chin. Parlee scratched at a mosquito bite on the back of his left shoulder as he made his way across the driveway. A blue tinted dusk-to-dawn yard light mounted on each end of the motor lodge's shower and office building was all that lit the entire area, save for the singular yellow neon light tubes that ran the roof peek of each unit. Most were blinking, some didn't work at all.

As Parlee made his way to unit eight, he could see a shadowy figure by the Impala. He trained his eye on the figure as he quickened his step. When he got closer, Parlee could see from the light coming through the window of 8A the figure was that of Colton. He was barefoot, in his sleeping shorts and t-shirt, pissing a stream that went under the Impala.

"What the hell you doin'?"

"Woke up, had to piss, couldn't find the light switch," Colton said.

"Or the bathroom. For shit's sake, the room ain't that big."

"This seemed closer."

"How about next time goin' a little further away from the car?"

"Sure thing Skip. How was your shower?"

"Exactly how I pictured it."

Parlee pushed open 8A. Deke was still propped up in his bed, asleep, beer can in hand. Parlee put his stuff down at the foot of the bed, grabbed the can out of Deke's hand and took his own off the night stand. Both were more than half full as he turned them upside down in the sink. He crawled into bed and switched off the light.

Parlee settled his head on the pillow in the darkness thinking about everything that happened on that busy day. He thought about what having to use Clay against Lebanon means to how things could go south in a hurry this weekend. He configured lineups for the weekend, based on what kind of players he thought Schmidty rustled up. He hoped they had enough pitching and that big guy they call Heidi who can catch and hits the shit out of the ball. He thought about the sparse crowd at last night's game and how he anticipates that to be the norm in coming games and seasons. He thought about how nice it would be for once not to worry about that and just play. He thought about the drive up and how he felt himself nodding off just before Mayville. How long can he keep hanging curve balls to the fate of the road before having one get knocked out of the park on him? He thought about the Braves leaving Milwaukee and how his friend, Gene Oliver, was reacting to that by wanting to give up the game. He thought about his own deteriorating relationship with Ashippun in general and The Turk in particular. He thought about how it made him understand all too well what Oliver must be thinking. He thought about the mess in his trunk.

As he drifted off, Parlee turned his thoughts to the triple he'd hit against Lebanon – about getting the fastball he expected. About the ball hitting the sweet spot of the bat in that rare place where he didn't even feel, in his hands or arms, the ball hitting the bat. About turning his hips on the pitch and sending the ball up the right-centerfield gap, the sketches of two shadowy runners in the outfield heading toward the same spot on the warning track as Parlee hit first. The way his heart skipped up a notch when he turned second at a full sprint, deciding on the fly to get to third. The way the catcher's shout of "Three!" bounced off the trees behind the diamond -- a distressed cry in the woods. The way he felt himself become airborne as he dove headfirst toward the bag as the Lebanon third baseman leapt to pull in a high relay throw. The way the Lebanon player's spikes grazed his hand when he landed as Parlee pulled the bag to his chest with a fresh load of dirt and clay down the front of his pants, his knee scab reopened, right hand rasp berried anew. Thank god he didn't break a finger on that spike.

That was the image that drifted Parlee off to sleep, the echoes of a dozen or so pairs of clapping hands breaking the dewy stillness of Ashippun Fireman's Park.

CHAPTER 6

Parlee woke from a dead sleep to the sounds of the paint coming off the walls from Deke's snoring. Once again, Parlee forgot about the elevated audibility of Deke's snoring from the effects of a deviated septum, the result of a bench-clearer in Horicon when the two played for Neosho three years back. Had Parlee remembered, he'd have paired Clay with Deke when they rolled in.

It was about seven, Parlee figured, too soon to get up. But there was no use in staying in the room with that band saw running full tilt. Parlee thought about the trunk of the Impala and it became clear that he couldn't get back to sleep no matter how much noise Deke was or wasn't making.

Parlee tossed back the covers and threw his feet over the side of the bed facing the snoring third baseman with the most natural swing anyone had seen. As Parlee rose, his sore joints made the sounds of a lit pack of lady finger firecrackers. Two ankles, a knee, neck and the right elbow all cracked in a syncopated progression. The head was heavy from six beers and road hypnotics, the body stiff and sore from the week's four games. He wondered if he had four more in him over the next three days.

Parlee brushed his teeth, put on his shoes and sweats and went out to the Impala. The morning was as still as the dead of night when they arrived five hours before. He backed the black beast around the lodge's driveway, searching for the laundry entrance of the main building. It was on the far side and Parlee backed the Impala's trunk right up to the door.

Parlee reached into the glove compartment and pulled out a rubber oval-shaped change purse that opened when placed in the palm of one's hand and the ends are squeezed. Standing behind the car he popped the trunk and turned his head away, toward the building. The pungently heavy air of the trunk circled his head. Parlee took a breath, turned to the trunk and scooped up the wet mound of jerseys, pants, undershirts and socks in both arms. He got about three-fourths of the pile, Parlee figured, and he turned to grab the latch of the laundry room's screen door with a hand held firm to his body, the arm levered against the damp pile of clothes.

Parlee staggered into the laundry room, making a beeline with quick steps toward a stainless steel side-load washer. He'd left, between the door and washer, a telltale trail of one pair of pants, several socks, a jock strap and an Ashippun Platers jersey top. Parlee filled the washer with what was left in his arms. He filled the washer next to it with the remaining clothes in the trunk and the trail remnants. He popped open his change purse to buy a small box of Borax from a wall dispenser and put half the powdered soap in each washer. He slotted a quarter in each of the machines and watched to make sure they began filling with water.

"Twenty Mule Team, do your stuff," Parlee muttered, urging on the Borax.

He went out to look for the pop machine he thought he remembered seeing as he circled the building when they landed at two that morning. He found a Coke machine on the side of the building near the office and delighted when he opened the machine's narrow display door to see Sun Drop.

"Ahh, the elixir of the gods," said Parlee of his favored hangover companion.

Parlee put two dimes in the slot and turned down the lever on the front of the machine that released the ten-ounce green bottle of Sun Drop that he pulled from the vertical row of various sodas.

"Refreshing as a Cup of Coffee" read the bottle in white letters under a small portrait of a steaming cup. Parlee opened the bottle and chugged about half its contents in the first pull. He set the bottle on top of the machine, plugged in two more dimes and pulled out a second bottle. He grabbed up both bottles and went back into the laundry room to sit in an armless chair at a wooden laundry table and stared through the glass domes of the working machines to the suds and water washing away last night's game.

At certain times, one of the jerseys would make its way to the front of the machine and show its letters to Parlee in the rhythmic turning of the agitator.

A-s-h-i-p.

And it'd be gone in a maelstrom of white bubbles.

p-u-n.

Then socks, suds, and pants with the water showing a pink tinge from the diamond's red clay.

Most days, Parlee would page through the two-day-old *Sheboygan Press* on the table next to his chair. On this morning, he stared into the machines and mused with the clarity that at times found his mind on mornings when he was a little hung over but not to the stomach sick extreme.

He thought about what he had told Clay on the drive early this morning while Deke and Colton slept in the back of the Impala. Parlee thought about how when he's teaching history lessons to his high school students, he's the one who's actually learning things from himself for no other reason than he's saying the lesson out loud— and he's listening

So it was with his lesson with Clay this morning as he recited the history of the beginnings of his friendship with Gene Oliver.

A-s-h-i-p.

Then suds.

In that clearing he was reaching in his mind, Parlee realized he'd yet to understand the things Gene had said to him earlier this spring. Nor had he come to terms with the Braves leaving town and now, his feelings about the Ashippun Trap.

So he recited the history to himself while that clarity perused his mind.

p-u-n.

Suds.

In April while Parlee was working himself into shape for the upcoming Rock River League season and counting the days until the end of school at Jefferson High, he went to Milwaukee to see his major league pal, Gene Oliver. Oliver made it big in baseball after he and Parlee spent portions of two summers together on the Downing farm in Iowa. The summer after Parlee had first met the Oliver boy at the Downing's, the two used their penpalship to coordinate a more extended stay at the Downing farm in the summer of 1947.

Having made it through ninth grade, Parlee was turning the corner on adolescence. But that didn't stop his mother from crying as Parlee stepped onto a bus in Madison that would take him for a two-week stay at the Downing farm. The rolling, bumpy, dirt diesel bus wound its way across southwest Wisconsin, crossing the Mississippi River to Dubuque. From there it snaked south through a series of small Iowa towns that somehow seemed familiar to him. Parlee realized the route must have been the same taken by his family when he was about nine and headed toward a Parsons College reunion for Gramps a couple years after his wife passed.

After some eleven hours on the bus, it finally stopped outside of a fold-up Quonset DX service station at the edge of Mount Pleasant. Parlee used the pay phone to call the Downing farmhouse.

For two weeks Parlee and Gene helped work the Downing farm, baling hay, milking cows, slopping feeder pigs and cultivating corn.

There was plenty of farm adventure and mischief for the two youths away at their own make-shift summer camp. One hot, sticky afternoon, the fearless Gene tumbled from his perch high atop a wagon load of hay bales. Parlee was driving the orange wide-front Allis 45 tractor that was pulling the load out of the newly-stubbled hayfield when the front wheel of the wagon struck a rock nestled on the side of a small hill. Stacked five bales high in two rows the width of the wagon with a top sixth row down the middle, the load of some 90 bales jumped in place when the wheel abruptly lurched over the rock before the gravitational forces of the hill went to work, shifting the load forward. Gene had perched himself on the top row of bales, leaning with the deliberate sway of the wagon, not unlike a surfer riding a slow wave as Parlee crept the Allis out of the field toward the barn. When the wagon wheel hit the rock, Gene and about ten of the top front bales were hurled toward the pulling tractor. Gene anticipated the throw and sprung to his left to avoid hitting the rear tire of the Allis. Parlee had pulled the hand clutch of the Allis and hit the duel brake pedals to stop as Gene flew off the wagon, controlling his fall with two summersaults, racing with a half-dozen tumbling green, ripe bales that made their way past the stationary tractor. On his last tumble, Gene kipped to his feet and faced up to Parlee, a gymnast saluting a judge at the end of a difficult routine.

The two laughed and awed for several minutes, retelling the tale to one another. They looked out over the field to see if Donnie, who was driving the baler, or Dennis loading the wagon, had seen the event. The baler made its way toward the far end of the field and Parlee and Gene were relieved to know the mishap was yet undetected.

Then they went to work, as best they could, to restack the bales onto the wagon. They soon learned the old farm lesson that when a load of bales comes undone, there's no recreating the tightness of the original stack. They had to reload the wagon twice more on their way to the barn as they crept down the narrow lane between the fence lines. Bales slid off the wagon at every suggestion of an incline or wagon rut.

Two days later, the younger Gene came to Parlee's rescue while the two were slopping the hogs and Parlee slipped off the fence he'd been showing off from and landed in the middle of the feed the hogs were greedily devouring. Gene pulled Parlee free of the fray, but not before a large chunk of Parlee's left boot became part of the feast. The retelling of the feeding frenzy got quite a laugh around the supper table that evening and Donnie and Dennis referred to Parlee as "One Boot" the rest of the week.

But the real reason Parlee and Gene came back to the farm was for the baseball. Dennis and Donnie again obliged, making Parlee and Gene pick up a bat and glove anytime there weren't farm chores to be done. On Sundays the four would find a pickup game somewhere and play all day. It was the last summer the Downing brothers would spend together. Donnie made it through high school the previous spring and was reporting for duty with the air force in September about the same time Dennis would be heading back for his senior year in high school.

Parlee learned more about playing baseball during those two weeks than any other time of his life. After that, Parlee and Gene fell out of touch the way of most teenage boys when they find other things to do besides write letters

Gene stopped spending his summers at the Downing farm after he began playing with an American Legion team out of Moline. The following summer, he was the youngest player in the league -- a thirteen-year old playing with kids sixteen and seventeen. Parlee found his own baseball pursuits to be less rewarding, being an end-of-the-bench kid on his high school and Legion teams.

But Parlee kept playing, even after being cut following one try out with the La Crosse State University team his first year in college. He'd play on any town ball team that needed a player. Parlee was one of those kids who took time to physically mature. He didn't out-grow his high school wiriness until well into his twenties and that's when his baseball skills began to mature as well.

Gene was a high school star who went on to play at Northwestern University, where he was recruited for a football scholarship. Baseball remained his first love. It didn't surprise Parlee when he heard Gene was drafted by the Cardinals in 1956. He remembered how Gene stood out even among the older players during those long days on the make-shift diamonds in southeast Iowa. There wasn't anything on those diamonds Gene couldn't do. Most days he was one of the fastest kids in any game they played, but Gene always found his way behind the plate, where he seemed most at home in a catcher's squat, controlling the game.

Oliver spent the summer of his twenty-first year with two Class D teams in the Cardinal organization. He moved up to Class B ball in Winston-Salem the following year and then settled in with the Cardinals Triple A team in Rochester, New York for four seasons. It was in Rochester where Oliver first caught the blazing fastball of Bob Gibson.

Parlee had no way to track Oliver's progression through seven seasons of minor league baseball. He'd get incomplete updates or curious looks from any of the Cardinal scouts he'd run into at whatever game he might happen to be watching or playing in during the summer.

Finally, in June of 1959, he saw the name "Oliver" in a Cardinal box score in a two-day-old Chicago Tribune he'd happened upon at the Squeeze Inn café in Milton Junction. It was a nine-seat lunch counter and Parlee interrupted every conversation in the joint with a whoop of glee when he read Oliver's name in the box score's small agate print. Parlee knew his once pen pal -- the kid from Rock Island who could out-throw, out-run and out-hit everyone who ever attended any Ottumwa, Iowa family picnic -- had made the big leagues.

It wasn't for a couple of years until Parlee had the opportunity to see Oliver live in a Major League uniform. He'd tried to get into County Stadium when the Cardinals were in town but just never made the connection.

Then in June of the 1963 season, the Braves traded popular right hander Lew Burdette, a star of the 1957 World Series team and one of the last remaining Braves who first came to Milwaukee from Boston in 1953, to St. Louis for pitcher Bob Sadowski and catcher Gene Oliver.

Parlee went to County Stadium one Tuesday night in late July of '63 when the Braves were hosting the Cardinals. Milwaukee was coming off a tough, twenty-game road trip out west, finally returning home the previous Friday for a four-game set with the Dodgers that culminated with Sunday's double-header sweep for Milwaukee.

After batting practice about thirty minutes before game time, the Braves players were starting to filter out of the first base dugout and onto the field to throw, stretch, jog and warm up.

Parlee made his way down the aisle toward the rail next to the Braves dugout as a handsome crowd of about 25,000 was starting to settle in around him. Parlee recognized most of the Braves by face. Del Crandall, Eddie Mathews, Roy McMillian and Frank Bolling had paired up to play catch in front of where Parlee was standing. Hank Aaron and Rico Carty emerged from the dugout and jogged toward the outfield where they began stretching along the right field line before getting up to run from the foul line out toward centerfield and back.

Seeing Crandall made Parlee think for a moment that Oliver might be catching and was out in the bullpen warming up Wade Blasingame, the evening's starting pitcher. When Parlee looked out toward the bullpen beyond right field, he saw Blasingame on the mound, working out of the stretch. He then caught a glimpse of the familiar number 15 worn by Joe Torre squatting sixty feet to Blasingame's left.

Parlee again wondered how much catching Oliver was going to be doing in Milwaukee with Torre, an emerging star, and Crandall, a multiple all-star, on the roster along with local boy Bob Uecker.

Then Parlee heard a familiar voice that had grown deep, rich and healthy.

"I'll be damned," the voice bellowed. "Hey One Boot, I thought the pigs ate you up!"

Parlee turned to see Gene Oliver for the first time in a big league uniform. He wore it as if it were a birth right – natural and deserved. The jersey had the familiar red tomahawk angled across the zippered front under the scripted "Braves." The number 12 was handsomely stitched on the lower left side just above the belt. Oliver had a catcher's mitt and began throwing with Denis Menke alongside their teammates.

Oliver didn't play that night and the Braves beat the Cards, 5-1. After the game, Parlee met Oliver at the National Avenue Liquor Bar for a few beers and the two caught each other up on their baseball lives of the sixteen years since their last meeting on the Iowa farm.

Parlee and Oliver rekindled their adolescent friendship during similar pow-wows about a half dozen times through the remainder of the season. Last year, the summer of 1964, Parlee kept Oliver updated on Ashippun's push toward the Rock River League title. When Parlee was finished recounting how he'd hit a three-run homer up in Brownsville to push the Platers into the championship game, Oliver talked about the Braves successes and failures through a roller-coaster 88-74 season. The Braves ultimately finished just five games behind the Cardinals, who chased down the Phillies to win the pennant. That pennant was all but conceded to the Phillies when they held a twelve-game, first-place lead as late as mid-August. After Philadelphia's unforeseen and monumental collapse, Oliver and his Braves teammates were left to ask themselves "why wasn't it us?" who ran down the Phillies to the World Series.

Bigger than that question was the fact the Braves had been sold to some Chicago interests in 1962 and two years later the new owners seemed determined to make good on a promise to move the Braves to greener pastures. In November, 1964, the team's ownership announced the Braves would be relocating to Atlanta for the 1965 season. A bitter, complex dispute involving Major League Baseball's long-standing antitrust status played out in local courts and resulted in the Braves having to honor the last year of their lease of County Stadium. In 1965, and the Braves returned for one final, awkward lame duck season in Milwaukee.

So when Parlee next saw Oliver at County Stadium in April, the baseball landscape had been altered for good and was still changing dramatically and rapidly in front of everyone's eyes. It couldn't have come at a worse time for Oliver, who felt as though he'd found a home in Milwaukee. In '64 he'd played a lot of first base. Now with Crandall traded it appeared as though Oliver would catch on the days Torre didn't and play first when he did.

Parlee had followed the tumultuous off-season in heart-broken horror and couldn't believe Milwaukee was losing its big-leaguers. Parlee had been on the Braves bandwagon since it rolled into town from Boston in 1953. Parlee was in his second year of college, home for the summer and working at the Cities Service station up in Milton Junction to pay his way through school. Throughout the week he pumped gas and wrestled with tires – big, heavy split-rim wheels off the trucks, wagons and tractors of area farmers doing a busy, if not profitable, dairy business. On weekends Parlee played with the Milton Merchants in the Central Wisconsin League. It was a team made up of some local guys like Parlee but was good because of the players from Milton College who hung around for the summer.

Like many Wisconsin folk, Parlee saw his first Major League baseball game in the spring of 1953. No one knew for sure Milwaukee was going to become a big-league city until it was announced in March the Braves would be moving from Boston for the upcoming season, which was just a month away. The Braves had drawn just over 280,000 fans in all of the 1952 season in Boston and Braves' owner Lou Perini wanted out of town, willing to cede the Boston market to the more popular Red Sox. Perini chose Milwaukee in a hastily-arranged deal facilitated by Milwaukee beer Barron Fred Miller. Months earlier, Miller's group came close to bringing the Cardinals to Milwaukee. But the team's owner had sold to Gussie Busch to keep the team in St.Louis, despite the fact Miller's group offered more money.

The finishing touches were just being completed on Milwaukee's brand new County Stadium and it wasn't until mid-May when the new Braves had their first extended home stand. The defending National League champion Dodgers from Brooklyn were part of that home stand and Parlee made a Braves matchup with the Brooklyn Bums his first major league experience.

The freeways were jammed around the new stadium and the parking lots full to capacity as Parlee made his way into the Major League's newest ball park that Tuesday afternoon. His heart went into his throat as Parlee walked from the concourse of the new stadium up through a gradient galley-way and he got his first glimpse of the rich, green infield grass between the heads of the new Braves fans he followed up the concrete ramp. His view expanded to breathless when he stepped out onto the aisle with the diamond and scoreboard in full view, a green ocean of seats rising up behind him and the red torrent of box seats expanding to his front.

The diamond was the lushest green he'd ever seen. The scoreboard had the look to Parlee of a giant illuminated chalk board, dominating the view beyond the right field fence. A long, black rectangle with "MILLER HIGH LIFE" block lettering across its top, the main part of the board had ten innings worth of score squares for the visiting team and the Braves, followed by squares each for runs, hits and errors. Below were tallies for balls, strikes and outs. Down the left side of the board was listing for National League scores, to the right, American League. Rising above the center of the board, out of the "HIGH" lettering was a large, square Longines clock with hands and Roman numerals.

A bevy of excitement encompassed Parlee. Agitated vendors squeezed past his stationary gawking pose as they impatiently hawked red hots, peanuts and cotton candy. Busy fans with scorecards scurried to their seats. It was a new and exciting experience for everyone in Milwaukee. He was part of a crowd of 36,000 and Parlee had never been with so many people in his life.

Parlee got out of the way, eventually locating his lower-grandstand seat – one of the green ones for three bucks. Parlee felt like he was ten, half his real age. He couldn't believe he was finally going to see, in the flesh, legends such as Spahn, Burdette, Mathews and Adcock. They were names that until now had merely appeared to Parlee in newspaper box scores and faces in black and white photos in *Look*, *Life* or *Post* magazines. Parlee had no reason to have followed Boston's floundering National League team and was far better-acquainted with the more famous names of the visiting Brooklyn Dodgers – Furillo, Hodges, Snider, Reese and, of course, Jackie Robinson. Duke Snider hit a two-run homer in the eighth, using the familiar, left-handed swing Parlee had seen on newsreel highlights before movies at the Rialto Theatre in Edgerton. Snider's smooth stroke put away a 4-1 win for Brooklyn but the new Braves fans were unfettered. They deliriously cheered everything in sight. They cheered infield pop flies that looked from their new perspective to be destined to go out of the park. They cheered foul balls and routine grounders. They cheered the grounds crew. They even cheered the Bums from Brooklyn.

Parlee's love affair with the Braves was born that day. He was among the Milwaukee baseball lovers who set new attendance records when the Braves were the first big league team to draw two million fans in 1954. He was also among the ten-deep that lined Wisconsin Avenue with cases of Schlitz to be part of the victory parade after the Braves from Bushville dispatched the mighty Yankees from New York to win the '57 Series.

Halfway through the parade a drunken Parlee bounced off the brand new '57 Chevrolet convertible carrying Eddie Mathews and Wes Covington. Parlee bolted from the crowd and ran into the street to hand Mathews his Neosho hat. Parlee misplayed the slow speed of the convertible and was knocked to the street when he hit the car at full stride after pushing his way past three rows of revelers and out to the parade. As he lay on his back, looking up from the hard grime of Wisconsin Avenue – the world turning above him – he saw Mathews rise to stand in the back of the convertible as it continued to ease its way in front of the cheering, and now laughing, throng. Still standing, Mathews put the Neosho hat on his head, turned backwards in the convertible and issued the fallen Parlee a military salute.

Parlee continued to lay spread-eagle on his back in the street, the sky circling above him. He'd never felt such elation, joy and pure satisfaction in his life. The feeling lasted until Parlee realized the convertible carrying Johnny Logan and Joe Adcock had stopped the parade to avoid running him over.

The Braves had wrestled the attention of the National Pastime away from the big east coast teams. They had been the team to break the eight-year strangle hold on the World Series trophy by teams from New York. In 1956, the Braves finished a game out of first in the National League pennant chase behind the Dodgers. They won the Series in '57 and in 1958 were beaten in the seventh game of the Series by the Yanks. In 1959, the Braves lost a best- of- three playoff series with the Dodgers after tying Los Angeles for the National League pennant.

The Braves were just a handful of games away from a four-championship dynasty and Milwaukee fans couldn't get enough. The Braves were also living proof of the success and financial gain that could be tapped in new markets. Within a few short years of the Braves leaving Boston for Milwaukee, other teams followed the lead, seeking new fortune. The Browns moved from St. Louis to Baltimore, the Giants and Dodgers from New York to California, the Senators from Washington to Minnesota and the A's from Philly to Kansas City. New teams sprouted in Los Angeles, New York, Washington and Houston.

It became clear to Parlee that the Braves succeeded too well as baseball's first relocation experiment. Just nine years after the Braves came here their new owners began seeking ways to make them the first franchise to move a second time.

Perini was a hero when he brought the Braves to town in 1953. But his refusal to sell the team to local interests made him the adulterer in a state-wide love affair with the Braves that was still blossoming. Once the new owners took over in 1962, rumors spread about an impending move and Braves fans were quick to file for divorce.

Parlee knew full well Walt Jaeger and his Ashippun ilk spoke for a large majority of the baseball fans in Wisconsin who weren't interested in giving one dime to the carpetbaggers. Still, Parlee just wanted big league baseball to be a part of his community and it broke his heart that the Braves would be moving, no matter who was to blame.

All through the off-season, baseball took a backseat to the news of the messy divorce. Braves ownership announced right after the '64 season concluded that they fully intended to play the next season in Atlanta. News of the court fight soon began, dividing Milwaukee fans into two camps: those who wanted to fight to hang onto the Braves until their dying breath, and those who wanted nothing to do with a team that didn't want to be here. As the off-season wore on, the latter camp grew larger and increasingly bitter.

Parlee couldn't find one bit of good baseball news through the off-season. In November the Braves sold Warren Spahn to the New York Mets where he would be a player-coach for a team some said couldn't compete in the Rock River League. Soon Spahn began making assertions that Braves manager Bobby Bragan was "managing to lose games" in 1964 at the direction of the owners who knew it'd be difficult to relocate a team that had just won the pennant.

Many fans believed Spahn's outrageous accusations because of

Bragan's constant and seemingly guideless tinkering with the lineup through the summer of 1964. In March, Spahn's criminations grew new life when Oshkosh native Billy Hoeft, a relief pitcher for the Braves in '64 and out of baseball the next year, made the same claim. Between the accusations and the court fight, the divorce became final.

The divorce may have been final but the separation was not. Milwaukee County won the court battle to keep the Braves in Milwaukee for the '65 season, but it was clear no one would show up to watch.

The Braves players, some scattered throughout the country during the off-season, followed the stories the best they could through the papers. They gathered for spring training in Florida with only a little understanding about the odd season that lay in store.

Braves management all but moved the entire operation to Atlanta during the off-season. A skeleton staff remained in Milwaukee to handle operations for a business whose mind, heart and wallet lay eight hundred miles to the south. The name "Milwaukee" appeared nowhere on any jerseys or souvenirs during the 1965 season.

In the face of threatened fan ticket boycotts, a local business group headed by Bud Selig, a young car dealer, promoted opening day tickets as a gesture to baseball to show Milwaukee was still a Major League city and deserved a Major League team. The group, called Teams Inc., sold more than 30,000 tickets for opening day, keeping a portion of the ticket revenue for efforts to land Milwaukee another big league team.

There was no guarantee how many fans would show up after opening day, but the prospects looked grim. Even Walt Jaeger went to opening day to support Teams Inc., he said, but promised to ignore the Braves for the remainder of the season.

Far away from the clamor and bitterness, the Braves players were finishing preparations for the season in sunny Florida. The team broke camp in early April and had one stop to make before opening the season on April 12, a Monday in Cincinnati. The Braves closed out their exhibition season with a weekend, three-game set with Detroit in Atlanta's new $18 million stadium.

When the Braves players flew into Atlanta that Friday, they were met at the airport by ownership and scores of Atlanta civic leaders and dignitaries. They rode in a long motorcade on the seat backrests of new convertibles through streets lined with waving people holding signs welcoming them to the city. Overpasses were full of kids and empty school busses that had brought students from school to hold class-project signs welcoming their soon-to-be new heroes.

None of the players knew where they were going, how long they'd be on the road in this strange parade or why everyone was making such a fuss. The motorcade finally stopped somewhere downtown for a luncheon. An endless number of speeches were given – Atlanta dignitaries thumping their civic pride, Braves owners saying how delighted they are to be there. "Wait 'til next year!" This, despite the fact the current season had yet to begin

Manager Bobby Bragan, in uniform, got up to say he and his team were from the north, here to surrender one hundred years to the day after General Lee gave in to U.S. Grant at the Appomattox Courthouse. To applause and laughs from everyone in the room except the team, Bragan apologized to the City of Atlanta for the rudeness of that General Sherman.

Once all of that silliness was out of the way the Braves got down to the business of sweeping the Tigers in a three-game series. More than 118,000 brand new baseball fans turned out for the three games.

Gene Oliver and his teammates didn't know that it would take until late May before more than 100,000 fans would go through the turnstiles at County Stadium that year.

The Braves opened the season by splitting a two-game series in Cincinnati on Monday and Tuesday and then headed to Milwaukee for Thursday's home opener against the Cubs, all wondering if the reception there could top what they saw in Atlanta.

There were no civic dignitaries to greet the Braves when their plane arrived from Cincinnati at the airport on Milwaukee's south side. There was no motorcade, no luncheon for braggarts topped off by a bad Bragan joke. Kids weren't allowed to skip school to line overpasses. Hell, Parlee read that kids weren't even allowed to skip school to attend the game – something that had become an opening-day tradition among Milwaukee schools.

None from the Braves' ownership group, in fact, even bothered to come to Milwaukee for their team's home opener.

What the Braves did find was a polite crowd of more than 33,000, some 5,000 more than the Reds drew for their opening gate on Monday. The crowd received the Braves, cheering an Eddie Mathews double and Sadowski's four-hitter in a 5-1 win over Chicago. The loudest cheers were reserved for the pre-game ceremonies in which members of the 1953 team, the original Milwaukee Braves, were introduced. Even the new Met Warren Spahn was there to take in the adulation. So, too, was Lew Burdette, now in his Cubs uniform. The biggest cheer went to Mathews, the only original Milwaukee Brave still on the roster.

Parlee couldn't make opening day on a Thursday school day and headed into County Stadium on Saturday for the second home game of the season. With temperatures hovering in the high thirties, it was a miserable day for baseball.

"It was a bad day for baseball and we played bad baseball," Bragan said after a 9-4 loss that saw the Braves commit four errors.

Parlee felt as though he had the run of the place to himself. Just over 3,000 people rattled around in the concrete ice box that was County Stadium on that day.

Parlee had all he could do to stay warm as the game dragged on for over three hours. His teeth chattered and he stomped his feet as he tried to sip a frosty beer from the prime and vacant box seat behind home plate he moved into during the bottom of the first, his green-seat ticket stub in his coat pocket. Finally, in the fifth inning, Parlee went up to the concourse and made the switch to hot chocolate, wishing he'd brought a flask of bourbon. The Cubs pounded out sixteen hits against five Braves pitchers, leaving what crowd was there little to cheer.

Instead, the crowd warmed itself by booing Bragan at every turn. They booed him when he exchanged the line-up card. They booed him throughout all four pitching changes. They even booed him when he went out to check on second baseman Sandy Alomar after a minor collision at the bag.

Oliver didn't play the field but pinch hit in the bottom of the eighth, grounding out to second. Before the game, through chattering teeth, Oliver and Parlee agreed to meet after the game at The Castle Inn over on Greenfield Avenue. It was a small joint some of the Braves players had been frequenting since the middle of the '64 season. It was a neighborhood place and the owners lived in an attached house. Even with the Medieval décor, which consisted largely of a European family shield on the back bar wall, Parlee couldn't shake the feeling he was drinking in the owner's living room. There were trinkets in the bathroom, fragrant soaps, a lighted candle and neatly-folded towels and wash cloths more suited for a wealthy person's guest house. The tavern was seemingly secluded from the busy Milwaukee bar business and that's why it had become a favorite place of some players. Other than the Braves, it seemed to Parlee, no one outside of a two-block radius frequented The Castle.

Parlee arrived at The Castle about the time the Impala's heater started to kick in. The horseshoe bar left little room between its stools and the wall for two-thirds of its semi-circle configuration. On the far side of the bar was a small area for three tables and a juke box. Parlee squeezed between two entrenched regulars and the wall and took a seat at the bar, facing the door, his back to the tables. Parlee nodded at the two men he thought to be brewery workers but got no response. He rubbed his cold hands together and blew moist, warm breath into his cupped palms.

The bartender, familiar to Parlee from last season's meetings with Oliver here, appeared behind the bar from a darken hallway that led into the home. Parlee thought he remembered her name to be Irma. She was a short, brawny middle-aged woman with a thick European accent with origins Parlee couldn't finger— not quite German, and not Poland sounding. Some sort of Slavic hybrid, Parlee guessed.

"What's youse havin'?" she asked Parlee as she flipped a coaster on the bar in front of him. The cardboard square sported the familiar brown Blatz triangle.

"A tapper of Blatz is fine," said Parlee as he struggled out of his coat.

"Honey, you look like you could use something to warm your belly," she said.

"I'll have a shot of brandy, too," Parlee said through his hands when he stopped rubbing them together. "Get these two gentlemen whatever they want."

"What say you?" as she turned to the two at the bar.

"We'll have what he's got," said the bigger and older of the two, ordering for both. "I thank ya."

The woman poured the beer and shots and asked Parlee where he'd been to get so cold?

"Over at the Braves game."

"I tought der season was over width," she said with a smirk as she placed the shot and a seven ounce glass of beer in front of Parlee. "Width theirs dat's two twenty five hon."

Parlee pulled out three singles to pay for the drinks.

"Anybody there?" the big one asked.

"Not more than a couple of thousand. Half that by the sixth."

"You won't catch me there," the big guy said as he and the other each raised their shot glasses toward Parlee. "But I'll drink to you dumb shits."

"Salud!" and the three knocked back the shot.

Parlee felt the sweet, stinging brandy burn down his throat to warm the pit of his empty stomach. Vendors gave up hawking cold hotdogs after the third inning. He felt his body spring back to life and Parlee grabbed one of the quarters Irma placed in front of him and went over to the jukebox.

He scanned the thin white labels of song listings, pleased to find they were unchanged from the previous summer. Parlee pushed "Big River" by Johnny Cash, "The Hanging Tree" by Marty Robbins and the Ray Charles version of "You Don't Know Me."

"I don't know how anybody can give their hard-earned money to those dirty damn Rovers," the big guy said as Parlee returned from the juke box. The "Roving Boys" is the name the local press gave the Braves' new ownership team.

"I thought I got a pretty good deal today," Parlee said. "Bought an upper grandstand seat for three bucks and watched the entire game from right behind home plate. Even had my own personal beer vendor."

Irma grabbed two empty Pabst bottles from long-gone drinkers to Parlee's right. She set the bottles on a shelf behind the bar and grabbed the family shield that decorated the wall. She slid the bottom of the shield up to the right and it pivoted, revealing a hole in the wall. She grabbed each bottle one at a time and slid them into the hole where they disappeared down a chute to The Castle's dungeon below. Irma let the shield slide back into place.

"I couldn't stand to give those assholes one dime," the man said.

"By the looks of things, I don't think they're going to be making very many dimes this year," said Parlee and he ordered up another Blatz.

The door opened. With no breezeway, the warmth of the small bar was sucked outside and replaced with the damp coldness of early Wisconsin lakefront spring. Parlee was chilled to the bone again but shook it off when he saw Eddie Mathews come through the door. Frank Bolling followed, then Denny Lemaster. Finally, Gene Oliver came in from the cold, pulling the door shut behind him, trapping in a whole new kind of warmth for Parlee.

Baseball was at last back for a new year.

Bolling and Lemaster trailed Mathews as he made his way between the wall and the brewery workers to one of the tables as Johnny Cash sang *"And I followed you, Big River, when you called."*

Oliver stood in the doorway shaking his hands and squinting into the bar's dim lighting. When he saw Parlee, his face lit up in a springtime smile.

Oliver came around the bar as Parlee got up from his stool. They shook hands and gave each other a one-arm hug, Oliver still in his

Braves' team warm-up jacket.

"How are ya, One Boot?" Oliver asked as he started to shed his jacket.

"Doin' okay Big Time." Parlee sat back down. "Shit, you might as well have left that jacket on when you hit in the eighth. Would have covered up the shitty swing you took."

"Yeah, I topped that one good. Don't care where you're from, you never get used to hitting on a day like this.

"You still drivin that big black Impala out front?" Oliver nodded toward the door.

"Yeah," Parlee said. "Irma, get these four new gents what they're havin'."

"I left you a little something on your trunk."

"What? Another dent?

"You'll see. A gift from down south."

"How was spring training, anyway?"

"Florida was fine, as always," Oliver said as he pointed Irma to the Blatz tapper. "It was our little stop off in Georgia that was the strangest damn thing any of us had ever seen."

"I read a little bit about that," Parlee said as he handed Irma a five for the round of drinks. "Sounded like they rolled out the red carpet for you bunch of carpetbaggers."

"Hey, we aint the carpetbaggers," Oliver said as Marty Robbins cranked up, "I *came to town, to search for gold.*"

"I don't know if there's a guy on the team who wants to go down there next year," said Oliver, settling on the stool with his beer. "I know I'm thinking of quitting after this year."

"You gotta be shittin' me."

"This whole off-season was a mess, I don't know if it's worth it anymore," Oliver said, his eyes getting distant thinking about the recent past. "When they said in November they were moving to Atlanta for this year, I made up my mind right then and there I wasn't gonna report for spring training. Just quit. I only decided to report after they said they had to play one more year here.

"Parlee, everybody likes it here," Oliver waved at Irma for another round. "You talk to any of them, especially Eddie and any of the guys who've been here a while, and they'll tell you how much they hate having to leave. Aaron, Frankie over there. This town's been good to them. Its home. Hell, I just played here a year and a half and know what they mean. This is where I want to be. It's close enough for family to come, not as close as St. Louie was but I like it here. I'm gonna catch a lot this year with Crandall gone and play first most days when Torre's there. This is going to be my last big go-around."

"What about Atlanta and the new stadium and all the people they drew when you were there?"

"That was a goddamn dog and pony show," Oliver spit as he worked a rogue bit of a tobacco leaf from between his teeth -- a leftover from the day's game. "We didn't know what to make of all the fuss. They met our plane at the airport. We had this parade that went on forever to the downtown for a lunch. We were all in these new convertibles and some of the streets were lined three deep with people waving and cheering.

"Hell, what have we ever done for them? They didn't know us from the Mets or Colt 45's. You'd had thought we'd single handily killed Hitler or stopped Pearl Harbor. Overpasses lined with school kids holding up signs."

Ray Charles moaned *"Well, you don't know me."*

"It was kind of cold to be riding that long in a convertible, waving to a bunch of strangers but we finally get downtown to this big hall, and every big shot in Georgia is there." Oliver grabbed a package of Blind Robbins off a cardboard display rack attached to the back of the bar's tappers and slid a quarter toward Irma. "We get there and they give us our name tags. Eddie takes his and swaps it with Alomar's and all the press guys and these senators and shit are all over Sandy asking him about how he feels being one of the original Braves who came from Boston and now he's got to move again.

"'Course, Sandy doesn't speak much English and couldn't figure out what the hell they were saying. Bragan got really pissed."

"What a bunch of dipshits," Parlee chuckled and whirled on his stool to look at Mathews. He was in the middle of a story as Lemaster and Bolling laughed and tossed back the last of their beer. Mathews got up and came over to where Oliver and Parlee sat at the bar and yelled for Irma. He looked at Parlee.

"I suppose you still want that hat you said you gave me in the parade."

"Naw, you go ahead and keep that. Give it to some poor Atlanta fan down on his luck," Parlee feeling his juice as he gave it back to one of the National League's premiere sluggers. "Nice job on the name tags at the lunch down there."

"This guy talks too much," said Mathews, punching Oliver in the back. "You get down below the Mason-Dumbass Line and its pretty easy pickin's."

"Spoken like a true Texan," Oliver added.

"I know my kind."

Irma came out of the dark hallway back to the confines of the bar.

"Irma, now I told you," Mathews said. "You can't be doing your laundry and ironing back there on my time. Get us a round, would ya?"

Irma went to work on the empty glasses.

"I read where youse guys aren't going to be around much longer," Irma said. "I've got real customers to take care of."

"Irma, I could never leave you," Mathews said and then turned to Parlee. "You still the mayor of Ashippun or where ever in the hell it is you play?"

"Yeah, I'm a pretty big deal in Ashippun."

"I'll bet you are," said Mathews, paying Irma for the round. "You and the snowplow driver."

Mathews punched Oliver again. "Can't be too long here Beefalo. We got that team dinner with Selig tonight."

Mathews went back to the table with beer for Bolling and Lemaster, leaving a couple of full glasses at the bar for Parlee and Oliver.

"You're not really thinking of giving up the game are ya?"

"Yeah, I am," Oliver said, looking down at his glass of beer. "The whole thing down there was a bunch of crap. We get off the plane and they have these beauty contest winners, Miss Macomb County and her friends or what the shit. We're no sooner off the plane and they're greeting us like the Hula girls do in Hawaii. Only they aint giving us leis."

"What the hell did they give ya?

"Little Dogwood trees."

"You're shittin'."

"Hell, no," said Oliver, holding his hand about a foot off the bar. "They gave us little Dogwood saplings in these little pots."

"What the hell were you suppose to do with that?" Parlee asked.

"I know what I did with mine," Oliver said as he turned to the table. "Hey Lemaster, what'd you do with your tree?"

Lemaster was up playing the juke box.

"I did what they told me to do with it," said Lemaster, keeping his eyes fixed the song selections in front of him.

"At the luncheon, the mayor of Atlanta's giving a speech and starts talking about the history of Dogwood trees," Oliver said. "About how farmers down there don't plant their crops until after the Dogwoods bloom in the spring."

"Jesus, that's some interesting shit," said Parlee, rolling his eyes as he pried one of Oliver's salty Blind Robins from its brittle cellophane wrapping.

"Yeah, yeah," Oliver said. "Anyway, the mayor says if we want to have the trees planted somewhere at the stadium, they'd be here when we get back next year."

Oliver bellowed his voice as a politician would deliver a big line, adding "So the Braves and these trees can grow together in the Atlanta community."

"We all about fucking puked," Lemaster said from across the room at the juke box playing *"Glad All Over"* by the Dave Clark Five.

Oliver turned to Parlee, lowering his voice as if sharing a well-kept secret. "So on Sunday after the last game when we're supposed to be packing up to head to Cincinnati, Denny tips a clubhouse guy for a shovel, waits for the grounds crew to get done and takes his tree out to the field. He digs this big-ass hole right at the base of the mound on the infield grass toward the plate and plants his tree."

"I don't think we'll be growing up with that one," said Lemaster as he reclaimed his seat at the table with Bolling and Mathews.

"It was hilarious," Oliver said. "He damned near missed the bus to the airport. Bragan gets a call from Atlanta when we get to Cincinnati. He was pissed again. Said we acted like a bunch of ungrateful spoiled little brats."

"What's Bragan think about moving?"

"You heard the crowd today," Oliver said. "I think he'd rather be anywhere but Milwaukee.

"I don't know," Oliver said as he spun in his chair to face his teammates. "The whole thing was a bunch of bullshit. The stadium's nice but not much better than here. They filled it up all three games for the Tigers but it was like they didn't know what they were looking at. They cheered foul balls and pop-ups. They went nuts when Lolich threw one back to the screen and then they all clapped when our guy struck out on the next pitch."

"Ya know," Parlee said "it was like that here in '53 when you guys first came to town."

"Yeah, well I don't like it. I'm gonna be done before I have to go there and play."

Mathews had gathered up his money, empty glasses, Bolling and Lemaster from the table. He put the glasses on the bar.

"We gotta go," Oliver said to Parlee.

"I'll walk out with ya."

Mathews led the group, sliding sideways between the wall and the now empty stools at the end of the bar. He glanced down the darkened hallway behind the bar.

"Nighty, night Irma," Mathews called. "We'll be back. We aint gone to Atlanta yet!"

Outside the chilly gray afternoon was giving way to cold, dark twilight. Mathews, Lemaster and Bolling headed toward a '65 Chrysler 300. It was common for area dealerships like Selig's or Wally Rank's to provide players of Mathews' stature free use of a new car through the season.

Oliver trailed Parlee toward the Impala parked on the street. Through the dim twilight, Parlee could see the silhouette of a growth on the trunk of his car—a foot-high stalk of southern spring hope reaching from a small pot on the trunk of Parlee's Impala.

"I'll bet that's what a Dogwood looks like," Parlee said.

"In all its glory."

"I know exactly where to plant it."

"So when's your season start? Same deal as last year?"

"First week of May," Parlee said. "Less than two weeks now. Same deal. We won the title last year so people kept coming out and all is well. I'll play about forty or fifty games. Sixteen Rock league games."

"Out of all them, how many you get paid for?"

"For sure, eight home Rock games," Parlee said as Mathews fired up the new Chrysler. "I split half the home gate with three other guys."

"What do you play the other games for?"

"We're in a night league that's mostly just for playing, not a lot of fans come out during the week anymore," Parlee said. "We play some exhibitions with teams in other leagues. For the guys who do it, keeps 'em sharp. Gets ya to the diamond to hit. It's the only way to get better."

"Better for what?" Oliver asked, Parlee pretending not to hear.

"Then we've got some tourneys lined up with decent pay days if we win. Even all together it aint much but I haven't had to work during the summer for three years now."

"Why do you do it Parlee?"

The question stopped Parlee. It was one he'd never pondered.

"Do what?"

"Why do ya play?" Oliver asked, a tone of sincerity in his voice. "I've played all my life too and make a living doing it. But now. . . but now it looks like we aint going to be playing in front of anyone all this year with everything that's going on. Then we're supposed to go play in a town I don't want anything to do with. I guess I'm looking for a reason to keep playing.

"You've never played for anything," Oliver stated, "but still you keep playing. It aint like when we were young, got something to prove. Kicking ass in Ottumwa."

"I don't know," Parlee said, not really knowing what to say. "I guess I just play because of the game."

The horn of the Chrysler blared.

"What the hell does that mean?"

"Damned if I know."

The Chrysler horn pierced the cool evening stillness again.

"I gotta go. You coming in tomorrow? Denny's starting."

"Can't," Parlee said as he circled the trunk to grab the sapling. "We're hitting and might have a scrimmage game with a bunch of guys from Helenville."

"Helenville? Where the hell do you find these places?"

Oliver trotted off to the new Chrysler, hopped in the back seat and headed off to his big league dinner and Sunday date with the Chicago Cubs. Parlee turned the switch on the Impala trying to think of the best way to get to that burger joint in Oconomowoc on the way home and wondering if the boys from Helenville would bring enough tomorrow for a full-blown scrimmage.

CHAPTER 7

Parlee shook himself back to the Trail's End laundry room. The washing machines had finished their work how long ago? Parlee finished the backwash of the second Sun Drop and began moving the clothes into three driers to speed the process. He fed the driers a dime each.

Parlee pretended to page through the *Sheboygan Press* but couldn't shake Oliver's question. Why was he still playing? It's a question he'd never asked of his self. But now, he was beginning to wonder. His whole baseball world was being shaken. The Braves were leaving Milwaukee, if the Platers don't turn things around, he was probably through in Ashippun and now he was questioning his own reasons for playing. Was it for money? It better not be. The limited opportunities to make a few bucks at this level were rapidly getting more evasive for a player like Parlee.

He fed the driers another dime each and went out to grab one more morning Sun Drop. The clarity of his thinking was becoming more elusive. On the way back, he looked to the front of unit eight to see Colton and Clay playing catch. He watched in silence without announcing his presence. They were not a contrast in styles, Colton and Clay, as players seperated only by the nearly fifteen-year age difference.

Clay would snatch the ball from his glove, turn the ball in his hand to feel different grips and then fire the ball back to Colton in an easy motion. Parlee figured Clay was imagining throwing different pitches to batters he's seen in games over the past couple of weeks.

Each time he threw, the ball would explode from Clay's hand through his natural delivery and Colton maneuvered his body to receive the ball at various positions, some with his hands closer to his body than others. He'd catch the ball and gather it from his glove in one motion and fire it back to Clay using different arm angles. Sometimes he'd crow-hop, sometimes he'd pivot, dragging his right foot across an imaginary second base bag.

"That one right there," Parlee thought to himself after watching one of Colton's animated return throws, "was the double play that got us out of the third-inning jam in Clyman. . .

"Maybe this is why we play."

Parlee returned to the driers with the Sun Drop, a new sense of clarity and the need to get to Milwaukee and talk to Oliver.

Deke came out of 8A in a groggy half-sleep. Hair a mess. Sweat pants disheveled.

"Jesus Christ," he said. "Can't you guys do that without making noise?"

"Grab your glove, we'll get a round of pepper going," said Colton, stopping to light a Lucky.

"Ah what the Christ," said Deke as he turned back into the room, scratching his ass.

"That a yes or no?"

"Time will be our interpreter," Colton said.

After about four more throws, Deke shuffled out of 8A, squeezing his oversized hand into his undersized mitt.

"What are we, ten?" Deke said as he took a stance next to Clay. Colton grabbed a bat that was leaning against the cabin and hit a sharp two-hopper off the asphalt toward Clay and Deke. Clay fielded the ball and pitched it back to Colton, who pulled his hands in toward his body to guide the ball back toward Deke.

"Give ya a quarter if you hit that can," said Deke pointing toward the Gettleman can halfway between.

Deke fielded the one-hopper as the three heard the Impala fire up on the other side of the office building.

Parlee rounded the office building in time to see Colton swing at a delivery from Deke, the ball came off Colton's bat directly to the Gettleman can that had rolled under the Impala at 2:30 a.m. The impact carried the can further into the parking lot and the ball caromed toward the base of the cabin unit. Clay, Deke and Colton each threw their hands up and cheered.

"You owe me a quarter!"

Parlee rolled the Impala around the drive and backed up to the cabin.

"Our laundry bitch is here," said Deke, gathering up the ball.

"Proud to serve," said Parlee as he looked at Clay. "You ever get that test pattern memorized?"

"Huh?"

Parlee popped the trunk and the four began sorting through the warm pile of clothes.

"You get the stains out of Clay's after he shit his pants last night when he almost got beaned?"

"Fuck you Deke," and then Clay thought for a moment. "You think they did that on purpose?"

"Let me see," Parlee said. "You struck out twelve and you hit a homer that you seemed to really admire from the batter's box. What would Drysdale do?"

"I gotta get out of this shit league."

"Careful what you wish for," Colton said. "In better leagues they don't miss when they throw at your head."

Parlee took time to dig into his duffel bag to grab his Nokona glove, remembering it'd still be wet from last night's game. He took the glove and tossed it on the shelf of the Impala's back window where the afternoon sun would bake it dry.

"Get this squared away and then let's get something to eat," Parlee said. "I'll go over to the office and settle up. Meet me over there."

Parlee grabbed his clean baseball gear, went in 8A and put on some real clothes for the first time in three days – blue jeans, t-shirt, cleaner hat. Over breakfast at a downtown café recommended by the Trail's End hosts, Parlee sat in silence pouring over the box scores in the *Milwaukee Sentinel* while Deke and Colton traded friendly and witty -- so they thought -- flirtations with the waitress. She was not the least bit impressed when Deke made a point to tell her he'd be spending the evening at the Trail's End.

Parlee read the Braves game story and box score from the Thursday night game against the Phillies. The Braves had shared the same rain with the Ashippun Platers and beat Philly, 4-2, on a five-hitter by Ken Johnson, who'd just come over from the Astros, and Billy O'Dell. Joe Torre had a two-run single when the Braves scored three in the eighth to take the lead. Parlee noted to the table that Oliver didn't play but pinch hit.

"He was oh for one," Parlee said.

The Braves began a three-game series with the Cardinals Friday night that included a single game Sunday. Parlee began calculating the drive time between Plymouth and County Stadium – or The Castle.

It was early afternoon when the four returned to Trail's End. There was a note jammed into 8A's door crack. Parlee grabbed the three-by-five piece of paper and unfolded it. One side was a blank receipt from the Plymouth Dairy Co-op, where Schmidty worked. The other side was full of pencil scribbling.

Parlee read: "Glad you made it up safe. Come on over to the park around 4. Schmidty."

Parlee fell asleep on the bed watching The Merv Griffin Show. The Rifleman, Chuck Connors, was the guest and Parlee wasn't surprised to hear him say he played professional basketball and baseball.

"I always thought he looked like he can play," Parlee said. No response came from Deke, who was asleep on the other bed.

CHAPTER 8

By midafternoon, the four were in their pants and long-sleeved undershirts, itching to get to the ball park. Three had on long black sleeves. Colton was in red.

"Didn't I say three or nine times we're wearing black this weekend?"

"Wife packed," Colton said without any embarrassment or apologies. "Must have gone with Ashippun colors."

Parlee navigated through downtown Plymouth, a task that took but a couple of minutes through the town of about five thousand. He tried remembering the best way to get to the ball park, located on the north east side of town.

"Am I pitching tonight" Clay asked from the back seat.

"Shit, I hope not," Parlee said. "We don't want to burn you up tonight."

"Hell, I'm ready to go, arm feels great," Clay said, looking out at the small side streets of Plymouth. "There going to be scouts here?"

"There usually are," Colton said. "Some kid off Felch's team got signed out of here last year."

"Twins got him, that guy could mash," Parlee said. "Big kid from the mining country up in the UP."

"I'll throw every inning if it'll get me signed."

"Easy big boy," Parlee said. "It's quality, not quantity."

Parlee spotted the field's lights over the roofs of some neighborhood houses and steered the Impala down what was becoming a familiar street.

"Here we are," Parlee said as he turned the Impala into the Loede Field parking lot.

The stadium seating and dugouts at Loede Field were built with WPA money during the 1930s. It had been the on-again, off-again home of several low-level minor league teams during its lifetime but now fielded teams in local leagues and youth baseball. It remained a destination diamond for youth players throughout the area, many of whom still thrilled in playing there for the first time. The seating and dugout facilities weren't overly nice but unique in how extensive the construction project had become back in the thirties. Schmidty had two uncles who worked two full years on the project. Despite being about thirty years old or less, the diamond had a true old-time feel to it.

The four light standards, two in the outfield and one each at the end of the dugouts, looked as though they'd been built with huge erector sets. Each stood about seventy feet in height and represented a geometric maze of narrow metal girders arranged at trapezoidal angles. The standards were all contained within the fences of the diamond and presented obstacles to outfielders chasing deep fly balls or infielders sprinting for foul pop ups.

Wooden bleachers on the terraced concrete grandstand make a nice backdrop for fielders reading the ball off the bat. The advertising placards on the eight-foot high outfield fence gave the park a closed-in feel from home plate and the grandstand. Gem Razor Blades, Plymouth Chevrolet and Cadillac, Hub City Hardware and a half-dozen area cafes and bars were among the advertisers.

"You'd think Plymouth Chevrolet would sell Plymouths," Deke quipped as he scanned the outfield fence, judging its distance from home plate.

"You said that last year," Colton said as he flicked a Lucky butt out the car and cranked up the window.

Each dugout had a tunnel that went up an incline with a low ceiling that expanded into a make-shift locker room and latrine outfitted merely with a urinal trough, an unpartitioned toilet and a shower head. The floor was contoured toward a three-inch circular drain. Parlee went back through the tunnel just once before his first game at Loebe. On his way back down the sloping tunnel his metal spikes went out from under him on the slick concrete floor. Parlee cracked the back of his head on that floor and his day was done before the game started. In four subsequent trips back to Loebe, Parlee never went back up the tunnel.

Parlee parked at a gate down the left field line, at the back of the third base dugout. The gate of the cyclone fence was open, but wouldn't be for long when the crowd begins arriving.

"If you gotta piss, I suggest you get it done outside the dugout before people start getting here."

"Still too chicken to use in the indoor facilities?" Deke kidded.

"I never did learn how to skate downhill."

Parlee popped the trunk. The four each reached in all at once to grab their gear. Parlee remembered his glove in the back window and grabbed it while for the melee at the trunk cleared. He reached into the trunk and grabbed his duffel bag the pine tar rag and the two remaining bats. He followed Colton, Clay and Deke through the fence and around to the top of the dugout steps. Seated in the dugout were three Flames players Parlee recognized from last year. He was pretty sure of their names—Heidenreiter, Krahn and Medved.

"Heidi, Krahner," Parlee said as he made his way down the dugout steps. "What do ya say Meds?"

"Hey boys, glad you could make it," said Medved as he got up to get a quick drink from the bubbler at the home plate end of the dugout and went back to tying his spikes. "We can sure use the help this year."

"Schmidty said you guys have been up and down this year," Parlee said as he took a seat and began shuffling through his duffel bag at his feet. "Where is he anyway?"

"A lot more down than up," said Krahn as he began shaking hands with the new arrivals. "He's getting things ready at the concession stand."

"Always trying to make a buck."

Parlee pulled out his Nokona glove from his bag. He felt it in both hands. It was warm from the window bake and mostly dry, but for the creases. He hated when equipment got wet, especially his Nokona. He'd had the glove for nine seasons. He bought it because the leather was thicker and a better quality than any glove he'd ever held. It took him two full seasons to break in, but once he'd come to grips with the Nokona, and it to him, the glove was like an appendage with which he'd been born. Parlee popped a tin of mink oil and began rubbing the oily paste into the glove the way a cobbler might oil a fine pair of boots he'd just finished assembling with great care and pride.

Without saying a word Parlee and Deke hopped out of the dugout at the same time from opposite ends and Deke lobbed a ball Parlee's way. Clay and Colton followed suit and then the Plymouth boys paired off as more players began filtering into the dugout. Parlee felt the back of his shoulder pop on his first throw as the snap of balls hitting mitts began to echo off the grandstand. Banter started picking up as a work day now turned into play for the latest arrivals. Soon almost a full squad was out between the foul line and dugout stretching, jogging or playing catch.

Parlee, once again, was taken aback by the youthful look of the Flames players – even though all were probably in their early twenties with jobs and families they'd just started.

"How come every year everyone gets younger except us," Parlee said to Colton, five feet to his right, throwing grounders to Clay.

"You just figuring that shit out?"

"Let's get this show on the road," hollered Deke as he went to the dugout steps to grab the bucket of balls left by Schmidty. He walked the bucket toward home plate. Two Plymouth guys who had jogged down the left field line a ways came back with an L-shaped screen that was stowed near the cyclone fence. They placed the L-screen about five feet in front of home plate.

"Right handed or left handed?" one of them said to Deke.

"I'm a righty,"

The two positioned the screen and Deke dumped the bucket of balls behind it.

"Who's up?"

"I'll hit first," a smallish, gangly kid, no more than nineteen walked a bat with a thick handle toward the front of the grandstand.

"I'm Deke."

"I'm Scott," the kid said. It was as if his hands wouldn't go all the way around the grip of the bat. "Whole team calls me Scooter. I'm hitting .292 this year."

"We'll see about that Scott," Deke said as he grabbed and kicked at the L-screen to square it up with the imaginary home plate in front of the grandstand and its chicken wire netting.

Parlee came jogging toward Deke, three balls in his glove. He caught Deke's glance and rolled his eyes. Parlee dropped the balls at the base of the L-screen and they both shuffled their feet, kicking the stray balls into the screen while each looked down.

"Jesus Christ," Deke said softly. "Schmidty give us the Legion team? You look at some of these guys?"

"We'll be all right. We know Heidi and Krohner can hit," Parlee said. "Any of these guys we don't know come up, work them a little so we can get a look at their swings."

Parlee started jogging out to right, picking up stray balls as he went and rolling them toward Deke. He had his back to home plate and was almost onto the infield dirt when he heard the crack of the bat.

"Lookout!" someone shouted from the dugout.

Parlee heard the buzzing of a ball with loose stitches zing over his head and land at the outfield lip then skip out toward right. Parlee turned and looked at Deke.

"Heads up, I think he goes that way,"

Parlee looked in at little Scooter. He choked up on the thick-handled bat about four inches above the nob. He faced Deke with a closed stance, his hands hung out over the glove he'd dropped at his feet to serve as a plate. He reminded Parlee of Pittsburg shortstop Ducky Schofield.

"I guess with that stance he has no other choice." Parlee said to Deke.

Scooter took Deke's next offering and buzzed it off the L-screen, level with Deke's knees. Parlee was still back pedaling on the infield dirt when he casually reached up to catch one of Scooter's soft liners in the Nokona and rolled the ball back to Deke's feet. Parlee knew Scooter wanted to line one over his head in the worst way. Parlee wasn't too far out on the outfield grass when he figured he was out of range and turned his back to the infield and jogged toward the outfield fence.

He sprinted hard the final fifty feet to the fence and not once looked back when he heard the crack of the self-proclaimed .292 hitter's bat. He pushed against the fence to stretch his calves and walked about twenty feet back onto the outfield grass from the warning track. There he sat and did some stretches while surveying the park.

Parlee loved six o'clock starts on a diamond like this, in a town like Plymouth – still small but large enough to get a lot of fans to the park. It was going to be calm and still. The sun was still hanging about three hours before dusk. The nice, warm evening would be inviting for a good crowd that, at about game time, would be settling into the grandstand after Friday night fish fry and a handful of Brandy Old Fashions, wanting a good show out of their Flames

There was a little more activity in the grandstand and the boys from Sparta began bobbing in the first base dugout. Scooter finally finished up hitting. About nine or ten balls lay on the edge of the right field grass, one hundred fifty feet or so in front of where Parlee stretched.

Deke pitched to three more Plymouth guys before Parlee saw Clay had grabbed a bat and was swinging it near the dugout. The best of the three was Heidi who squared up about half of Deke's pitches and drove several up the left-center gap to the warning track.

Clay stepped in against Deke and the ball hitting the bat made a whole different sound. It was a resounding crack of authority. Clay shot hard liners from the left field line to the right-center gap, each time sending a reverberating smack that echoed off the empty grandstand seats. The Plymouth guys shagging on that side of the outfield, at once, were made busy chasing balls that skipped fast on the outfield grass toward the fence. Clay broke up their buddy conversations and put them to work. Clay hit deep drives to the warning track and sent three over the left field wall.

Parlee could see that with each hard crack of Clay's bat, the few fans getting themselves settled in the grandstand stopped what they were doing to watch Clay hit. The six guys playing catch in front of the Sparta dugout all paused their throwing to see what they faced.

When Clay finished, Colton strode up to hit from the right side. Parlee got up from stretching as Colton bunted the first three offers. He sprinted to a spot medium-deep in the right-center gap. On Colton's first swing the ball was rocketed on a line toward Parlee. The slicing line drive came out the size of a pea and Parlee tracked it as the ball became larger and smacked into his Nokona, chest high. He didn't have to move one step. Colton's next swing sent one the same depth into the left-center gap – this time the ball hooking.

Parlee had moved close to Scooter and Heidi, could hear their conversation. Heidi was sitting on the grass, stretching, and Scooter appeared anxious to run down Colton's next drive.

"Man, these guys can hit," Scooter said. "Where'd Schmidty come up with them?"

"Ashippun," Heidi said. "Wait 'til you see the guy throwing hit. I think Schmidty went to college with one of them."

"I thought a couple of them looked older. Where the hell is Ashippun?"

Parlee sprinted to the right field line to cut off a hard grounder Colton sent that way. He scooped up the ball on the run and began sprinting into the infield, across the diamond behind Deke. He stooped to grab several balls and guided them to the L-screen, all the while keeping an eye on Colton in case he sent one his way.

Parlee went down the dugout steps and put the Nokona on his bag. One of the Plymouth players who had already hit relieved Deke and he and Colton came toward the dugout.

"Nice swinging, as always," Deke said.

"Felt pretty good," Colton said. "I think not playing last night actually helped. I'm sure as hell not as sore as I usually am."

"You know what it means when you feel better by not playing, don't ya?" Deke, grabbing a bat.

"It's time to retire?"

"Yep, getting old aint for pussies," said Deke as he turned a bat in his hands and started swinging. "Man I gotta get up there and hit, you mind? Its pitching that's for pussies."

"Go ahead, I need a couple," Parlee said

Colton grabbed his glove and jogged out toward second base where he slickly fielded a couple grounders hit by the last of the Plymouth guys. He took throws from the outfield and rolled the balls into the L-screen.

Parlee reached into the side pocket of his duffel bag and pulled out two pieces of Bazooka bubble gum, unwrapped them, set the comics aside for later and popped the hard gum into his mouth. He began chewing hard as he watched Deke bunt three pitches. Parlee wished they were in the first base dugout with Deke up, especially with him swinging from back by the grandstand. Parlee got up, grabbed a bat and came back to his seat with the pine tar rag, all the while working the gum in his mouth.

He started rubbing the bat handle with the sticky, black rag. The tar had put a black blotch on the bill of every cap Parlee had owned after it smeared on his hands and his hands adjusted his cap. Deke had hit a couple of deep drives to left and Parlee continued to keep a keen eye. On his third swing, Deke turned his quick wrists and hips on the ball and sent it whistling toward the third base dugout, right at Parlee.

Parlee hit the dugout floor and could hear the ball smack into someone's water thermos that was on the shelf behind the bench. The top exploded off the thermos and the ball caromed twice more off the dugout wall and ceiling before bouncing out toward the field.

As Parlee lay on the floor he grabbed a white towel off someone's bag and kneeled to wave it as a truce flag out of the dugout. Parlee could hear laughter from the outfield and looked across the diamond to see the Sparta guys laughing and pointing.

"Goddamn you Deke," Parlee yelled. "Get some lift on the ball, you don't want to hit weak grounders all night."

"Whatever you say, Skip."

Parlee settled back down on the bench as Deke stroked four liners out to left. He reached into the duffel bag and brought out a leather pouch with a draw string. Parlee took the gum out of his mouth and pancaked it on the top of his pant leg. Parlee pulled the draw string to open the pouch he figured could be nearing one hundred years old. Parlee reached in and pinched a good amount of Applejack leaf tobacco and placed it on the flattened gum.

Parlee folded the gum over the tobacco and placed the concoction inside the right cheek of his mouth. Now he was ready to play, knowing full well that by the third inning, that gum and tobacco mixture will form something of a juicy rubber ball to be worked around in his mouth to the slow rhythm of the game, exploding occasionally in a stream of spit the same way the game is certain to flare up on each big hit, strikeout, snared liner or high drive over the fence.

Deke lost five balls in all during his at-bat. Two were long, hooking drives foul that hit the parking lot asphalt and skipped down the street, out of site. Two others were howitzer shots that everyone in the park stopped to watch until each disappeared well beyond the left field fence. The last high drive grazed off the light standard in left, far above a yellow homerun line before ricocheting out of sight beyond the fence.

As Parlee went to take his cuts, he saw a familiar gate shamble down the grandstand steps.

"Still got these guys playing old man?" Schmidty, about twenty pounds heavier than last year, carefully took the short aisle steps one at a time. "When are you guys giving up the life?"

"Hey Schmidty, good to see ya. Be right up, I'm the last to hit."

Schmidty seemed relieved to be able to stop and take a seat about six rows up. Schmidty had been the best catcher in the State University Conference during his days at La Crosse. A hard collision at the plate his senior year tore up his knee and kept Schmidty out of pro ball. He came back to his hometown to play with and run the Flames, guiding them to becoming a major force in the Lakes League. Parlee couldn't remember how many titles the Flames won with Schmidty catching, hitting fourth and making out the lineup. But it was a few.

Schmidty was a couple years ahead of Parlee at La Crosse and stayed in the program as an assistant coach for two spring seasons after he got hurt. He spent his summers on the diamonds of Coulee

Region baseball and in La Crosse taverns before coming home to Plymouth. He and Parlee played a summer together on the team from Bangor, a small road dot east of La Crosse that prided itself with the town ball teams it fielded each summer with the help of a handful of college players.

Schmidty was fond of telling the home folk he did his knee rehab on a La Crosse barstool, all the while turning himself into a local baseball legend. For years Schmidty was one of the best catchers and hitters in the Lakes League. He eventually submitted to the grinding pain in his knees and stopped playing about five years ago. The agonizing process was no doubt hastened by Schimdty's large appetites for life in general and food and drink in particular.

When some guys finally give up the game, Parlee had observed, they feel compelled to leave their spikes, glove or some other piece of their baseball past out on the diamond or in the dugout somewhere after their final game. Addie Pruefer's hat hung in the Jefferson dugout for several years after his last game there. Parlee played centerfield behind Shorty Kuehl during his last season and game in Neosho a few years back. Shorty, a six-foot, four-inch rangy lefty, pitched for Neosho for fifteen years and was pushing forty when he took off his spikes for the last time. By the time Shorty was thirty, he'd lost whatever fastball he might have had and relied on a creative array of well-placed deception to get hitters out. After his final game, a 5-3 loss to Rubicon of no consequence, Shorty tied his spikes together with the laces and left them out on the pitching rubber. The Neosho diamond was carved out of farm land that bordered the west end of the small village of about four hundred people at the confluence of Highway 67 and a large mill pond fed by smallish tributaries of the Rock River. It wasn't much of a baseball facility. There were no lights or dugouts, only wooden benches where the players baked in the sun on hot summer days. The outfield, from center over to the right field foul line, had a dramatic uphill pitch. Shorty's spikes were still on the mound when the snow melted the next spring.

Freddy Lauersdorf, whose family farmed some of the land around the Neosho diamond, was a second baseman for a few years when Parlee played there. Shorty never came to the diamond the next entire season. Not once did he come out to see his old teammates. But Parlee remembered Freddy saying during spring practices of that next year how several times during the winter he'd driven past the diamond on the tractor and there was Shorty, sitting on the home bench, staring out at the snow covered mound.

It was not unlike someone going to a cemetery, Freddy told Parlee, and sit the gravesite of a recently-deceased loved one.

Parlee didn't know if Schmidty left his spikes or catcher's mitt out on the field after his last game. But he was certain that just like Shorty, Schmidty left a big chunk of his heart behind that day.

Parlee threw his glove between the cleat marks left by the right-handed and left-handed hitters before him. He took his left-handed stance and looked out at the Flames batting practice thrower.

"This one of the guys gonna throw this weekend?" Parlee said just loud enough for Schmidty to hear.

"Only in an emergency. Pretty good outfielder."

Parlee dug in, then leaned back and tipped his hat out to the pitcher.

"Parlee," he said.

"I know, I played for Slinger a couple years back."

"Oh shit, you're Drago," Parlee said as he straightened back up, cocked his head and spit some gumbacco juice. "Thought you looked familiar."

"That's me," Drago laughed. "I had to get out of that league, everyone got too familiar with me. Especially your guys."

Parlee dug back in remembering the three-run homer Deke sent out of sight off Drago in a rout a few years back. Parlee thought Drago to be a pretty good player, just not a good pitcher. Parlee bunted the first five pitches and then settled in to get his timing, sending liners to left and liners to right. He especially worked at rolling his wrists on all locations of pitches, trying to pull hard grounders between first and second.

After about fifteen swings, Parlee was satisfied and grabbed up his Nokona and headed toward the dugout. He looked up at Schmidty, told him he'd be right up.

When Parlee came back out of the dugout he had a clean Plymouth jersey in his hand and Schmidty had moved over and down to a third-row seat on the end aisle nearest to the third base dugout. Parlee climbed into the grandstand from the field and shook hands with Schmidty. He sat on the ledge separating the stands from the infield and faced Schmidty. Parlee had his back to the diamond as the Sparta team began taking hitting. He sat on the ledge and leaned back against the chicken wire.

"How is it Schmidty?"

"Same," Schmidty said. "Still tough not playing. I guess it's as good as it's ever going to get again."

"I hear ya, Schmidty," Parlee said as he leaned back and turned his head to spit through the chicken wire. The sweet gum and the harsh tobacco juice were working their magic in his mouth. "I don't know if I could ever just manage. Young guys drive ya nuts. At least while I'm still playing I can try to make 'em be like me, good or bad. Try to teach them some respect."

"What? For their elders? Good luck with that."

"No, not like that. For their teammates. For their opponents. For themselves," Parlee said as he turned to look out at the field. "For the game, I guess. Pisses me off being on the diamond with guys who don't respect the game."

"I know what you mean, but you gotta have the young guys," Schmidty said. "It's their game. The future on the field ain't with guys like you and me. Hell, I was looking around this year and I don't think there's anybody left in our league as old as you and Deke and Colt."

"Same down by us."

"But you guys think nothing of playing last night, jumping in the car, probably gettin' drunker than shit, and driving all the way up here to play with guys you don't know."

"You left out the part where it rained down there last night."

"I don't think I've got one guy on my roster would do that." Schmidty said. "But we do alright. Still drawing good crowds. Should be good this weekend. You know the deal, we win, I'll give ya the prize money. We don't, I gotta give the prize money to some other team."

"Ya, I know, we'll do what we can to get ya a good crowd on Sunday," said Parlee as he turned to take note of a Sparta player, a lefty, drive a ball off the right field fence. "I imagine the big cash prize drew some good teams."

"Shit, I wound up having to go with two diamonds," said Schmidty, puffing his chest. "Got games going over across town. Split it off in two brackets. I'm being told this might be the best amateur tourney in the state this summer. Couple of scouts will be here.

"Got two games after you tonight and start back up at ten Saturday. Got the Blue Ribbons out of Green Bay, Old Styles from La Crosse, Avenue Bar from Madison."

"Avenue Bar? You shittin' me?" Parlee turned to spit again. "Shit they'll have the whole Badger team. We ran into them a couple years back and they had Richter and Rick Reichart and Hackbart. They can play with most minor league teams."

"Those guys are either in the NFL or Reichart's with the Angels," Schmidty said with a half smirk.

"Go ahead and laugh, those are the kind of guys they'll bring."

"I tried to put all the good teams in the other bracket so you won't have to see them until Sunday."

"What, so we can get our asses handed to us in front of a lot of people?"

"I can fudge with the second-place money," Schmidty winked. "Give that to ya, make it worth your while. You got Sparta tonight, probably Sheboygan Saturday afternoon and then most likely Horicon Saturday night to get to the finals."

"We'll make it work." Parlee said. "We got enough pitching?

"You tell me. How's Clay?"

"Clay's as good as anyone we've seen this summer," Parlee looked down past the third base dugout to see one of the Flames warming off a side mound. "Had to use him last night, though. Turk stuck his nose in our shit."

"That dumbass. Game probably didn't matter to anyone except his concession stand," Schmidty said. "I got ya three pretty solid arms

I think. Kid tonight's decent, young. Tries to throw it through the catcher."

Parlee saw two umpires come through a field gate beyond the Sparta dugout. He spit.

"You're gonna be in the dugout aren't ya?"

"I figured I'd better," Schmidty said. "This is a pretty big deal for our young guys. Don't want them to think I'm completely turning the team over to a bunch of guys from a place none of them heard of."

"Even though that's what you're doing," Parlee said. He got up to turn and face the field. "From what I saw during hitting, you probably better lead off Clay, then go me to move him, Colt, Deke, then whatever. Put Clay at short, I'll go to right. . ."

"Colt at second, Deke at third," interrupted Schmidty as he got up to make his way to the field. "Right field? Gettin' old there pardner?"

"If one of your young bucks can't out-run me in the outfield, we're in trouble."

"Ain't the runnin' I worry about," Schmidty started ambling up the steps, his back to Parlee. "It's what they do when they get where they're going that always concerns me."

"See ya in the dugout, Skip," said Parlee as he climbed back onto the field. It was about fifteen minutes before game time. A good crowd was beginning to settle in and the Sparta boys were just finishing up infield. Parlee went back down into the dugout. He put on his Plymouth jersey, a sleeveless gray, button down vest with black lettering to match the long sleeves of Parlee's undershirt. The name "Plymouth" was scripted across the front, mirroring the way the automobile uses it in chrome across the tail fins of its Fury.

CHAPTER 9

Colton was the only player in the dugout with red sleeves.

"No doubt who the ringer is," Parlee said to Colton, who took one last drag off a Lucky before he threw it onto the concrete dugout floor. Scooter was seated next to Deke and stared at the smoldering butt as if a great debate was raging in his head on the merits of him coming off the bench to step it out.

Parlee finally noticed that Scooter, unbeknownst to him, had a Bazooka blown bubble perched on the top of his hat. It was the size of a tennis ball.

Deke looked at Parlee and grinned. Parlee saw one of the umpires walking toward home plate with two new baseballs provided by the Sparta boys. Parlee grabbed the two new balls Schmidty must have left with the clean jerseys and handed them toward Scooter.

"Hey Scooter, the ump's coming for the new balls, hop out and get them to him before he gets here," Parlee said. "Maybe he'll give us a call."

"Go get 'em, Scott," Deke said.

Scooter gave an excited smile, grabbed the balls and stepped on the smoke before heading up the dugout steps. He walked toward the umpire with an authoritative stride, the bubble still perched atop his cap.

"You gotta be shittin' me," said Deke, nudging Colton "Look at this shit."

"Hey look at Scooter!" Heidi yelled. "That's beautiful, who did that?"

Schmidty was just getting to the dugout steps. He and everyone in the dugout turned to look toward home plate. All the Flames began to hoot and laugh. Guffaws could be heard coming from the grandstand. Some of the Sparta players were smiling and pointing in Scooter's direction.

The umpire took the balls from Scooter and leaned in to say

something. Scooter turned and walked quickly back to the dugout with a bewildered look on his face as he first glanced up into the laughing faces in the grandstand and then those of his teammates. Schmidty stopped him at the top of the dugout.

"What'd the ump have to say tonight?"

"He said somebody's playing a joke on me."

Schmidty reached and grabbed the bill of Scooter's cap. He raised it off Scooter's head and then slowly lowered it in front of his eyes. Scooter was finally in on the joke.

"You bunch of assholes!" he said grabbing the hat from Schmidty with one hand and taking the gum bubble with the other. He spiked the gum on the ground outside the dugout.

The dugout again exploded in laughter and Scooter came down the steps, his teammates tossing gum wrappers, crumpled paper cups and little balls of athletic tape in his direction.

Scooter returned to his spot next to Deke.

"What do ya say you get a couple hits tonight, Scooter?" Deke said.

Scooter finally broke into a smile and shook his head up and down in a gleeful gesture of assent.

Schmidty read off the lineup from the top of the dugout steps and sent the team out to the field. Schmidty not only made sure the Flames had a favorable draw, but also secured the home advantage, at least for the first game.

Parlee half-sprinted out to right feeling a pretty good spring in his step. He turned to view the infield and stands to see the grandstand behind home plate filling in nicely. The bleachers down each line were starting to crowd up as well and Parlee thought Schmidty should be pleased. Clay threw a strike to first from the hole at short and Krohner tossed grounders to Colton and Deke.

Parlee heard a whistle from his right where Scooter was poised to lob a warm-up ball. Scooter let go a high pop up back toward the fence that Parlee glided under and caught, returning a hard throw on a line to Scooter. He turned and lobbed a pop-fly throw to Drago in left.

Heidi was behind the plate, receiving throws from a strong right hander named Whitehouse. His Flames teammates naturally called him Whitey. Parlee wondered what Deke might be calling him, at least until he marks his first strikeout. "Outhouse" was a good bet and Parlee chuckled to himself.

Parlee counted four guys in the dugout with Schmidty and wondered if any of them were pissed to have had to give up their opportunity to play in front of a nice, big tournament Friday night crowd to four strangers from Southern Dodge County.

Heidi threw the ball down to Colton at second and it went around the horn with three more slaps of leather as the ump deliberately walked in front of the plate, turned his back to the mound and bent at the waist to sweep the plate with a stubby whisk broom. He stood, circled behind a crouching Heidi and pointed out to Whitey.

The infield chatter began in earnest as Whitey set himself on the mound for the evening's first delivery. It was a knee-high fastball strike to Sparta's right-handed leadoff hitter. The crowd responded with a rousing cheer.

It seemed to Parlee that Whitey threw with good velocity. Whitey backed up that notion on the first two batters. The leadoff hitter grounded weakly to Colton and then the number two hitter, a lefty, also had a defensive swing to ground out to Clay. Whitey struck out the three hitter on a 2-2 fast ball. The crowd cheered and urged the Flames to get some runs as they ran toward the dugout.

By the time Parlee got to the dugout and tossed the Nokona on the shelf behind the bench, Clay was already on the on-deck circle swinging a bat. Parlee stepped down into the dugout, grabbed his bat and tried on a helmet. He popped back out of the dugout and joined Clay at the circle, grabbing the tar rag from him. They both looked back to see Colton and Deke swinging bats at the top of the dugout.

"Feels like home," Clay said. "Too bad we ain't splitting this gate."

"No shit," Parlee said. "I love playing up here. Let's give 'em a show.

"Listen, same as always. You get on I'll take two pitches, you get your ass to second. You get there, I'll just try. . ."

"Yeah, I got it," Clay interrupted. "You'll try to shoot a grounder toward right, get me to third."

"Get after him."

Clay strolled toward the plate and Parlee first realized there was no PA announcer. The home crowd, unfamiliar with its own leadoff hitter, didn't know what to say.

"C'mon thirteen!" someone finally yelled. "Get a hit!"

Parlee tossed the tar rag back toward the fence and looked at Schmidty.

"No announcer tonight?"

"Had to work late, we usually start at seven thirty." Schmidty said. "He'll get here."

"What kind of a horse shit tournsament you runnin'?"

"Blow me."

As Clay stepped into the right handed batter's box, Parlee settled into his stance near the fence. Parlee started his swing as he cocked his head and spit a stream of brown juice. He swung the bat through the juice, coating the barrel with slippery goo.

Now he felt ready to hit.

Clay took two pitches off the three-quarter righty. The first was some kind off an off-speed pitch that didn't appear to move, missing the outside corner about belt high. The second pitch was a very hittable fast ball that crossed the plate at thigh level. Whatever the third pitch was called, Clay turned it right back where it came from, lining a seed over the pitcher's head and into center field.

The crowd cheered as Clay took a wide turn at first before retreating to the bag.

"C'mon Parlee move him around!" Parlee heard his name from a couple places in the grandstand, Flames faithful who must have recognized him from past years.

Parlee dug into the left-handed batter's box and looked to the third base coach he didn't know. It was only then he also realized he didn't know the signs, a pregame detail that must have gotten lost in Scooter's gum incident. The kid in the third base coaching box was one of the bench guys and he went through a long gyration of signs, touching himself here and there with such speed and veracity that the meaning would be lost on even the longest tenured regular Flames player. He concluded the barrage of secrets with a deliberate grip of the bill of his cap followed by a demonstrative swipe across his chest from left shoulder to right.

Parlee called time and stepped out of the box, pretending to wipe a speck of dirt from his eye. He stepped back and looked up at the umpire, saying under his breath "I think whatever in hell he was telling us to do, he just wiped away."

Parlee looked down at Clay who was staring across the diamond with a dumbfounded look equal to Parlee's. Parlee faced Clay and grabbed the bill of his hat. Clay responded by doing the same.

"Now we're set," said Parlee as he dug back into the box. He heard the umpire chuckle.

The pitcher came off his stretch to deliver the same off-speed pitch he threw to open the game, missing the strike zone at the same spot, inside to Parlee. Parlee acted ready for the next pitch at which he had no intention of swinging. The pitcher came set, gave a quick glance at Clay, and delivered.

Clay bolted for second on the pitcher's first move. Parlee took a thigh-high fastball for a strike and the catcher snapped a throw toward second that Parlee felt whiz past his helmet. Clay slid safely into second as the second baseman took a high throw and didn't even bother to swipe a tag toward the base.

"Sumbitch can run," the catcher muttered as he replaced his mask and regained his crouch behind the plate.

"Bring him around Parlee!" A shout from the grandstand as the applause died down.

Parlee was pretty sure he knew what was coming next. He sat fastball even though Clay's hand didn't go up as he took his lead from second. So he patiently stayed off an off-speed pitch that again missed inside. This time when Clay took his lead he extended his right arm parallel to the ground as he inched toward third. Parlee got his fastball on the next pitch, rolled his wrists as he swung, jerked his hips open and shot a bounding grounder to the right side.

Parlee got more of it than he first thought and the ball zipped between the first and second basemen and out into right field. Parlee knew Clay would have no problem scoring and was surprised when the right fielder charged the ball, gathered it off the grass and fired toward the plate. When Parlee saw that the first baseman had no chance of cutting the ball, he clipped the bag hard at first and lit out for second. Parlee slid safely into second without a throw as the catcher went to his knees up the third baseline to block the ball.

The crowd cheered its excited satisfaction, so loud, it was, that Parlee couldn't hear what the angry catcher was yelling toward the right fielder as he pointed to the first baseman and walked the ball to the mound. No interpretation needed. Parlee had delivered that lecture with increasing frequency in recent years and he gave a sarcastic and satisfied chuckle only he heard as he slapped the dirt off his pants and took his lead when Colton stepped into the batter's box.

The catcher was still seething from the outfielder's throw that allowed Parlee to take second when he quickly and deliberately put down one finger as the pitcher and Parlee leered in at the sign. Parlee extended his lead by another step and held out his right arm for Colton to see. The pitcher set in his stretch, looked back at Parlee and delivered the fast ball Parlee, and now Colton, knew was coming.

The ball came to the plate about thigh-high to Colton, and his quick swing shot a liner up the right-center gap that Parlee could see was slicing away from the centerfielder. With no need to hurry, Parlee waited to make sure the ball hit the ground before turning to run at not quite a full sprint toward third. As he rounded third and headed home, Parlee turned to see Colton hit the bag at first and make toward second, his body upright, spine arched and shoulders back, the same way Colton has run on every double he'd ever hit.

Parlee touched the plate with the Flames second run as the crowd delighted in their home-town out-of-towners. Deke came toward the plate and slapped at Parlee's hand.

"Sit fastball second pitch and try not to hit it into the fucking dugout," Parlee said.

"Whatever you say, Skip."

Parlee went down the dugout steps, taking in the congratulations of the young Flames. He took a seat down at the end of the bench by Clay.

"Nice job," Clay said as the pitcher missed with an off-speed pitch to Deke.

"You got the catcher so rattled he forgot to change up the signs when you got to second" Parlee said. "Then the right fielder got him so pissed he forgot again."

"If he even knows," said Clay as he wiped his face with a towel.

"Watch this," Parlee said.

The Sparta pitcher delivered and Deke timed up the thigh-high fastball and sent it high and deep over the left field fence. The crowd gasped and breathlessly gave out an "oooh" before erupting into a unison cheer when the ball cleared the fence, disappearing about ten feet behind the 355-foot sign. Deke took his time around the bases and was greeted at the plate by Colton. The Flames emptied the dugout and greeted Deke as he turned away from home plate. Scooter was at the head of the line.

The Sparta pitcher took a seat trailing by four without getting an out. A tall lefty came in and held the Flames in check the rest of the game by mixing a decent fastball with a slider and big curve that gave fits to the Flames' three left handed hitters, Parlee included. The Flames couldn't cash in a couple of opportunities, including a two-out double by Clay in the fourth. Parlee ended that inning by popping to short on a weak swing.

The Flames finally got their fifth run in the seventh when Scooter walked, stole second, went to third on a grounder and scored on a deep sacrifice fly to left by Clay.

Staked to an early lead, Whitey cruised easily, relying almost exclusively on his fastball. He allowed a run in the third when he walked two. He pitched himself into a little more trouble in the eighth when he hit a batter and walked two more to load the bases with one out. But Colton made a pretty good play to grab a bouncer up the middle. With a four-run lead Colton made sure to carefully feed Clay coming toward the bag, expecting just to get one out. But Clay came across the bag so quickly and unleashed a dart to Krohn at first that he doubled up the speedy batter. The crowd loved the play and it preserved a 5-1 win for the Flames.

From his vantage point in right, Parlee guessed that the crowd had reached about seven hundred by the fourth inning. A good portion of the crowd missed the first inning fireworks. Parlee figured that those who saw Deke's homer no doubt added at least fifty feet to its travels when they let the late-arrivals know what they had missed.

After shaking hands with the Sparta team, Schmidty reminded the Flames they'd play again at two o'clock Saturday, followed by an eight o'clock game to get into Sunday's finals. Parlee, Deke, Clay and Colton quickly gathered up their gear to make room for the next game and to get over to the beer tent.

"What's your average now Scooter?" Deke said to his newest fan.

"I was one-for-three plus a walk," Scooter smiled. "Still .292."

"What's your average with gum on your hat?"

Heidi flashed a smile at Deke and pushed Scooter's cap down over his face.

Schmidty walked down toward the Ashippun boys to say thanks for the win.

"It was your guy who pitched a hell of a game," Colton said.

"I assume you guys are sticking around."

"It's either here or the Trail's End," Parlee said. "You assume correctly."

"I got someone wants to talk to you."

The four turned toward the gate with their equipment as some of the Sheboygan players hovered on the field, waiting to get into the dugout. Parlee led the way back to the Impala. They stowed the equipment, Parlee emptied his mouth of the remnant of his chaw and the four readied to head around the stadium to the beer tent. Colton leaned against the rear tail fin of the Impala and lit a cigarette. Parlee appreciated the set up in Plymouth that allowed people to come and go to watch the game being played or mingle in the tent. Most the town came out on Friday night for the beer tent, band and baseball. They treated their Flames like celebrities and Parlee couldn't help but notice that all the younger players kept on their Plymouth jerseys so they'd be recognized, especially, they preferred, by the young girls.

CHAPTER 10

First time I ever played with the coloreds was down in Cuba with Teddy and the Rough Riders. Damned awful place, temperature like nothin' anybody'd ever seen. Humid, skeeters, malaria. We played anyway, keep the morale up. At least the ones who weren't in the infirmary tent shitting the bed would play. They weren't that many of us down there to begin with. The big mustering hadn't come in yet after the Maine blew up. Everbody on edge. We just kept playing amongst ourselves over and over. One Sunday this bunch of colored plantation workers showed up wanting to play. They'd learned their own version of the game one way or 'nother and come wanting to play. Least that's what the guys who spoke Spanish said they was saying. Our company, what was healthy, was divided on the idea. Half didn't wanna play with no negras, the other half wanted to play against anyone different than who'd they been playin'. We played. Ones who didn't want to be with the Negras went back to the barracks tents.

They played different than us, them colored fellas did. Never seen a bunch have so much fun than them fellas. We couldn't understand anything they was saying, but it was about the most joyous chatter I can ever remember hearing. Some of our guys tried to get rough with 'em. Hittin' 'em at bat, sliding hard into 'em in the field. Didn't matter to them, they just thought that was how we played. All us white fellas we always played so business-like no matter where I've played. These colored fellas played with a joy and happiness the likes I ain't never seen since. They celebrated everything.

Seemed like there wadn't a ball that went up in the air that didn't get caught. And their infielders had the quickest hands and feet we'd ever seen. Most of 'em were bean poles, like they didn't get 'nuf to eat. But they could run and throw better'n any of us. What they couldn't do was hit. The bats they brung were just skinny sticks and our older guys wouldn't let 'em use our'n. "Ain't no negra gonna touch my Hickory." What they had that was better'n us was a ball. They had a ball wound real nice and tight that had some sort of leather cover stitched over it. That ball flew a long ways when it met up with one of the Hickories. After the game, one of their players showed our grub sergeant -- he was the one what dressed the hides from the cattle we'd slaughter for food -- he showed him how to cover a ball wound with hemp or twine or what have ya. After that we always had a good ball to play with.

Another one of their players had seen the cuts and scrapes I had on my arms and knees from slidin' and divin' on that rough infield. He led me off to the bush of the jungle and found me an Aloe plant and showed me how to break it open and use the sticky juice to treat the sores.

Couldn't tell ya who won that day, but I'll never forget the feelin' we all had after treating those fellas so mean and poorly to begin with and then the kindness they showed us afterward.

***

The four at the Impala were the only Flames who had peeled off their dirty jerseys. The parking lot around the beer tent was cordoned off with a snow fence. Picnic tables instead of cars were parked inside the fence. Off to the left near the stadium were a food stand and a separate stand that sold beer. The beer stand was simply a series 55-gallon drums connected by scrap lumber for a make-shift counter. Members of the Plymouth fire department were behind the counter, pulling cans of Pabst, Blatz and Schlitz that bobbed in galvanized cow tanks half full of water and large blocks of ice. From the back pocket of his ball pants, Parlee pulled the envelope the Turk had given him Thursday night.

"Who wants to make a run?" said Parlee as he separated out seven dollar bills. "I gotta catch up with Schmidty."

"I'll go," said Clay, grabbing the ones. "But that's too much."

Parlee looked at the sign posted behind the beer stand to see a can of beer was fifty cents. He dug three more bucks out of the envelope to make an even ten.

"Keep 'em coming 'til that dries up."

Clay set out for the beer stand as Deke, Colton and Parlee surveyed the small town doings.

The band was tuning up under the tent. Three guys with guitars plus a drummer. People were starting to congregate around picnic tables. Three of the younger Flames players were at one table talking to a gaggle of five young women that Parlee didn't think were even eighteen let alone old enough to be in the beer tent.

"Clay's gonna have to watch his ass tonight," Colton said. "A lot of jail bait."

"What about me?" Deke said.

"Cops would never buy it," Colton said. "Probably write you a commendation for your effort."

"Either that or a lifetime service award," responded Deke as he nodded Parlee toward a table where sat Schmidty and two guys he didn't recognize. The older of the two was about forty-five and wore a light zippered jacket and a baseball hat with a scripted "WR" on front. The younger of the two looked to be in his early thirties or late twenties and sported a pull over jacket and the same hat as the older man. The hat was much newer and he looked as if he could have just taken hitting.

"If I'm not mistaken, those are baseball guys," Parlee said. "I'll be right back."

Just as Parlee took a step, Clay got back with four beers clamped together in his hands, two Pabst and two Schlitz. Parlee grabbed a Schlitz and headed over to Schmidty's table. As Parlee approached, Schmidty stood to make introductions.

"Parlee, this is Jack Shepherd," Schmidty said as he swept his hand toward the older of the two. "And this is Barry Frietag."

Parlee shook hands with each, circled the picnic table and straddled the bench, facing his Ashippun crew. He drew an opener from his back pocket and opened the beer.

"So you're the ring leader of the Ashippun gang, Schmidty tells me," Shepherd said.

"I don't know if I'm the ring leader but I make out the line up and get bitched at if we run out of beer."

"Brother I've been there and back," said Shepherd, sipping a bottle of Coke. "I been with the Twins since before the Griffith family moved us west from Washington. Barry, here, just got done playing last year and joined our scouting staff."

"Glad you guys could make it, there's some pretty good talent here this weekend," said Parlee, glancing at Schmidty. "I know it's more than I bargained for.

"You lookin' for someone to manage the big club?" Parlee took a gulp of beer and reached around to his hip pocket again, this time to grab his tobacco pouch. He set it on the table. "I got the whole summer off."

Shepherd and Frietag laughed and watched as Parlee pulled on the rawhide draw strings of the pouch and reach in for a chew of leafy, brown tobacco.

"Not my department," Shepherd said. "Sammy Melee's got them in first place so I'm not sure we'd be taking applications. Hey, that is an interesting pouch, you mind?"

Shepherd picked up the pouch and held it in both hands, feeling its suppleness.

"What the hell is this?" He passed it to Frietag who handled the pouch as if it were made of fine lace.

"It's from the bladder of a really long-dead buffalo."

"You're shitting me."

"There's a story there but I'd be certain you don't have time to hear it."

"You're probably right," Shepherd said. "We got to get in and catch some of the next game. But I wanted to ask you about the Mize kid. We're here looking at four or five guys and he's one of them.

"You probably know about our team in Rapids," said Shepherd as he again picked up the pouch and fingered its uniquely smooth texture.

"Yeah, I've played up at the park in Wisconsin Rapids."

"What you might not know is that Rapids is just one of five single

A teams we have now." Shepherd appeared to have ended his fascination with the pouch and pushed it back toward Parlee. "We've had a lot of movement in our organization in recent weeks. Guys getting hurt at higher levels. Guys moving up, guys getting cut, guys giving it up. Always happens this time of year. We're looking for some warm bodies to fill in the Rapids roster."

"You think Clay might fit the bill," Parlee said, working the fresh chaw in his mouth.

"We've heard good things about him from people who've seen him play in the Rock," Shepherd said. "What we saw tonight backs that up. We hear he's also throwing the ball well."

"I think he's the best player in the Rock," Parlee said. "He might have been the best pitcher in the league last year. He came back this year with a fork ball he commands real well. Now there's no doubt he's the best pitcher in the league."

"You're going to throw him sometime tomorrow I assume?"

"That's the plan. Thing is, he didn't come in this weekend with a fresh arm. Had to use him last night during a league game."

"Whose dumbass idea was that?" Shepherd looked astonished. "Unless you draw bigger crowds than this for your weeknight games."

"Sure as hell wasn't my idea."

"What's his home life like?"

"Comes from an athletic family in Janesville," Parlee said. "Dad played football at Northwestern before the war. Clay and his older brother were both war babies while the dad was in the Pacific. So the mom's kind of a doter.

"The older brother was a better athlete than Clay," Parlee said as he looked over where some of the younger Flames were starting to congregate with Clay, Deke and Colton. "Looked like he was going to play football at Wisconsin. Summer of his senior year in high school he was swinging off a rope at a swimming hole in Janesville and wrecked his knee. His ma had the goddamn tree cut down. Pissed off every other kid Janesville."

"Clay is what? Twenty, twenty-one?"

"Twenty-one," Parlee said as he spit off to one side. "He won't be overmatched at Rapids or where ever you put him. He's the real deal."

"We're looking for local guys that can come on board right away," Shepherd explained. "Thing is, Rapids is A ball but they're a bunch of older guys for that level. Guys are all twenty-two, twenty-three, twenty-four years old. Some of 'em been in pro ball for three, four years. He a pretty mature kid for his age?"

Parlee looked over to from where he had come. Four or five of the younger Flames guys had circled Colton, Deke and Clay. One had brought a batting helmet out of which Deke was chugging beer. Deke, beer dripping down his chin and onto his shirt, passed the helmet to Clay. Clay took his turn with the helmet, the Flames players chanting "Go! Go!" Colton was pouring his beer into the up-turned helmet as fast as Clay could slug it down.

Parlee closed his eyes and leaned to spit again, trying not to laugh.

"He's always fit in real well with our older guys," Parlee said.

"The other thing is," Shepherd lowered his voice a bit and spoke into the table. "I never see any negroes when I scout these town ball teams in this state. You get in pro ball and you play with all kinds. Our organization is one of the first to do a lot of recruiting out of the Caribbean. Tony Oliva, Zoilo Versalles. What's his attitude toward those types of people?"

Parlee worked the chaw in his mouth as he looked around the all-white Plymouth beer tent. He tried to remember the last time he played a team that had colored players. Last season they'd run into a team of Puerto Ricans out of Milwaukee but he knew Shepherd was right.

Parlee sipped his beer and began telling Shepherd about their trip the previous spring to the Selma Civil Rights March.

"I'm a high school history teacher," Parlee began. "Last March I took some students to the Selma march. Clay came with."

"You went down to a goddamn race riot with high school kids?" Shepherd was taken back.

"Wasn't quite like that," Parlee said. "The first one in early March was when all the shit happened. This was the one later, the third one when twenty-five thousand people marched to the courthouse in Montgomery."

Parlee had a college buddy who went on to graduate school at Vanderbilt in Nashville and had become a part of the Student Nonviolent Coordinating Committee, one of the groups involved with voting rights in the south, and had helped organize the march. Parlee's buddy, now a professor, wanted white bodies at the event and guaranteed him the march would be safe this time. He convinced Parlee his students would have a rare opportunity to see history being made up close.

"I took three students down," Parlee said. "Just happened to be our spring break. Could have taken at least ten or fifteen more but that's all I could fit in the backseat of my car. School wouldn't have anything to do with it so a bus was out of the question. Our principal just told me I needed another adult to go along and Clay went. It was an eye-opener for all of us."

Schmidty perked up.

"I told you that made the papers up here didn't I?"

"Yeah ya did," Parlee said as he turned back to Shepherd. "The shit hit the fan when we got back and the school board found out. Newspapers made a big deal out of it and I damn near got fired. Only thing that saved my ass was the parents of the students finally spoke up and said it was a great learning thing for their kids."

Shepherd drew a breath and swig of his Coke.

"That's taking the long way around the barn," he said. "But what I'm hearing you say is that this kid won't have any problem using a drinking fountain after a colored."

"That's about right," Parlee said.

Shepherd made some notes and looked at Frietag before turning back to Parlee.

"I just wanted to give you a little courtesy heads-up" said Shepherd as he turned to look behind him at the fracas the Flames were making. One of the local Flames was taking his turn with the helmet. "We're going to make a decision by the end of the day tomorrow. If he agrees to join us, he's ours. He's no longer yours. He probably won't even go home with you. Rapids has a Sunday double-header. We'll take him right over there and plug him in somewhere."

"I think that's great," Parlee said. "Clay's up to any challenge you've got.

"The only thing I'd ask is that you not look at him as a 'warm body,'" Parlee said quietly. "You take a good look at him, pitcher, infielder, outfielder. You give him a fair shake."

"I appreciate that," Shepherd said as he looked at Frietag. "Barry can tell you that once we've got a player, it's pretty much up to him. You perform, you move up. There's not a lot of politics at this level. You either make the most of your opportunity or you don't."

Frietag looked at Parlee then turned to look at Clay.

"My old man's worked for the Griffiths all his life," Frietag said. "That fact might have got me this job but it didn't help me as a player. I worked my ass off for five years but never made it above double A ball. It ain't like I was shitty. But just from what I saw tonight, I was never as good as that kid."

"That makes me feel better," Parlee said. "I want him to have a clean shot."

Shepherd and Frietag stood and shook Parlee's hand. "Like I said, it'll be up to him," Shepherd said. And they worked their way back into the stadium.

Schmidty looked at Parlee.

"That's a pretty neat thing," he said, "having some kid signed off your team."

"It is," Parlee said as he spit a stream of tobacco juice. "It's gonna fuck up the rest of my summer, but that's okay. It's been a long time coming."

Schmidty went behind the food counter to tend to business and Parlee rejoined the Flames. They were standing in a circle, seven in all. A galvanized milk pail of icy water with floating cans of beer sat in the middle of the human orb. Parlee reached in and grabbed two beers.

Clay was outside the circle talking to two of the young girls Parlee thought might not be twenty-one. He tossed a beer to Clay.

"Let's take a walk."

Clay followed Parlee into the stadium. They walked up a concrete tunnel and came out into the stands behind home plate of Sheboygan's game with Norwalk. The grandstands were still pretty full but Parlee and Clay landed in a couple of seats about fifteen rows up.

"I'm thinking you should start the second game tomorrow," Parlee said as he settled in to see that Sheboygan, hitting in the bottom of the second, had a 2-1 lead. He spotted Shepherd and Frietag seated down in the third row behind the screen.

"I told ya I'd pitch every inning but I just assumed you'd save my start for the championship game Sunday," Clay said. "Thought I might close some tomorrow but I'll do whatever, Skip."

"You still might close the first game tomorrow if we need ya," Parlee said. "Thing about Sunday is, you might not be here."

"Where the hell would I go?"

"Maybe Rapids," said Parlee as he hoisted his beer to raise a toast. "Those guys I was talking to are from the Twins. You're in their line of fire."

Clay's eyes lit the way they do when a hanging breaking ball is heading his way. He took his beer and clanked it with Parlee's.

"You're not bull shittin me are ya?"

"Not on something like that," Parlee pointed down at Shepherd and Frietag. "That's them down there in the third row. Said you were one of four or five guys they were looking at this weekend. I'm pretty sure that if they said something to me, they're pretty serious. Guys like that usually like it better if no one knows they're here."

"Jesus, Parlee this is what I've been wanting. Just when you think no one's paying attention. . ." Clay stopped, excitedly searching for more words. "What'd they ask ya? What'd you tell them?"

"I told them you look clean cut but you're really a part of that whole beatnik revolution and a card-carrying commy on our own old Senator McCarthy's list," Parlee said as he blew out another stream of tobacco juice that pooled on the concrete between his feet. "Told 'em how you like other men, that sort of thing."

"The fuck you did," said Clay, now laughing, relaxed.

Parlee looked down on the field where the game had stopped. The Sheboygan catcher, a young guy, maybe nineteen but tall and strong, had his mask off and was screaming in the face of the home plate umpire. Parlee paused and took note before turning back to Clay.

"You should probably take it easy tonight," Parlee said. They could hear the band start up outside, leading off with a Buddy Holly tune. "You're gonna want to play your best tomorrow so knock off the beer. And stay away from those underage Bangme Sisters out there. Two of them are a dozen. They look like they could keep you up all night."

"I'll be all right."

"Clay, you don't want to screw this up," said Parlee as he grabbed Clay's beer, turned the can upside down and set it top down on the concrete under their seats. Its contents emptied and began running like a waterfall down the grandstand steps.

"You don't want to wind up like me and Deke, thirty some years old, drivin' around drinking beer, chasing games in shit leagues on shit diamonds," Parlee said. "Deke kickin' himself in the ass all the time, wondering what it could have been like.

"Just this one night. A week from now you won't even know you missed anything, especially if they're payin' ya to play."

Clay watched his beer wash away and looked up bright-eyed.

"Gimme a ride?"

"Hell yeah, let me grab a burger and another beer," Parlee said. "See what trouble Deke's getting into and we'll head back."

"Sorry to make ya go early."

"I don't like to over-do it when we have a game the next day," Parlee said. "Suppose to be hot tomorrow. Baseball's a game best played when you're not miserable."

They went out. The parking lot had filled up between the snow fences with seemingly all of Plymouth and the band was at full throat, covering the Beatles' "She Loves You."

"Yeah, yeah, yeah!" Clay yelled with a melodic twang as he bounced ahead of Parlee into the crowd. Parlee broke off and bought two hamburgers and one beer. He corralled Clay and steered him toward an empty table on the outskirts of the fenced-in area where they could sit and look for Deke and Colton.

They ate the burgers and watched the crowd. Parlee reached around to his back pocket for his opener and popped his Schlitz. Clay pointed out Colton. He was by the fence on the far side of the beer corral, thick, horned rim glasses, a beer in one hand, cigarette in the other. Looking at him now wouldn't give any of the young pitchers who might be in the tent any clue that they couldn't get a fast ball by him. Colton was talking to a big guy in a pull-over windbreaker and ball cap. About fortyish. Parlee recognized him to be Bobby Munby, a lefty first baseman with a Duke Snider type swing who'd forever played for West Bend in the Lakes League. Probably still does, Parlee thought.

Parlee was about half way finished with his beer and they'd polished off the hamburgers when he saw Deke come out of the crowd, shuffling with his heels not leaving the ground as he made his way to the beer stand. He bought two beers, turned and walked back toward the crowd. Parlee tried to track Deke through the crowd but lost him. He stood on the bench of the picnic table and tried to pick up Deke.

From his high vantage point, Parlee saw a small clearing in the crowd and Deke came through to it and handed a beer to a woman who looked to be in her late twenties, long, strawberry brown hair she wore down. Parlee realized she was the waitress from the late-morning café breakfast. She wore jeans that rode high and hugged her figure and a sweater that flattered her topside.

"Oh shit," Parlee said.

"What?"

"It's bad enough we might lose you to the Twins," Parlee said as he stepped down from his perch. "We might lose Deke to the twin peaks."

CHAPTER 11

Parlee and Clay got back to the Trail's End at about eleven. When Colton hitched a ride back an hour later, Parlee was sitting in the thick-metal out-door spring rocking chair outside of 8A. Parlee, in a t-shirt and shorts, was sipping the last of the two beers he'd left out with from the beer tent. His thinning hair was wet from the shower over in the Chief's Sweat Lodge and his knee wound was glistening fresh secretions highlighted by the yellow neon lights buzzing at the top of the cabin unit.

Colton had been dropped off by the road and Parlee recognized his gate as he made his way across the driveway. He was still in his ball pants and red sleeves. The ember of his smoke glowed in a right hand that Parlee yet could see, a small red beacon detached from its shadowy carrier.

"Street dance done?" Parlee said as Colton approached.

"Still goin' pretty good." Colton walked into the yellow light and Parlee could see he had a can of Pabst in his left hand. "You guys left early."

"About three beers later than I'd promised Clay," Parlee said.

Colton put the half-burned smoke in his mouth and used his empty hand to drag 8B's metal chair closer to Parlee. The runners of the metal rocker bounced atop the pea gravel that buffered the parking lot's asphalt and the foundation of the cabin. When the chair hit the asphalt, the screeching sound echoed off the quiet homes and trees across Highway 67.

"What news of Deke?" Parlee reached down to the ground to grab his tobacco pouch for one last chaw now that Colton was here. He wouldn't be waiting up for Deke.

"You know that waitress we had this morning?"

"Yeah, I saw him drinking with her. Not a bad looking woman."

"Last I seen of him before I left, he was slow dancing with her," said Colton as he settled into the chair.

"That's some good work."

"Especially since the band was playing 'Rock Around the Clock' at the time," Colton said. "I figured Clay'd be competing with him tonight."

Parlee gave a snort and fit a small chew in his mouth. "You ever get the feeling there's something going on you don't know about?" Parlee leaned back in his chair as he studied Colton, contemplating. "You see those two guys I was talking to after the game?"

"Munby said they were from the Twins." Colton said. "But he's usually so full of shit I never know what to believe."

"They are," Parlee said as he carefully closed up his tobacco pouch and placed it atop his thigh, petting it with his right hand as if it were a sleeping kitten. "I'd be pretty sure they're gonna sign Clay before we start for home Sunday."

Colton's eyes got big and went distant. He paused, took a drag off his Lucky, remembering the day some fifteen years prior when a guy dressed in a suit coat, tie, and bowler hat came up to he and his father after Colton's last high school game at the state tournament and produced a contract form from the Philadelphia A's organization.

"Holy shit." Colton rocked back and forth in the chair, staring into the asphalt driveway.

After a while, Parlee thought he'd break the silence.

"So," he said, pausing, not really wanting to interrupt the nostalgia trip he knew Colton was on. "I've sequestered him. He's sleeping. Or at least he's laying down and not drinking beer and out making little mistake Clays."

Colton shook himself back to the Trail's End. "That's probably a pretty good idea."

Colton took one final drag off his smoke, turned the can of Pabst upside down in his mouth for the last of it, and looked at Parlee with that old twinkle in his eyes that often gets hidden behind his thick glasses.

"We were pretty good tonight, that Plymouth kid can throw.

"Ya know," Colton continued, "I was standing in the beer tent and I heard these guys saying that one of the Plymouth guys hit a four hundred-fifty-foot bomb. That damn thing's gonna be five-fifty by the time we get Deke home."

They laughed, Parlee finished up his beer and let the can fall out of his hand and onto the asphalt. There was more air in the conversation before Colton leaned forward on his chair and pensively steepled his fingers in his lap.

"Here's the other thing Munby told me," Colton said. "Horicon's got a guy since we last played them. Two guys, actually. One's a pitcher who's pretty decent, but they got this other guy who Munby says can mash. Big guy, about thirty. From Moline. Was working down there in the John Deere plant and all of a sudden he's working in the Horicon Deere plant this summer."

"Most their team gets summer jobs at the Deere plant. That's how they keep being good," Parlee said. "Guys will play as long as they're getting a Deere paycheck during the week. This somebody we're supposed to be pissing down our leg about? He play pro ball somewhere?"

"Munby says no one seems to know much of anything about him," said Colton, blowing out the side of his mouth. Parlee could see a hint of smoke. "Said he looks like a professional hitter. He's played six games for them, hit five homers. They're callin' him 'The Marsh Monster.' Guess he hit one up in Brownsville about a hundred feet into the corn off Morgan."

"Yeah, and Deke's went four-fifty tonight," said Parlee, as he looked down at the tobacco juice puddle he'd proffered to the asphalt between his feet. "No matter. It's a poke just to get one out of there and Morgan's always been tough on us."

"I guess we'll find out tomorrow," said Colton as he rose off the chair. "I'm hittin' it. You ain't gonna sit here like the den mother you are waiting for Deke are ya?"

Colton got up and went into 8B. Parlee rocked a little, thinking about Ashippun's soon-to-be deduction and Horicon's addition. He went in 8A and fell asleep to the murmuring of Colton's conversation with Clay.

CHAPTER 12

In the morning, Parlee woke to welcome silence and eventually screwed up enough courage to activate his sore joints and lift his aching body off the bed. He went into the bathroom, came out, brushed his teeth and turned on the TV. He flipped through the three channels before settling on Rocky and Bullwinkle. He lay back down and stared mindlessly at the fluttering picture on the TV, chuckling now and again at the Jay Ward puns. Parlee didn't move when the Ward venue changed from Moose and Squirrel to Hoppity Hooper, set in Foggy Bog, Wisconsin. A place Parlee knew well on mornings like these.

It was about eight-thirty when Parlee went out to grab a Sun Drop. On the way past the office, the woman behind the counter waved him in and handed Parlee a phone message. Deke was at the café. Parlee rousted Colton and Clay and within twenty minutes the three were heading downtown for breakfast. Parlee whistled the theme to Dudley Do-Right as he drove.

They arrived at the café to find Deke half asleep in a booth, a pot of coffee on the table. Colton slid in alongside Deke. Clay and Parlee sat opposite. A waitress unfamiliar to the group brought menus and more coffee.

"Where's your night friend?" Colton asked.

Deke yawned and nodded toward the front of the café.

"She's working the counter." All four heads in the booth shot glances toward the waitress pouring coffee at the counter. At the same moment she peered over at the booth. She stopped her pour to give Deke a look.

"It's a good thing we don't have her," Deke said. "She'd probably pour coffee in our laps. She's a little pissed. I made her late for work. She'd only give me a ride this far."

"So how'd you, ah. . ." a wide-eyed Clay started, "how'd you land her?"

"Wasn't too hard," Deke said. "She came up and said someone told her I hit five hundred-foot homeruns. Then I told her I used to be a smoke jumper."

"A smoke jumper?" Clay, learning by the minute.

"Yeah, told her I was Airborne in Korea, which ain't too far off the truth, and then signed on to be a real live forest fire-fighting smoke jumper in Montana."

"Which is total bullshit," Colton said.

"You use your Pulaski on her?" Parlee asked.

"What?"

"If you're going to use the line," Parlee said, "you'd best brush up on the terminology."

The four ordered and ate their meals with little conversation. No one mentioned the Twins scouts. When he was finished eating Parlee rifled through a fresh *Milwaukee Sentinel*, the big city's morning paper that was left at the counter.

"Braves lost, 5-4," Parlee announced to the table. "Cards got a run in the ninth after Milwaukee got two in the eighth to tie it."

"Who gave it up?" Colton wanted to know.

"Let's see," Parlee said as he scanned the box score. "Looks like Niekro. Walked three and gave up three hits in two and a third."

Parlee saw that Oliver played first and caught and went two- for- three. He didn't say it out loud.

"They had a crowd of ten thousand," Parlee said. "Not bad considering what they usually play in front of."

"I went in about three weeks ago on a Friday," Colton said. "Pittsburg was in. There was just over two thousand people there. Jesus. Upper deck's never open."

"Place is a god damn tomb these days," Parlee, folding up the paper. He grabbed the check, pulled out the Turk envelope and went up to the counter cash register to pay.

Parlee finished up at the register and left a healthy tip on the table. Deke was down the counter having a couple of friendly words with the counter waitress.

"Come on Smokey!" Parlee raised his voice loud enough for most of the patrons to hear and went out.

***

The black Impala wheeled into the Loube Field parking lot just after one. Horicon was finishing up its second win of the tournament, a drubbing of Saukville. The four pulled their gear and game-ripe jerseys from the trunk and lingered behind the third base dugout until the game finished up, Horicon 9, Saukville 2.

Schmidty lumbered across the parking lot from the direction of the beer tent to talk about the lineup and pitching with Parlee.

"You have to use a fire hose to empty the beer tent again?"

"Why, Deke show up all wet this morning?"

The game time temperature pushed 90 degrees and Parlee was happy he didn't stay late the night before. Nonetheless he was pleased there wouldn't be time to expend energy on batting and infield practice.

"Gonna be a long day," Parlee said to Colton as they played catch in front of the dugout. Deke sat at the end of the bench looking like a member of the French Foreign Legion. A wet towel was draped over his head, hat askew on top of the towel. Clay jogged in the outfield, Scooter right on his heels.

After getting three hits and making plays all game long last night, Clay couldn't shake Scooter. He followed Clay around the dugout and field like a spring colt trailing its mother who'd just won the big race.

Heidi warmed a lefty off the side mound and Parlee looked across the diamond to see Sheboygan was also warming a short, stocky left hander. Parlee and Colton stepped down into the dugout and Parlee could tell that Schmidty was agitated about some irritant unseen by any of the Flames. Schmidty took two new baseballs and stomped them out toward home plate where stood the two umpires.

Clay came into the dugout and squeezed on to the bench between Parlee and Colton, leaving Scooter to find a seat down the line.

"What the hell's going on there?" Parlee nodded toward home plate as he opened two pieces of Bazooka. Schmidty was having an animated conversation with the umps, putting a finger in the face of the home plate barrister.

"He's pretty riled up," Colton said.

Deke remained motionless at the end of the dugout, arms crossed, towel still draped over his head. He'd yet to play catch.

"Schmidty was saying the home plate ump is from Sheboygan," said Deke, not moving, looking straight ahead. "Claims the guy used to play there and ran the team."

"Jesus shit," Parlee said to Colton, "I'm getting that feeling again. Something's going on we ain't in on."

"Every time we come here!" Colton yelled from the dugout of the tournament's host team. "Give 'em hell Schmidty!"

The crowd was just settling into the seats behind home plate and began to stir. Schmidty was pounding a fist into an open hand, his head moving side to side as he loudly and angrily made whatever point he thought had to be made.

"You tell 'em, Schmidty!" an elderly voice from the grandstand. Parlee popped the gum in his mouth, reached into his duffel bag for his pouch of Applejack and traded it to the dugout shelf for the Nokona.

"Deke, throw?"

Deke was wiping his face with the towel. He put his hat on proper and fit his hand into his glove.

"That time isn't it?"

Parlee trotted out in front of the home plate side of the dugout. One of the umps was removing his chest protector and dropped it on the ground on top of his mask. He knelt to undo the straps of his shin guards.

The other ump knelt and began strapping on the shin guards. Schmidty walked back to the dugout to a spattering of applause by the crowd. Parlee was pretty certain most of the crowd didn't know why they were clapping. They, like Parlee, knew only that Schmidty just won his argument.

Parlee was tossing the ball back and forth quickly with Deke, working hard on the gum in his mouth.

"What got you so pissed off?" Parlee said as Schmidty arrived back at the dugout.

"That dirty rat bastard," said Schmidty, still fuming. "That's Freddie Klements. He was still managing Sheboygan two years ago. Gave it up to make money umping. And he's a good god damn ump. I hired him to schedule the umps for the tourney and told him he needed to stay away from any Sheboygan game. We show up and he's behind the goddamn plate?"

"He's still going to ump, it looks like," Parlee said.

"Where the hell we gonna find another ump five minutes before game time?" Schmidty barked. "I told him there's no goddamn way he's calling balls and strikes."

"Atta boy, Skip."

Parlee finished throwing with Deke, went down into the dugout and grabbed his pouch, thinking they'd be taking the field.

"We're hitting first," Schmidty announced.

Parlee was surprised but didn't want to further agitate Schmidty by bringing it up. So he nestled the gum chaw, tarred up the bat, grabbed a helmet and went out to the on-deck circle. Clay followed and Parlee could tell he was nervous.

"Just do what you do," Parlee said. "Everything will take care of itself."

Clay tapped the barrel of his bat with Parlee's and walked to the batter's box as the home plate ump hollered "Play ball!"

Parlee turned to scan the crowd. He saw a nice gathering seeking refuge in the grandstand shade from the hot mid-afternoon sun. Parlee spotted Shepherd and Frietag about six rows up, right back of home plate. Their gaze shifted from Clay to Parlee as he swung his bat from right hand to left in the on deck circle. Parlee and the scouts did not acknowledge one another.

Parlee knelt on one knee to the side of the pea gravel on- deck circle, his hand cupping the knob of the bat as he leaned into it. Clay stayed off a first-pitch breaking ball from the stout, short-armed lefty. On the next pitch, Clay sent a hard liner to left for a single.

Parlee stepped in against the lefty not expecting to see a big break in the curve ball he figured was coming. He was right, there wasn't much break to it but the pitch dropped in for a strike. Parlee still thought he'd take one more pitch. But before the lefty delivered he snapped a throw to first. Clay dove back late and the first baseman slapped a hard tag up on Clay's shoulder and then hopped on one leg away from the bag as he held up the ball in his over-sized mitt and looked at the first base ump, whom Parlee thought was most likely the hulking first sacker's former manager.

Good move, Parlee thought. It'd be best not to get the over anxious Clay picked off and called out by an ump that's probably itching to give his old team a hand. So Parlee stepped out of the box to touch his hat and then moved his hand to his belt to show Clay he was going to bunt. The third base coach was probably giving the bunt sign in a different language that Parlee and Clay again failed to learn.

The lefty came set again and Parlee squared, expecting another breaking ball he could easily guide to the ground. Instead he got a good fast ball high in the zone, couldn't adjust in time and fouled the ball straight back on the bunt attempt.

"Shit!" Parlee said as he backed away from the plate to recompose himself.

After two more quick throws to first, Parlee took two more breaking pitches inside to run the count to 2-2. Parlee got jammed when the lefty busted a fastball on his hands and Parlee shot a two-hopper right at the second baseman. The young, lanky Sheboygan infielder took his time in squaring himself to deliver an overhand throw to the shortstop coming across second base. A quick, fluid relay throw, unencumbered by Clay's slide, got Parlee by three steps at first for a double play.

Parlee jogged back to the dugout, helmet in hand as the excited Sheboygan infield snapped the ball around the diamond. Colton ended the inning by hitting a fly to center.

"Fuck, fuck, fuck," Parlee clucked under his breath as he trotted out to right.

The starter for the Flames could easily be mistaken for the Sheboygan pitcher's first cousin. He was also a stocky twenty-five-year-old lefty named Thompson, called "Tommy" by his regular mates and "Mommy" by Deke when he didn't think anyone could hear. Parlee could see from his vantage point in right that Tommy appeared to throw too much with his shoulder to last too far into the game, let alone much past his late twenties for his career. Tommy kept the A's off the base paths through the first three innings, save for a second-inning close play at first when the runner was called safe.

On that play, Deke had used a back-handed snatch to grab a high two-hopper, set himself and threw across the diamond to Krohner. Parlee was running at an angle toward foul ground to back up and didn't get a clear view of the play at first but saw enough to know it was a bang-bang play.

Parlee was surprised when Schmidty stormed out of the dugout on his bad knees to engage the first base ump in a heated exchange that lasted far too long for the play's impact on the game. Tommy got out of the inning by throwing a pop-up to the next hitter. When Parlee got into the dugout he made a point to pass next to Schmidty.

"You got pretty spun up there Skip," Parlee said as he grabbed a bat and headed down the dugout with the pine tar rag.

"I knew this would happen with that bastard," Schmidty snorted. "There's other umps in the park now. I should sit his ass down."

"That's an interesting concept," Colton said to Parlee as they sat down together. Parlee went to work on the bat as the Flames hit in the top of the fourth with a 2-0 lead. Deke and Heidi hit back-to-back doubles to lead off the second for one run and Scooter hustled a second run in the third, scoring on an error after walking and swiping second.

Parlee rubbed the tar rag on the bat as his jaw worked the rubbery chaw in his mouth. He knew the Flames had been just a key hit or two away from blowing the game open.

"We gotta quit leaving guys all over the bases," Parlee said to Colton as he headed out to the on-deck circle after Tommy's bloop single moved Scooter, who drew another walk, from first to third with two out.

"Gotta get at least one out of this Clay," Parlee yelled as Clay made his deliberate walk to the plate. Finishing the thought, Parlee said to himself, "This is where we win it."

Parlee knelt alongside the on-deck circle and glanced back into the stands to find Shepherd and Frietag. The two looked on with the cold indifference Parlee had seen in scouts at other games.

Clay stayed off an outside breaking pitch for ball one and Tommy and Scooter worked an age-old baseball play when Scooter broke down the line from third and Tommy busted toward second. The catcher faked a throw to second and snapped the ball to third to try to get Scooter. Scooter had no intention of stealing home and broke back to third, easily beating the throw. The Flames had runners on second and third and Parlee was certain Sheboygan would intentionally walk Clay. Because it could take the bat away from Clay, Parlee questioned the thinking of the steal.

Parlee was surprised when there was no indication Sheboygan intended to pitch around Clay as the base ump trotted across the infield to reposition his self at first.

The second pitch was a fast ball on which Clay pounced with the meat of the bat, sending a hump-back liner just foul into the left field corner.

"Straighten it out!" An indignant demand came from the grandstand.

Parlee rocked back and forth on his right knee, the bat, its nob cupped under Parlee's right hand, moving in rhythm like a metronome on top of a piano playing a slow waltz. Clay stayed off another breaking ball outside. On the next pitch he timed up the fastball but clipped it foul straight back with a mighty cut. The crowd let out a gasp that explained just how close the swing was from resulting in a three-run homer instead of a second-strike foul.

The cocky catcher stood and held out his right hand expecting the ump to load it with a fresh ball. He held his mitt hand toward the mound and pumped it downward urging caution to his tiring pitcher.

Parlee wondered if the catcher was smart enough to consider two more breaking pitches in the dirt that would, at worst, set up a lefty-on-lefty matchup with the bases loaded. He spit and watched as the lefty threw a low, off-speed pitch that dove toward the dirt behind home plate. Clay leaned into his swing but didn't come close to moving his hands or bat through the hitting zone.

Parlee heard the plate ump call "ball" as the catcher picked the pitch off the dirt. Right in Parlee's line of sight, however, was the first base ump who was pointing toward home plate and, in a fit, made a sweeping fist to ring up Clay.

Parlee came unglued. He shot off his knee to the home plate ump who was holding both hands in the air to kill the play.

"He can't make that call unless you ask him!" Parlee screamed as he bolted toward home plate. Parlee got right in front of the home plate ump, the bill of his cap clipping the ump's mask. "You never asked for help. That's not his call!"

"He made a call," the stunned plate ump tried to explain. Parlee couldn't see the ump's lips moving behind the bars of the mask.

"But that's not his call! He just can't call fucking balls and strikes from the outfield unless you ask for help!" Parlee threw his bat down at the feet of the ump and now the catcher who, instead of retreating into his own dugout with a minor victory, moved closer to the fray. "Jesus Christ!" Parlee screamed. "He can't over-rule you from ninety feet away! For chrissake, the catcher didn't even ask you for an appeal!"

Clay had thrown down his helmet and was screaming toward the ump. None besides curse words were audible. Schmidty had gotten between Clay and home plate, pushing Clay away from Parlee, the ump and the Sheboygan catcher.

"If it makes you feel better," the catcher, in a smart-ass tone voiced in Parlee's direction, "I'd like to appeal that last swing to the first base ump."

Parlee's eyes remained fixed on the ump, just inches away from his mask.

"You'd better tell him he doesn't have a seat at the big table," Parlee said as he pointed toward the catcher. Then he turned to face the young buck. "The adults are talking here!"

"Why you old prick!" the maskless catcher put his mitt into Parlee's left shoulder, grabbed a right handful of Parlee's jersey up around his left collar and heaved. Parlee reeled backward, stumbled but maintained his balance. Colton and Clay both grabbed the catcher but were interrupted in their final intentions when the home plate ump wedged his self between the three. The ump turned to the catcher and let out a growl.

"You're out of here!" he bellowed as his right arm extended toward the sky.

Schmidty stalked toward the base ump who was only then arriving at the disturbance.

"That was a bullshit call and you know it," Schmidty said in a measured, stern voice. "You get your ass off this diamond right now!"

Schmidty turned and walked toward the grandstand, motioning to two men seated in the front row near the Flames dugout. The base ump followed close behind.

"You can't kick me out of a game!" the base ump yelled, trying to be heard over the boos and catcalls cascading from the stands.

Parlee wanted nothing to do with the big catcher so he stood back and watched Schmidty begin a conversation with two guys Parlee figured were to ump the next game. All of the Flames and A's had come out of their dugouts and were congregating around home plate.

Tom Gustafson, the Sheboygan manager, was in a heated conversation with the home plate ump. As he argued, Gustafson kept his back to the catcher, serving as a moving, human fence as he tried to detain the catcher from getting closer to the ump.

As the catcher tried to get through his manager to the ump, Parlee could see Colton holding Clay who was trying to get at the catcher. Every player on both teams shouted and cursed to no one in particular.

Parlee looked for Deke, hoping he hadn't laid out one of the A's. Parlee couldn't see him in the scrum. He turned toward the dugout and there was Deke, seated at the end of the bench, towel draped over his head. He hadn't moved.

Parlee worked his way through the hostile gathering to Colton and Clay.

"Come on, Clay," he said. "You have an audience. Let's get in the dugout."

The three turned in the close quarters and Parlee could feel bodies moving and pushing around him. He could hear the catcher's strained voice repeating "That's bullshit! That's bullshit! That's bullshit!" as if he knew no other words.

Parlee looked down as a mass of entangled bodies all but engulfed the three. Right in front of him, Parlee spied the back of a panted leg that was strapped with a shin guard. Parlee let go with a mouth full of tobacco juice that rained down and painted the back of the catcher's calf in expressionistic styling.

The three cleared the melee and headed toward the dugout. Parlee scanned the crowd and found Shepherd and Frietag looking into the mass at home plate with great amusement. Frietag spotted Parlee, Clay and Colton as they walked toward the dugout and pointed them out to Shepherd. When Shepherd joined Frietag's gaze, Parlee tipped his hat in their direction and offered a full-faced grin.

The three went into the dugout.

"Thanks for helping me out in my hour of need," Parlee said to Deke.

"I figured if you needed help with that big son of a bitch, you'd have called out," Deke continued to look straight out toward the gathering around home plate. Nothing seemed to be happening that would move the disturbance to some sort of resolution. "What the hell is going on, anyway?"

"I think Schmidty kicked the base ump out of the game," Parlee speculated.

"You gotta be shittin' me," Colton said. "I've seen a lot of guys get thrown out but I've never heard of an umpire getting tossed. Can Schmidty do that?"

"It's his tournament," Parlee said. "He can do whatever in the hell he wants."

Order came slowly to the field. The plate ump and Gustafson had escorted the catcher to the Sheboygan dugout and joined Schmidty and the base ump at the grandstand screen where the other two umpires stood at their seats. A lengthy discussion followed.

The excited Flames players returned to the dugout, eagerly recounting bloated stories of what they had just seen, did and should have done. Parlee saw the base ump taking on Schmidty in a heated conversation. One of the umpires who had been watching the game was now on the field.

"What the hell's the hold up?" Deke's gruff voice from under a towel.

"You don't just kick an umpire out of a game without figuring out what comes next," Colton said as he lit a Lucky.

Gustafson had joined the conclave by the screen and after about ten more minutes, it split up. The new ump stayed on the field. The banished base ump huffed off toward the Sheboygan dugout with Gustafson. Sheboygan fans cheered and the Plymouth faithful clapped and whistled. Schmidty came down into the dugout toward Parlee.

"Schmidty, you kick that ump out of the game?" Colton asked.

"I sure as hell did," Schmidty said as the young Flames broke into a loud cheer.

"But here's the deal," Schmidty said as he settled in front of Parlee and leaned against the shoulder-high dugout wall, his back to the field. "We got a different ump and their catcher's gone. Clay's out and the inning's over."

"That's a bunch of shit!" Clay yelled. "I didn't swing at that pitch!"

"I know that, everyone knows that but that was the call on the field before all this other shit," Schmidty looked at Parlee. "One more thing. Gus wouldn't agree to any of this unless one of our guys gets booted, too. Says they won't take the field unless. . . Says that someone's gotta be you."

"What? Me? What the hell did I do besides almost get knocked on my ass?" Parlee couldn't believe what he'd just heard.

"Parlee, look, I'm on uncharted thin ice here trying to kick an ump out of the game," Schmidty said. "Gus knows their guy's an asshole but they won't keep going unless we throw him a bone."

"And he wants me? I'm the pound of flesh?"

"Says you baited his guy."

"Baited?" Parlee surprised, indignant. "It sure as hell didn't take much. The guy's a fucking retard. If they're saying I baited their retard, then I'm guilty. But you make goddamn sure to tell Gus that."

"Don't worry, I will. Already called him worse to Gus," Schmidty said as he began heading toward the dugout steps. "So you're okay with that?"

"No, I'm not okay with that," Parlee said. "But we got to get out of here before Deke falls asleep."

The reality of Parlee's ego was that he was tickled to have achieved martyrdom by serving as the Flames' sacrifice. One by one, the young Flames made their way down the bench to offer Parlee condolences and appreciation.

"You got screwed man," Krohner offered.

"You're the best," Heidie said.

"I'd play with you guys any day," Drago said as he grabbed Parlee's pouch for a chew. "You mind?"

"We're going to win this one for you!" a bright eyed Scooter said as he patted Parlee on the shoulder.

Parlee rolled his eyes and turned to Deke.

"You are a piece of work," Deke said as he finally took the towel from his head. "You should run for mayor of goddamn Plymouth."

Parlee marinated in his ego the rest of the game, chirping non-stop encouragement to the Flames. He knew this would be a game the young players would carry with them for a long time. He wanted to show them how it could be handled with class and little drama.

During his new-found idle time, Parlee examined the crevices and cubby holes of the dugout. Above the bubbler, between two two-by-sixes that ran the length of the dugout about a foot apart to help hold up its roof, Parlee saw what looked to be the carcass of an old catcher's mitt. Parlee looked at Schmidty, who was wrapped up in the game, staring out at his struggling pitcher. It was the helpless look of a man handcuffed in the back of a squad car while his buddies take a bum rap. He wanted to be able to do so much more. He wanted to escape his situation.

Tommy pitched two more scoreless innings and the Flames made it a 4-0 lead in the sixth on Clay's two-run double. Tommy gave up a couple of runs in the bottom of the sixth and found himself in a full-blown jam in the seventh when the A's number eight hitter doubled with a guy on to put runners at second and third with one out.

"You'd better go to Clay," Parlee said to Schmidty. "You have anyone to play short?"

Schmidty popped out of the dugout and looked back to holler, "Fish! Come on."

One of the bench Flames, a young guy, small and quick, grabbed his glove and sprang out to the field. It wasn't what Parlee had in mind when he asked Schmidty about shortstop.

On his way to the mound, Schmidty pointed at Clay. He took the ball from Tommy, patted him on the butt and sent him toward the dugout. As Clay trotted to the mound, Schmidty waved Colton from second to short and Fish eagerly took Colton's place. Parlee threw a ball out to Krohner who tossed gentile grounders toward Fish and Colton.

Deke came to the dugout and had Parlee toss him somebody's water thermos. He took a big swig.

"Jesus Christ it's hot out there."

"This probably won't take very long, nine and the top," said Parlee, reciting the batting order in case Deke had dozed off.

Parlee was right. After Clay got ready to go, he threw two fast balls at the knees of Sheboygan's over-matched nine hitter for two quick strikes.

"Show 'em what they're up against," Parlee said to himself as he could tell Clay was gripping the fork ball hidden by his glove. Clay let it fly with velocity nearly equal to the fastball. But just as it got to the plate, the ball dove toward the ground and the Sheboygan batter swung over the top of it, missing the pitch by a foot.

Parlee sat at ease on the dugout bench, flanking Schmidty who was still standing nervously at the corner of the dugout. Parlee could feel Schmidty relax as he watched Clay's forkball do its work. Parlee was certain Schmidty wished more than ever that he was behind home plate, catching Clay's hot stuff.

"Jesus shit," Schmidty exhaled. "Where the hell did he get that pitch?"

Parlee looked into his own hands holding the tobacco pouch in his lap. "The Devil's Right Hand."

Clay used the exact same three-pitch sequence to strike out Plymouth's leadoff hitter to end the inning and incite the home crowd. Parlee saw the A's runner at third turn dejectedly to the third base coach, hand him his batting helmet and said "We're fucked."

Parlee shifted his gaze to Shepherd and Frietag. Both were diligently writing notes on the sheets attached to their clip boards.

The A's were done and everyone in the park knew it. Parlee's only regret was that the Sheboygan catcher was no longer in the game. Parlee would have had Clay hit him in the hip and Clay would have gladly obliged.

Clay retired the A's in order in the eighth and ninth, getting three more strike outs, a pop up back to Heidi and two weak grounders to Fish at second.

The Flames were in the semi-final against Horicon and had to wait through the other semi-final between Avenue Bar and Green Bay. The Avenue Bar players had impatiently waited for the Flames to exit the third base dugout. The winners of the two semi-finals would play for the big prize money Sunday afternoon. The losers would play in the morning consolation, a game Parlee wanted to avoid at all costs.

Parlee and Schmidty sat together in the grandstands and watched the Madison-Green Bay game with casual disinterest, dissecting the Sheboygan scrum and plotting the evening's game.

"You kicking out an umpire is a story I'm going to tell for a long time," Parlee said. He pointed at the Avenue Bar dugout. "I'd be surprised if we walk out of here tomorrow with the cash prize but coming away with that story makes it worthwhile."

Parlee and Schmidty watched as Avenue Bar rotated a seemingly endless roster of players, the next just as good as the last, into the game. Madison used three pitchers, each threw harder than anyone Parlee had seen all summer.

"Who the hell do you suppose they're saving for tomorrow?" Parlee asked Schmidty after they watched the third Madison pitcher's blazing fastball.

Along about the sixth inning a realization finally settled on Schmidty. "Our only chance tomorrow would be to throw the best Clay could ever offer."

"Even then, we'd have to score a run," Parlee said. "But we ain't going to have Clay, we gotta use him tonight or not at all," Parlee looked down about fifteen rows to the scouts. "Did you see Shepherd and Frietag going to town on their reports when Clay was pitching? If they think a guy's shitty, they don't bother writing it down."

Green Bay looked to Parlee to be about as good a team as he'd seen all summer. To a man they were older than Avenue Bar and took good swings off some real good pitchers. Still, Avenue Bar held a 5-2 lead in the seventh when Parlee got up, stretched and popped his joints to start getting ready to play.

"We gotta have Colt at short?" Parlee asked as the hometown crowd started settling into the grandstand for the Saturday evening main event. "Which one's your normal guy there?"

"Ain't here," Schmidty said in disgust. "We got a young stud, about twenty, first year with us. Our best player. Was all jazzed up to play and then when he heard we were picking up three infielders and you from out of town, all of a sudden he's got some family fishing trip he can't miss."

"What, he didn't think he'd play? Wouldn't get any at-bats? You tell him we're all really old and might not make it to Sunday?"

"He's a goddamn prima donna," Schmidty said. "One of the guys on the team told me instead of fishing he's got some cousin in Juneau and he'll be over there tomorrow playing in their league game. Don't ya love that open roster shit?"

"Juneau?" Parlee sat back down. "Jesus Christ that's where Ashippun is tomorrow."

"Ain't that a kick in the ass? Funny things happen in this game."

"That's a whole 'nother problem," Parlee said. "Thing is, Colt doesn't see well at night. He'd never not play there for ya but he might not feel too comfortable."

"Well," Schmidty said. "I'm open to suggestions."

***

After Avenue Bar played its way into the finals, the Flames ran and stretched around the Loube Field diamond as a large crowd settled into the grandstand and the red sun hung just above the western horizon. It would be issuing a challenge to Parlee in right field as it set in his eyes before fully disappearing by the fourth inning.

Clay was warming off the side mound as Parlee sat and stretched in front of the dugout and surveyed the Horicon team doing the same across the diamond. Parlee recognized most of the players as the Honkers' regular league team the past few seasons. Some could be assholes, he thought. He did not recognize the tall right hander warming up on the side mound or the big guy hitting balls into the fence down the right field line. The big right handed batter stood about six-three, Parlee guessed, with a thick chest and shoulders. He was pounding balls into the fence from about six feet away. The balls were being flipped underhanded into the hitting zone by one of the younger Honkers who knelt before the new Horicon warrior like an indentured squire before the champion jouster he is forced to serve.

Each year the Horicon team is in the running for the Rock River League title and competes for the purses of all the major amateur ball summer tournaments. The city of fifteen thousand is located at the southern tip of the expansive Horicon Marsh fifty miles below Lake Winnebago, Wisconsin's largest inland lake. Geese out-number

Horicon residents better than five-hundred to one and the City of Horicon wears its love of the large migrating fowl on its collective community sleeve, including the jerseys of the Honkers. The team is bank rolled by Fatsy Barber, a foreman at the Horicon John Deere plant who each year arranges jobs for any ball player he deems fit to settle on the Horicon diamond for the summer and help fill the stands. The round, cigar smoking Barber, who never comes out from behind a pair of aviator sunglasses or from under a floppy cloth fishing hat, is Horicon's version of Ashippun's Turk. A propensity to place large bets on the Honkers can make Barber an even more volatile baseball personality than the swinging temperament of the Turk.

Parlee got up to throw with Colton. He took a stance near Schmidty, who was at the edge of the dugout, filling out a lineup card.

"Must be Fatsy's new ringer," Parlee said as he nodded in the direction of the big hitter.

"Name's Blake Sheridan," said Schmidty, not looking up from his lineup card. "I talked to Tootsie last night about him and no one seems to know anything about him. Came up from the Moline plant to work in Horicon end of May."

Tootsie is Toots Hanrahan, the Horicon manager for at least ten seasons. Parlee liked Toots and considered his offer play with the Honkers three years back. Parlee always felt bad for Toots because he had to put up with Fatsy and his constant personnel changes. A Honker could go hitless over two games and Fatsy would have a new replacement he'd force Toots to stick into the lineup. Parlee wanted nothing to do with Fatsy's meddling. So bad it is that Parlee instead opted for the company of the Turk. The Turk's meddling was guided only by greed. Barber's behavior was driven by a combination of that same greed, misplaced pride and alternating wrath and envy toward Horicon's opponents. If Parlee had felt compelled to care enough for further contemplation, he was certain he could fill in the remaining seven deadly sins.

The grandstands filled in nicely with many of the same Plymouth faithful from the afternoon game. By game time, Parlee figured the crowd to be better than eight hundred. His buddy Schmidty had a nice thing going and Parlee wanted to help make sure he had another large crowd Sunday afternoon.

Clay seemed ready to go but Parlee wondered if he'd have the same zip and movement the Flames needed after pitching Thursday and then earlier in the day.

"What do ya think Skip?" said Colton after noticing Parlee was keeping a close eye on Clay while the two threw. "Would have been nice to give Clay an extra day."

"Yeah, but we ain't getting to Sunday without him today."

"I was thinking the same thing."

The summer air was still when the Flames took the field at the start of the game. The crowd was equal parts relaxed and excited, wanting their boys and the four from Ashippun to play their way into tomorrow's championship. Parlee guessed many in the crowd had already planned family barbecues after church services before heading over to the park for the grand finale.

"Let's not disappoint all these nice folks!" Parlee hollered over to Scooter as the two lobbed a ball back and forth in the outfield. One of the Plymouth bench guys was tossing with Drago over in left and Scooter started ticking off the names of relatives he had in the stands for the game. Parlee had tuned out by the time Scooter was naming cousins and watched Deke and Colton on the infield with Fish at second.

Deke had perked up considerably from the afternoon game after crawling into the bowels of the latrine and shower cave behind the Flames dugout for a nap that lasted nearly as long as the Avenue Bar's game -- but not quite. Deke had materialized from the sloping tunnel into the back of the Avenue Bar dugout in the eighth inning like a hibernating bear emerging from its lair. The startled Madison players, most of whom had no idea anyone was back up in the latrine area, moved aside to give Deke a wide berth as he stumbled up the dugout steps, yawning, farting and scratching his ass. As mysteriously as Deke had appeared, he was gone.

Colton looked good at short but there was still plenty of daylight.

Parlee heard Scooter say something about his uncle's family from Michicot when the public address announcer introduced a Miss Jenny Rosso from Ootsburg and a music student at Lakeland College in Sheboygan. The young woman stood behind home plate facing the grandstand with a microphone that did not work. She performed an a cappella version of the National Anthem that Parlee couldn't hear. He became aware of the song's conclusion by the polite applause of the crowd.

The centerfield chatterbox resumed his recital by naming shirt tail relations from Manitowoc and Heidie threw the ball down to Colton covering the bag at second. Parlee struggled to keep the sun he faced above the bill of his hat and Clay went through the first two hitters, getting a strikeout and a one-hopper back to the mound on a bad swing. Then the new Blake Sheridan made a slow walk to the plate. Parlee thought the bat looked small in his hands the way of Ted Kluszewski, the bare-armed beast who Parlee had seen at County Stadium a few years back when the Reds were in town, or Frank Howard last year with the Dodgers.

Parlee took a couple of steps back and told Scooter to do the same. Clay started Sheridan with a curve ball strike. On the next pitch, Sheridan went down and got a low outside pitch and drove it Parlee's way. Parlee instinctively tilted his head back to track the flight of the ball. When he did, the bill of his hat went above the sun and he was momentarily blinded. It didn't matter. Parlee's initial read of the ball told him he didn't have a chance to catch it. He turned toward center and sprinted with his back to the infield to the outfield fence. He could see Scooter doing the same. The ball smacked off the base of the outfield fence at the Plymouth Motors sign as though it'd been shot from cannon.

Parlee got to the warning track as the ball bulleted back to him. He scooped it and fired to Fish who had come out for the relay. Parlee had fully expected to see Sheridan chugging around second and on his way to third. Instead, the big man was jogging to a stop at second as Parlee got to the ball. He stood at second, looking out at Parlee, hands at his hips.

Scooter had converged with Parlee.

"Wow! Did he hit that one!"

"Fuck him," Parlee said as he stalked back to his spot, Sheridan watching his every stride.

Clay struck out the four hitter on four pitches to get out of the inning. The crowd cheered the Flames back into the dugout. Parlee swung a bat on the on-deck circle next to Clay.

"You might wanna save the good fork for that guy," Parlee said.

"I did."

The Horicon right hander was as good as any pitcher Parlee had seen all summer. He was around the plate with four pitches; fastball, curve, slider and a change. Parlee hit one ball hard all game. In the fifth with Clay at second and two outs, Parlee was looking fastball but got a change that wasn't enough off the fastball speed. Parlee turned on the pitch and pulled the ball hard down the right field line. Parlee initially thought the ball was destined for the right field corner to plate the game's first run. But Sheridan jumped to snatch the ball out of the air, his glove behind his head when he made the catch. He flipped the ball from his glove to throwing hand and rolled the ball to the mound. The last thing Parlee saw before pivoting to return to the dugout for his glove was Sheridan staring him down.

"That guy's a goddamn creep," Colton said as he tossed Parlee his Nokona.

Into the top of the sixth the game was still scoreless and fully under the lights. Clay didn't appear to have his best stuff, but kept racking up strikeouts. His forkball proved to be a dependable "out" pitch as the Honkers' repeatedly swung over the top of it. But with two outs, the Honkers' two hitter, a quick lefty, shot a bouncer to Colton. Parlee could tell Colton had a tough time reading the grounder when he stayed back on his heels. Colton didn't react in time to the ball's final hop and it smacked the wrist of his glove hand and rolled toward Deke at third.

Schmidty came out to say something to Clay as Sheridan slowly made his way to the plate. The crowd stirred and someone yelled "put him on!"

Not on your goddamn life, Parlee thought to himself. Make him earn his satisfaction.

Sheridan did just that, rocketing Clay's first offering deep into the left-center gap, the ball smacking halfway up the wall. Scooter got there in good shape and Parlee thought they may have a play at the plate. But Scooter's throw sailed over Colton's head and the runner from first scored standing up and Sheridan jogged into second with another double.

"Hit the goddamn cutoff!" The same expert voice from the crowd. Scooter was pounding his glove with his head down as he walked back to his place in center.

"You're okay Scooter," Parlee encouraged. "We weren't getting him anyway. Keep your head up, we need ya."

The Flames got the run back in the bottom of the sixth when Colton and Deke led off with singles, putting runners at the corners. Colton scored when Heidi bounced into a double play and the promising rally went no farther. The crowd that was buzzing like a dragon fly after Deke's hit, fell back on its hands as the game moved to the seventh, knowing the Flames missed a bigger opportunity against a good pitcher.

The game moved its 1-1 score to the top of the eighth and Clay got two quick outs. The Horicon leadoff hitter, an Oshkosh college player, drove a clean single to left. The two hitter, the lefty, again hit a sharp grounder toward short. Colton was late getting in front of the ball and in his anxiety slapped his bare hand too soon into the glove. The ball hit the ring finger of his throwing hand dead on, splintering it backwards.

What Parlee saw from right field was Colton flipping the glove off his left hand while clasping his right. The ball dropped at his feet. The crowd that at first cheered the grounder that was a sure out, pivoted quickly to an audible gasp as Colton grabbed at his hand in agony. Parlee ran to the infield at a full sprint.

The infielders and umpires had gathered around Colton by the time Parlee was close enough to hear what was going on. It didn't sound good.

"If you don't pass out, I will," Deke said.

"Goddamn it!" Colton growled. "I couldn't pick up that fucking ball off the bat."

Parlee pushed his way past Krohner and then Clay to get next to Colton. Several good-size drops of blood were on his pants. There was a smear of blood across the belly of his jersey.

"Let's see."

Colton held his left hand over his right, bent at the waist, not wanting to show Parlee.

A woman was walking across the infield with a dripping bag and a towel.

"C'mon. There's ice coming."

Both of Colton's hands were shaking as he held them out as one. He removed his left hand to show a compound fracture of his right hand ring finger. The nail was torn off, the tip of the finger purple. Between the first and second knuckle the bone protruded through the skin. What worried Colton the most was the hard lump and swelling at the knuckle of the hand, indicating the finger had been jammed straight back into the hand.

"Fuck, I might never be able to grip a bat again."

The woman with the ice and towel shouldered her way to Colton. She placed the ice and towel over his outstretched hand.

"Come on hon. You need to sit down."

Colton made the slow walk across the diamond toward the grandstand. The crowd and Horicon players clapped as he disappeared up the grandstand steps.

"He's in good hands," Schmidty said to Parlee. "My brother's wife. Works over at the clinic. What do we do now?"

"Jesus, Schmidty, I'm running out of brain here," said Parlee as he looked around the faces on the infield and into the Flames dugout.

"You can slide Deke over there if you got someone can stand at third."

Parlee and the rest of the Flames heard an impatient shout from the Honkers' dugout. "Come on, let's get this show on the road!" Parlee snapped his head the Horicon direction. The shout came from Sheridan. He was standing in front of the dugout, impatiently swinging his bat.

Parlee turned to Clay. "You put anything near the strike zone, it better be your good fork."

"That's what he's hit for two doubles."

"Well shit," Parlee said as he picked up the ball that fell at Colton's feet. He looked at it. A speck of blood melded the red stitching with the white horse hide. He began rubbing the ball with both hands, the Nokona under his left arm pit. "Like I told Schmidty, I'm all out of brain. If he hollers one more word like he just did, hit him in the fucking neck with it."

Parlee slammed the ball into Clay's open glove and trotted back out to right. He turned to see Deke and the new third baseman taking grounders from Krohner and throwing the ball back across to first. All three throws from the new third sacker short-hopped Krohner.

"Fucking lovely," Parlee said nearly loud enough for Scooter to hear.

The Honker runners took their leads at first and second. Clay started with two curve balls, the second for a strike. The next two pitches looked to be sliders off the outside corner. Clay came back with something hard up and in and Sheridan timed it up perfectly with fat part of the bat. The ball boomed high and deep to left, clearing the fence by plenty. Sheridan took his time around the bases and the jubilant Honkers flocked to meet him at the plate.

"Well, shit!" Parlee said loud enough for Scooter to hear.

Clay got the next out and the dejected Flames went quietly into the dugout, down, 4-1.

"What was that pitch?" Parlee asked Clay.

Clay wouldn't respond.

"We tried to bust him up and in with a fast ball after the two sliders away," Heidi said as he adjusted his gear and wiped his sweat laden face with a towel. "It wasn't even a strike. I don't know how he got the good part of the bat on it."

"I suppose that didn't look too good to the scouts," Clay finally said.

"They ain't looking at results so much as what ya got and how they can work with it," Parlee said. "What they won't like is if you go out there and roll over in the ninth. You've shown 'em plenty this weekend."

Three Flames batters made three quick outs in the bottom of the eighth. Clay got two more strike outs in the top of the ninth to finish with ten. In the bottom of the ninth, Clay flew to deep center for the second out and Parlee ended the game with a soft fly to left. The Honkers celebrated just a little bit too hard for Parlee's liking. The catcher, third baseman and shortstop mobbed the mound while Sheridan drew a crowd of teammates at first. Parlee went down into the dugout and didn't come back out to shake hands with the Honkers.

He packed up his gear and gathered Colton's things and set it all out on the field. Schmidty got everyone's attention and reminded the team of the consolation game to be played Sunday at ten against Green Bay. Parlee hadn't even considered the possibility of having to play Sunday morning. The idea sat him back down on the bench and he looked over at Deke. Deke was slapping his spikes together and considered the notion the same way a ten-year-old might contemplate beets at the dinner table.

"What do I do Parlee?" Clay's voice from behind.

Parlee considered Clay's meaning, then said "Help me get all this stuff in the car and then I gotta go find Colt. You wander out to the crowd and make yourself available, if you get my drift."

By the time the gear was thrown into the trunk of the Impala, the hour was after eleven. Clay went across the parking lot and into the stadium hoping to run into Shepherd and Frietag. When Parlee looked around after closing the trunk, he saw Colton coming toward the Impala. His right hand was bandaged and Parlee could see a splint that was taped along the ring finger.

"Nice move, Slick," Parlee said.

"I'll be goddamn if I can pick that ball up at night under lights like these."

"You okay Colt?"

Colton said he'd called his wife to come and pick him up and he'd have whatever needed to be done to his hand – most likely surgery of some kind – at home by his regular doctor.

"I don't trust anybody north of Madison with a scalpel," Colton said.

Parlee gave Colton a ride back to the Trail's End. His wife would be there in ninety minutes or so. Parlee went back to the field to check on Clay. He couldn't remember ever being so busy after an away game.

A much thinner crowd than Friday's was at the beer tent. There was no band and the crowd mainly consisted of ball players and a few younger women wearing over their sweaters the jerseys of their catch of the day. The evening air was cool but not uncomfortable for Parlee, who was still heated from the game. He had replaced his jersey with a button-down nylon Braves jacket. On his way back from the motel, the radio told Parlee that Aaron had hit a two-run homer, his eleventh, and the Braves beat the Cardinals, 6-5, to go ten games over .500 at 34-24. The news announcer said there were 6,186 people at County Stadium that evening. All season long, TV and radio news broadcasters made sure to include the attendance in each report, as if reporting the number of people attending a wake or funeral.

About half the tables in the fenced area of the parking lot were full. Parlee quickly found the one that held Clay, Shepherd and Frietag. On his way to the table, Deke shuffled over and put a beer in Parlee's hand.

"I'll be over there," Deke nodded toward the tent.

"They signing Clay?"

"I don't know. They've been talking to him since you left. Colt okay?"

"I guess. His wife's coming for him. He's pretty blue."

Parlee walked to the table, Shepherd and Frietag on one side, Clay the other. Clay was holding a bag of ice on his right shoulder. His face lit up when he saw Parlee. He stood.

"I'm signing Parlee!" Clay said as they shook hands and gave one another a one-arm hug. "I'm signing!"

"That's great! Congrats. You deserve it." Parlee shook hands with each of the scouts. "Thanks guys."

"We'll take him with us to Rapids in the morning," Shepherd said. "Sorry to steal him from ya."

Before Parlee sat he pulled the tobacco pouch and can opener from the hip pocket of his ball pants. He tossed the pouch on the table and opened the can of Schlitz.

"That's okay," Parlee said. "I was just ruining him anyway. Treating him like a rented mule. Sorry he won't be able to pitch for a few days."

"Don't worry about it," Shepherd said. He couldn't help but pick up Parlee's pouch and gently roll it in his hands. "Our reports are strongly recommending the organization play him as an infielder and look at him as a pitcher, too. My guess is they'll take a hard look at him as an infielder and get him some time on the mound as the season goes. After the season they'll decide which way to go and have him show up in the spring as one or the other."

"The spring?" Parlee said as he took his pouch away from Shepherd's hands. "That mean you're not just looking at him as a warm body?" Parlee opened the pouch and pinched out a small-size chew.

"If he plays like this the rest of the year, he'll be in Florida, come March."

"Hot damn," Parlee said as he grabbed Clay's left shoulder. He put the chew in his mouth, closed up the pouch and looked at Shepherd.

"I suppose if he was a few years younger, you'd be all over that Sheridan."

Shepherd let out a laugh and grabbed the pouch.

"Not on your ass," he said, holding up the pouch. "Just like this here there's a story there but we ain't got time for it."

"I gotta get back to the hotel, Parlee," Clay said. "They're coming by at five in the morning and I want to call my parents right away."

"Shit, I just came from there."

"We'll run him over," Shepherd said. "After those two games you probably need to drink some beer. When was the last time you got booted from a game for being a punching bag?"

"Thanks," said Parlee, smiling. He turned to Clay. "Make sure you call home right away. The phone rings much later than this and the first thing your mom's gonna think is that I ran us all into a telephone pole on some lonely back road. Colt's back there I think your news will cheer him up. He'll need that."

"Changing of the guard," Shepherd said. "You can tell by looking at that guy he must have been a hell of a player. Shit, he still is. Now it might be over for him, if that finger's as bad as it looked."

They left Parlee with that thought turning over in his mind like a dancing knuckle ball headed toward the plate. Parlee was certain he couldn't square up either of them.

Just as Parlee finished his beer, Deke, wearing three days of bristle and stink, sat down with a replacement Schlitz. Deke wore the same pants he'd put on for Friday's game. He had three days whisker growth and his shirt sported a weekend's worth of sweat, mustard, beer and diamond dirt. Parlee opened the beer and snuffled his nose in Deke's direction.

"I don't think you're getting laid tonight."

"Don't be scratching me out of the lineup yet there Skip. You want to head back to the motel?"

"Hell no. Let's stay here for a while and have one or five," said Parlee as he spit off to his right side. "I don't want to be there when Colt's wife shows up. Every time something like this happens, the wife or girlfriend or mother always looks at me like it's all my fault."

They sat on the same side of the picnic table, legs stretched out away from it, elbows back on top of it. Parlee studied the grounds. There were about forty people still mingling in the dimly-lit tent area. It was as if everyone there hoped not to miss something important. A few of the younger Flames and three young women were at one table. The prettiest of the women was sitting cross-legged on top of the table, making sure everyone faced her direction. About half of the Horicon team, Sheridan and the new pitcher among the missing, were gathered around another. Some of the Madison guys were at the make-shift bar but Parlee didn't see any of the Green Bay players. He took that as a bad sign and his mind continued to wander.

"Isn't it?" Deke said. Parlee's mind snapped back to the table.

"Isn't it what?"

"Isn't it all your fault?"

"Well, yeah." And then Parlee began to tell Deke of Clay's good fortune.

They were the last to leave.

CHAPTER 13

You ask me what was the most unforgettable lineup I was ever a part of? I can tell ya that one 'fore you draw yourself your next breath. It was Jack Rabbit in center, Buffalo Chief in left, Cloud Chief at third, Snake Hide at short, Little Buffalo at second, Lone Wolf played first. Our pitchers was Fleetfoot, Wild Deer, Scatter Cloud and Roaring Thunder. I put that one to memory, that lineup. It was Ben Harjo's Oklahoma Indians. That's what the posters said that would roll into a town 'bout three days 'fore we'd get there.

That was during my barnstormin' days after I quit out of the army. I'd play right, 'cept when Jim Thorpe was there. He'd show up when he could. Weren't no shame settin' the bench when he was there. Crowd was always twice the size when he would show and the papers called him the "greatest athlete of all time."

Old Ben used to put together some pretty good teams to play the barnstormin' circuit back in those days. Teams would travel around like circus acts. They was peppered with players Kennesaw wouldn't 'low in the big city league. Coloreds and whatnot. Ben used to get up a team of Indians ever year and off they'd go. I kept one of them posters for the longest time. That one read "Ben Harjo's Oklahoma Indians to do peaceful battle with Brown Hunter's Grays". That was a place called Middletown, somewhere's in New York on a hot Fourth of July, I recollect.

Ben made a lot of money puttin' that thing together. He'd built his own ball park on his farm in Oklahoma near where his ancestors was marched off to from Georgia. That's where he'd have 'em train and have tryouts. Play games against other barnstormers. The April I showed up they was fifty men wanting spots on the team. I was the only one picked what wasn't Indian. We'd go back east and them promoters wanted to play up the Indians for the crowd. Ben had all these Eagle feather headdresses the players would put on during introductions. 'Cept me. They make us do this skit 'fore the game *where they'd make me put on this cavalry hat and the rest of the team would run around me in a circle whilst the announcer tolt some story 'bout the Battle of Little Big Horn. The team hated doin' it and I was surprised Ben went along. But them eastern crowds couldn't get enough of that. Acting like they was honoring some Indian heritage. I never seen it that way.*

Ain't no honor in buffoonery.

***

Parlee woke up at the Trail's End and everything was different. He woke with that familiar hangover clarity that washed the team's jerseys Friday morning. He lay in bed thinking about everything that had happened since. Clay and Colt were no longer there and had gone in completely opposite directions. He thought about the fight and getting booted from the game. He thought about the hits he'd had in the tournament. There'd only been the three but he replayed them over in his mind knowing they'd face a pretty good Green Bay pitcher this morning. He thought about the meaning of losing Colt and Clay for league play while Horicon added Sheridan and another live arm. For reasons he couldn't ascertain, he got stuck on thinking about finding Schmidty's mitt in the dugout, about Shorty's spikes in Neosho, Pruefer's hat in Jefferson. He grappled for a meaning. He thought about the Braves final season, a muse that occupies his mind with greater frequency as their final game in Milwaukee gets closer with each passing day, each game played, each pitch thrown. What will Gene leave behind in the dugout after that last game? He thought about the fact that losing to Horicon means he'd be heading home without any booty or treasure after being so certain through the early part of the summer that the tournament represented a handsome pay day. Now they were stuck playing in the consolation. . .

"Holy Shit!" Parlee shrieked as he bolted upright in bed. He looked at the clock. "Deke, its quarter after nine! We gotta get the hell out of here!"

Parlee looked over at Deke, face down in the other bed. He began to stir. Parlee realized Deke hadn't been snoring. That must be why Parlee was able to stay in the room past nine. Parlee slipped on his shoes, went into the bathroom and then back out the door.

"Get your ass up!" he called as he shot the door and made his way across the parking lot to the office area, his morning clarity serving him well. He stopped in the office to report that they'd be back after the game to check out and gather their things, if that was okay. He then went around to the pop machine and gathered four Sun Drops.

Back in the small room, Deke and Parlee moved around in a buffoon's ballet as they stumbled over one another in search of missing elements of their uniforms. They took turns on the head and guzzled the Sun Drop. The room had taken on the dank and pungent odor expected when its occupants did little more than play baseball, drink beer and woof bad food for three days. It smelled of a cross between a locker room, an outhouse and the kruesening tanks at the Heilman Brewery in La Crosse where Parlee worked one summer after college.

"Cleaning lady's going to earn her keep," Deke said as he tossed an empty Sun Drop bottle in a corner where it clattered against two empty beer cans and some hamburger wrappers.

They went out. They got to the park just fifteen minutes before game time. The young Flames players were pretending to stretch and play catch in front of the dugout while comparing hangovers and stories from the previous night's beer tent.

Parlee and Deke slipped down the dugout steps to get ready to play. Parlee looked over at the dugout of the Green Bay Blue Ribbons, their players seemingly fresh, mature, big and strong as they warmed. He looked at the rag-tag Flames, who seemingly just came from a teen drinking party.

"This is the kind of shit I try to avoid," Parlee muttered as he twisted on his spikes.

"What?" said Deke, pulling his musky jersey from his bag. He gave it a whiff and reacted with a sour expression.

"We're in the wrong fuckin' dugout."

A tall righty threw hard off the side mound near the Green Bay dugout. The Flames' mound was empty as Everest.

"Beginnin' to worry you guys weren't showing," Schmidty said as he came down the dugout stairs.

"Deke picked a hell of a time to give up snoring. Who's throwin' for us?"

"Drago," Schmidty said. "He actually got here on time. All loose and ready to go."

Parlee grabbed his pouch and thought better of it. Dry mouth. He took a drink from the bubbler.

"Any Sun Drop around?"

"Gotta take the field boys!" Schmidty hollered.

Parlee took three or four quick throws with Deke as he began to trot out to right. The spring was gone from his stride as he jogged toward the outfield fence. When he ran out of room to run, Parlee didn't want to turn around, too afraid to look at what he would see. He turned anyway.

What a difference a day made. Not having Colton and Clay blew a couple of big holes on the infield, in the lineup and on the mound. Drago still threw with a three-quarter motion that was too much shoulder and not enough legs. It was the same motion someone would use to throw a pie.

The rout began early. Green Bay picked up three runs in the first during an inning that was mitigated by Scooter's running catch in the left-center gap with two on. It was one of five hard-hit balls that inning.

Parlee knew when not to vest too much emotion in winning these types of games – ones where his depleted team is over-matched in a game that has little meaning in the tournament. But he never lost sight of the fact that at-bats are a finite commodity. That's especially true for players his age. So he did the best he could to lock onto the hard-throwing righty, a pitcher he knew would be around the plate with decent speed.

Parlee hit him for three clean singles in his first at-bats—two liners to right and a seed over the pitcher's head and into center. Parlee's first hit followed Scooter's lead-off infield single to pose a mild threat in the bottom of the first. But after Deke flew to the warning track in left, two strikeouts ended the inning.

"We needed Colt there," Deke said as he trotted back onto the field with Parlee.

As he stood in right facing a 6-0 deficit, Parlee assessed the crowd during one of Schmidty's many trips to the mound. There'd been one per inning so far and Parlee couldn't help but believe Schmidty thought he was catching again when he could go for a mound visit any time he wanted. There were perhaps seventy-five people yawning their way through the morning game.

Hard telling how many will show for the championship game with the local team sent packing. Had the Flames made the finals, there could have been a thousand people on hand to see them get their asses handed to them by the Madison team. This was a more anonymous butt kicking, but Schmidty won't be too pleased with the day's gate.

The game and tournament for the Flames finally ended after two pitching changes by Schmidty. He purposely made them in the dugout between innings in order to save time. Parlee didn't get his fourth hit of the day but Deke cemented his legacy with the young Flames by lifting a towering fly ball to left that carried over the fence to break the shutout in an unceremonious 8-1 loss.

Parlee and Deke gathered up their gear, walked it to the trunk of the Impala and headed over to the beer tent to grab something to eat. They camped at a picnic table under the tent and Schmidty brought over a plateful of burgers and laid it on the table. He sat and handed Parlee an envelope.

"What's this?"

"Gas money," Schmidty said as he unwrapped a burger and dumped ketchup on the patty. "I appreciate you guys coming up. We wouldn't have won a game in this tournament without you guys."

"It was kind of a loaded field, but you don't have to do that."

"I do," Schmidty said. "The only good thing is you guys have enough time to get down to Juneau for your league game."

Drago and Heidi came to the table, each with a pail filled with cans of beer. Deke grabbed two, slid a Blatz down to Parlee hoping it was enough to convince him not to try making Juneau.

"Thanks, man," Deke said between bites of hamburger.

"Thank you guys for playing," Drago said. "That's the best we played all year."

"Really?" Parlee said, looking at Schmidty.

"Really."

More of the Flames showed up and surrounded the table. They drank and ate and twice retold the tale of the fight. At one point Scooter recounted how Deke had popped the Horicon catcher on the side of the head. Parlee looked at Deke.

"Let him go," Deke said, "he's on a roll."

Before anyone knew it, the day had slipped to one-thirty in the afternoon, a half hour before the championship game. It was already game time in Juneau.

"I could tell by that look in your eye you weren't heading to Juneau," said Schmidty as he got up to go back into the stadium for the championship game.

"That and the five or six beers," Parlee said. "Dead giveaway."

"You guys sticking around for the game?"

"I think the city of Plymouth has kicked my ass enough for one weekend," Deke said. They shook hands all around. Parlee looked in the envelope, four fives. He handed one to Deke.

"Go get us a bucket o' beer, I'll grab the Impala."

Parlee wheeled the Impala to the beer tent entrance. Deke came through the near-empty tent area with a galvanized pail full of ice chunks and three kinds of beer. He put the pail on the expansive floor board at his feet.

"Where to, Skip?"

"Home."

"Home? The hell?"

"We'll go home through Milwaukee."

Deke used the church key to open a beer, leaned back in the seat and pulled his cap down over his eyes.

"That's more like it."

CHAPTER 14

By the time Parlee and Deke checked out of the Trail's End and pointed the Impala south on Highway 57, it was well after two. Parlee brought up the Braves game on the radio and Deke sat back and drank beer and listened while Parlee sipped at one of the three Sun Drops he'd brought from the motel. They talked about the weekend and what might lay ahead for them as the season unfolds without Clay and Colton. They didn't bother to consider what may or may not be happening in Juneau as they drove south.

Highway 57 cut straight south, running parallel to Lake Michigan about ten miles inland. The highway led a direct route toward the city of Milwaukee through Saukville, Grafton and Cedarburg and eventually to Highway 100 where once he turned west the roads would become more familiar to Parlee.

When the Impala rolled through Saukville, the Cardinals were holding a 5-0 lead over the Braves. Mike Shannon hit a two-run double off Lemaster to cap a five-run second inning for the Cardinals. By the time Cedarburg came through the Impala's windshield, Aaron had made it a 5-1 game with a solo homer in the sixth.

In Cedarburg, Parlee spotted a Kroger grocery store just off the highway and pulled in.

"I'm gonna call the clubhouse, leave a message for Oliver that we're on our way to the Castle," Parlee told Deke. "Maybe get some bread and sandwich meat."

"Just in time, I gotta piss like a drunken camel."

Parlee didn't know what that meant as he dug through the glove box looking for a slip of paper Oliver had given him with the phone number for the Braves club house. Deke reeled into the store and headed off toward the meat department in back where a sack boy said he could find the washroom. Parlee found a wall pay phone at the front of the store. Two of the store's four checkout lines were open, each with a line of three or four customers.

It wasn't one of the new supermarkets that were springing up in urban areas and Parlee got the feeling the store was still family owned and operated. It was well-lit with narrow aisles and well-stocked shelves. The floor was made of thick, foot-square linoleum cubes that in high-traffic areas had worn through to the store's original wood floor. Parlee looked down one of the aisles to see a man with a butcher's apron and hat pointing Deke in a certain direction.

Parlee dropped a dime in the phone and dialed the number, not letting his finger out of the dial hole until it returned to position. When he finished dialing, Parlee turned toward the store as much as the phone's short, corrugated metal cord would allow. Every person in line and the sack boy were looking his direction. Parlee realized he looked exactly like what he was – a drunken old ball player.

Parlee left his message with a woman clubhouse attendant and gave a half-hearted attempt at convincing her to stop by the Castle. He hung up and turned to his small, indifferent audience. Parlee bent to slap the side of his right thigh and a cloud of dust and diamond dirt exploded off his baseball pants.

A stuffy woman with a small grocery sack in one hand led her small son past Parlee with the other. The boy, in a baseball hat a size too small with a patch that simply said "Little League," couldn't take his eyes from Parlee as his mother scurried him toward the door. Parlee was certain the boy, against his will, would be signed up for tennis lessons by late Monday morning.

He went in search of Deke and Braunschweiger. Deke wasn't hard to find. Parlee heard a commotion down one of the aisles to his right. He turned the corner on the aisle and there was Deke in the cereal section grabbing boxes of Post cereal one-by-one, scanning the back and then discarding the box on the aisle floor. Deke stood ankle deep in about fifteen cereal boxes that were on the floor.

"Deke, what the hell are you doing?" As the words left Parlee's mouth, he realized that all the boxes Deke was looking through were the Post brand that had baseball cards on the back of each box.

"I'm looking for a card of Oliver," Deke said, throwing two more boxes on the floor. "Help me look."

"You could be a little more orderly about it." Parlee started taking boxes off the shelves and search the eight baseball cards on the back of each. Once done, he'd place the box back on the shelf, cockeyed.

Dick Groat, Frank Robinson, Harvey Kuehn, Roger Maris, Jimmy Piersall, Juan Marichel, Jim Lefebvre, Ken Boyer. On his fourth box, Parlee found an Oliver card of Gene in a Cardinal uniform.

"Got one," he held it up for Deke to see.

"Already got one of those," said Deke as he continued to rifle through the boxes. "I'm looking for one in a Braves uniform."

Parlee looked at the Oliver card. The last stat line was from '63. He'd been traded midseason, 1963, but the card company must have reused his Cardinal photo for the next year's card. Parlee started looking more closely at other boxes.

"These are all from '63 Deke," Parlee said as he began to toss the boxes on the floor. "These are all two years old. We ain't gonna find one of Gene in a Braves uni."

"You mean these have all been sitting on the shelves for two years?"

"If not here, somewhere else," said Parlee as he continued to scan the boxes before throwing them on the floor.

"What the hell are you guys doing?" The words came off the gruff, throaty voice of the butcher, a short, broad-shouldered man in his early fifties, who stalked down the aisle toward the commotion. Black hair curled out the back of his butcher's hat and gray hairs speckled his dark beard. Parlee guessed him to be the store owner or a family member working the Sunday shift.

"What the hell are you doing selling two-year old food?" Deke said, holding up a box that had Roberto Clemente, Curt Flood, Clay Dalymple, Early Wynn, Al Kaline, Carl Yastrzemski, Don Drysdale and Vada Pinson. "Early Wynn hasn't pitched in two seasons. I bet he's older than you. We're just trying to get this shit off the shelves for you."

The butcher tried, but couldn't find any words at that moment. He turned red in the face, his bulbous nose afire from the heat of its tiny, angry veins.

Parlee held up a box and pointed to a Chicago Cub.

"You see this guy? That's Ken Hubbs," said Parlee, speaking in teacher mode. "Ken Hubbs died in a plane crash two off-seasons ago. How can you sell cereal to kids with a dead guy on the box?"

"Get the hell out of here before I call the cops!"

Deke and Parlee kicked through the boxes and got clear of the aisle. Parlee kept the box with Hubbs and Deke had two with Oliver.

"Half-price for this old shit?" Deke said over his shoulder as he followed Parlee through one of the closed checkout aisles past two lines of curious customers. The butcher was right on their heels. He stopped and watched Deke and Parlee push through the door to the parking lot. He looked at the bewildered sack boy.

"Need youse over by the cereal."

***

Parlee and Deke chuckled about the butcher all the way down to Highway 100. Deke opened one of the cereal boxes and began eating handfuls of the bran flakes, washing them down with gulps of Schlitz. As they headed west on 100, the radio said the Cardinals extended their lead to 6-1 with a run in the top of the eighth. Mack Jones hit a solo homer in the bottom of the inning to cut the lead to four.

The Impala was southbound again when the Braves' ninth-inning rally fizzled. Oliver singled and scored on Frank Bolling's double. Rico Carty singled to make it a more respectable 6-4 final. But that was it.

When they got to the Castle, Parlee and Deke sat at one of the tables by the juke box and talked Irma into cooking a couple of hamburgers off the kitchen stove in the living quarters. Just two of the neighborhood regulars were seated at the bar. Irma would cook only at certain times for certain people. It'd been a nice, June Sunday afternoon, the bar was slow and she knew Parlee to be a good tipper.

They had eaten the hamburgers and were on their second pitcher of beer and sixth quarter in the juke box when Oliver came in to the tune of Johnny Cash's "Ring of Fire." He was alone and stopped by Irma to grab a pitcher on his way across the room.

Oliver set down the pitcher on the table as Parlee stood. They shook and gave one another a one-arm hug. Parlee turned and said, "This is Deke, I might have mentioned him once or twice. Deke, Gene Oliver."

They shook hands, "You're the guy Parlee tells me should be in our dugout."

"Only if you got a keg set up in there," Deke laughed.

"Christ, look at you guys," Oliver stepped back. "You guys ever shower? Take your clothes down to the river and beat 'em with a rock?"

They settled in.

"Man, it was a tough one today," Oliver said. "Lemaster didn't have his stuff. That's been happening a lot. We got in a hole."

"Their guy tough?" asked Parlee as he topped off the three beer glasses.

"Purkey? Hell no. We had eleven hits. Scored twice on two solos through eight."

Bob Purkey was a thirty-six-year-old righty the Cardinals acquired from Cincinnati during the off-season.

"Heard you single and score in the eighth," Deke said.

"Ninth," Oliver corrected. "Shit I should have had at least three hits off him," We always hit him pretty good. Had an RBI double last night." Oliver raised his glass to Parlee and Deke.

"You win last night?" asked Parlee, forgetting he'd heard the score on radio on his way back to the park after taking Colton to the hotel. "We got a little busy last night and this morning and I guess I lost track."

"Won, 6-5 in front of a big Saturday night crowd of six thousand."

"That's a damn shame," Parlee said.

Parlee and Deke took turns telling Oliver about their weekend baseball adventure. When they got to the grocery store story, Deke reached down and pulled up an empty box of Post cereal with Oliver's card on the back.

"Holy shit!" Oliver said. "You found this in a store today? They quit doing that before last season."

"Yeah, the cereal was a little dry," Deke said. "Took me three or four beers to wash it down."

Oliver leaned back in his chair. Parlee couldn't remember the last time he'd seen him hatless. His brown hair was beginning to thin, too. Oliver wore dark slacks and a nice, western-style shirt. He examined the eight cards on the back of the cereal box, his card alongside Willie Mays. A smile curled his lips as the juke box played "Big Iron" by Marty Robbins. His eyes came off the cereal box to Parlee.

"Let me get this straight," he said, "you got tossed from a baseball game for nearly getting planted on your ass and then you got thrown out of a mom and pop grocery store all in the same twenty-four hours?"

"What? That shit don't happen in the Bigs?" Deke said.

"That's some weekend," Oliver said. "Too bad about the purse."

"This shit keeps up, I'll have to get a real summer job one of these years," Parlee emptied his glass. "Hey, you know a guy from down your Moline way name of Blake Sheridan? Gotta be close to your age."

Parlee slid one of the half-empty pitchers his direction and filled the three glasses. It emptied and he held it up for Irma to see.

"Blake Sheridan? Where the hell did you run into Blake Sheridan?" Oliver, unbelieving, took a drink of beer.

"Showed up about a month ago playing for Horicon ," Parlee said. "Hit one about four-twenty off our best pitcher Saturday night. Clay, the kid that got signed.

"Word around the campfire is he was working down in the Moline Deere factory and transferred up to the Horicon plant."

"Holy Christ," said Oliver, still not believing they were talking about Blake Sheridan. "Word around this camp fire is that he's a full-blown pedoass."

"You're shittin'," a smile came to Parlee.

"What?" Deke said between gulps of beer. "Pederass?"

"Yeah, swear to god, he did three years down in Marion for diddling a bunch of boy scouts."

"That's beautiful," Parlee said. "He did time in the Illinois federal pen?"

"Hard time," Oliver said. "You know what they do to child molesters in prison?"

"Probably get a pretty nasty taste of their own medicine," Deke speculated.

Oliver told the story about how he was best friends through high school with Sheridan's older brother, Blaine.

"Blake was the real thing on the diamond," Oliver said. "Big kid, played Legion ball with us even though he was a couple, maybe three years younger."

"He and Blaine anything alike?" Parlee asked.

"About as similar as grapes and gravel," Oliver said. "Blaine played too but wasn't real good. A great guy, class president and all. Blake was always kind of a loner and a lot of people around town thought he was a creep. By the time he was a senior, I was at Northwestern and didn't really see him much."

"What the hell happened?" Deke asked.

Blake Sheridan was an all-state baseball player his senior year in high school. Early that summer, he'd been drafted into the Cincinnati Reds organization. But before that he'd volunteered to help supervise a Boy Scout outing in the Ozarks.

"Everybody thought it was pretty neat," Oliver said. "This local baseball legend offers to help out the Boy Scouts. They get back from the trip and Sheridan goes off with the Reds. They put him in 'D' ball somewhere down in the Georgia-Florida League."

"About halfway through the summer, some of them kids began comparing notes about what happened and some of the parents got wind of it. Next thing you know they served him a summons right in the dugout someplace in Georgia. Big trial, papers had a field day. Got convicted and did three in Marion. A year for each kid."

"I'll be goddamn," said Parlee. He looked at Deke, could see the wheels turning inside.

"I heard a few years ago he was out," Oliver said. "How he got to Horicon, I couldn't tell ya."

"Maybe he likes geese now," Deke said.

Irma brought another pitcher. The juke box played out and no one stood to keep it going. Parlee and Deke sat, wondering if what they just heard should be considered funny, disturbing or disturbingly funny. Oliver got quiet, watching the bubbles of the beer race one another from the bottom of the pitcher to the foam deck on top.

Oliver broke the silence.

"Eddie says none of this would be happening if Fred Miller wouldn't have gotten killed in that plane crash." Miller was the baron of Miller Beer and worked behind the scenes with Lou Perini to bring the Braves to Milwaukee. Shortly before securing the Braves, Miller's group nearly brought the Cardinals to town. But Gussie Busch bought the team for less than Miller's group offered and kept the Cardinals in St. Louis.

"He and his kid were killed on that plane right before the '54 season," Parlee stated for Deke's benefit. "I remember when that happened. Someone said Billy Bruton was supposed to be on that plane but got sick or something at the last minute and didn't go."

"Yeah, Eddie got pretty tight with Miller right after the team moved here," Oliver said. "Eddie says that Miller had an agreement with Perini that if the team ever came up for sale, he'd get first crack. That would have been great. Local ownership. These new owners have made it real hard on everyone here.

"We're not having much fun," said Oliver, leaning back in his chair, looking from his beer glass to the wall over the silent juke box, fingers knitted behind his head. "This season's been tough on all of us, especially the guys who've been here for a long time. Eddie, Hank. I wasn't here in '57 but all they talk about are those days. What the '57 and '58 World Series meant to this town. . . And to them.

"Every day is like one day closer to a funeral you somehow know is coming."

Oliver kept leaning back in his chair. He looked again at the back of the cereal box with an expression of great personal satisfaction. His face soon returned to one of resignation.

"Home games have been eerie and almost scary," he said. "Especially the night games. It gets so dark and silent back up in there. You can't see the empty seats but you know they're there."

Parlee held his glass in his lap with both hands, considering the scene. "The silent ghosts of fans from '57," he said.

"Yeah," Oliver said. "You can't hear them or see 'em, but you can feel them there. Day games are somehow worse. It's not scary, just sad. You have a bright, sunny Sunday like today and you look around and there's forty thousand empty seats. People used to love coming out here on Sundays. Doubleheaders, people'd be here the whole damn day. Stick your head out of the dugout, early game one. Four hours later, late in the second game, see the same faces."

Deke and Parlee drank their beer in silence and digested the sad scene into which County Stadium had descended. Parlee remembered sitting in the outfield bleachers of game four of the '57 World Series. The green grass of the diamond contrasted the rich brown infield dirt. The stadium, decorated with bunting and forty-five thousand rabid fans in a view sprawled before him like a scene in a handheld Viewmaster stereoscope. When Mathews hit the two-run homer in the tenth to win it and set off a deafening roar, Parlee couldn't ever imagine what could possibly happen to silence County Stadium. It was a sound that should last forever.

"Biggest crowd we've had since opening day is when Spahn came with the Mets and got a start." Oliver's fact brought Parlee back to the reality of the present.

The day after Spahn pitched, Parlee saw the paper that told how some seventeen thousand fans showed up on a Thursday night a month ago to greet and say farewell to the greatest lefthander of all time. Spahn came with the Braves in '53 and had been a part of everything with the Milwaukee fans – the rise to two World Series and the fall toward Atlanta.

"That was the damnest thing, too," Oliver said. "We finally get a crowd over fifteen thousand and they're here to cheer the opposing pitcher. The fans were good to us, always have been through this. But Spahn would strike a guy out and they'd cheer. One of our guys would get a hit, and only some would cheer. Mathews hit a three-run homer off him in the fifth and it was as if the crowd didn't know what to do – cheer or sit on their hands."

"A lot of us felt sorry for the crowd that night."

Spahn finished the fifth inning that night but that was it. When he walked off the mound at the end of the inning, the crowd gave him a standing ovation in what everyone figured to be Spahn's final County Stadium start.

"We hit him for seven runs and no one liked doing it," Oliver said. "Especially Eddie. It was as if Spahn was attending his own wake and his old teammates showed up and were shitting on the food."

"Yeah, his arm was already dead," Deke said coldly.

Parlee let those last two lines hang there in the conversation for a moment. He poured some more beer and asked Oliver, "You still thinking of hanging them up?"

"Yeah, I am, no doubt. I'm thinking about opening a gym back in Rock Island," Oliver said. "Be around for the kids. Maybe do that full time. But before I decide for sure, I'm at least trying to figure out what makes a guy like Spahn keep playing and do what he's doing."

Oliver's revelation was news to Deke. Parlee hadn't told Deke that Oliver was considering quitting the game. Deke couldn't imagine why anyone would want to stop playing big league baseball.

"I can't even figure you guys out," Oliver said as he rolled his beer glass between his fingers, his index and ring fingers cocked and crooked from being broken through years of catching. "You guys are like feral ball players. You keep roaming around, trying to find games."

"It's because we still find games," Deke said without hesitation.

"We stop finding games that will have us and we'll stop playing."

Parlee chuckled at the notion. He and Deke had gone to great lengths over the last few years to play the game. Parlee wasn't so sure Oliver got it.

"Yeah, but why do you do it?" Oliver asked. "What do you get out of it?"

"Don't you play just because of the game?" Deke asked and stated.

"Your pal there said that to me the last time he was here," Oliver said. "What the hell's he talking about?"

"Half the time I don't have no idea what he's talking about," Deke said. "All I know is when I'm in that batter's box, there could be five people in the stands or five hundred or fifty thousand and I wouldn't know the difference. I do know that when I go to sleep every night this week, I'll be thinking of the two home runs I hit this weekend, even though they didn't mean shit."

"If I didn't have this game, I don't know what the hell I'd do," Deke said. "And I've never been able to make a living doing it.

"Shit, I'll trade you playing on that shithole diamond at Ashippun for the new stadium in Atlanta any day."

Oliver gave no clue that Deke's words caused him muse.

"I never saw baseball as work before until this season," he said. "It's a hard game to play and when no one's at your game or you have to go play somewhere you don't want to go, you wonder if all the work is worth it.

"All my life I worked to get to the Major Leagues," Oliver said. "Couldn't wait to get here. Then things happen where you get traded or your best friend goes, or this thing with the whole team going to Atlanta and it makes you wonder if it's worth it. I got traded from the Cardinals over to here couple of years ago and then they win the World Series last year. I would have never thought that was going to happen there. Now it's like I missed out."

Deke looked at Parlee. "We had good crowds this weekend, but how many were at our game Thursday?"

"Maybe thirty," Parlee said.

"How many of those were watching the game?"

"Maybe ten, counting the two umps."

"Shit, I didn't get the feeling they were watching too close," Deke turned back to Oliver. "If baseball wasn't a hard game, everyone would be playing," he said. "But it is hard and that's what makes playing it so goddamn special. Everybody tries to make it out to be some kind of magical game. People write goddamn poems about it for Christ sake. That's all bullshit -- grass under your feet, sun on your face and all that cheap shit. You ever see a poet try to pick up a groundball off the glare of the skinned infield at Clyman? Or bake on the bench in Neosho with the grass turned brown and crunches under your feet? Ball taking left turns when it hits a rock in the Ashippun outfield. It's a goddamn dirty game. And the only reason to quit playing is if you can't stand getting dirty anymore.

"You can get dirty a lot of different ways," Deke said. "We got Ashippun, you got Atlanta. Which Sally sittin' here has it better? You think guys like us are sitting around feeling sorry for you because you didn't play in the World Series last year?"

Deke had a weekend of diamond dirt, sweat and disappointment stuck up in his craw and he was spewing it at Oliver. He took time to take a breath, chuckle and fill everybody's beer. He raised a glass.

"If you don't want to play, get the fuck off the field," Deke toasted. "Who gives a shit? The game will go on without ya. You don't want to be here, I don't want to watch ya play and I sure as hell don't want ya on my team.

"You're the lucky one here," said Deke, still holding up his glass. "We fuck up our lives chasing baseball, but you Big Leaguers have baseball chasing you. Hell, I'm just happy Parlee knows how to work the system to pay for our beer and gas. But it sure don't cover the costs of losing wives or showing up sore and lame for work on Mondays. It's getting the chance to play the game that covers those expenses.

"I gotta piss," Deke concluded. He slugged down his beer in two long, sustained gulps and got up. He fumbled open the door to the small, decorated bathroom. Parlee hoped Deke wouldn't break anything in there.

"He got on a bit of a roll," Parlee said to Oliver. "Sorry about that."

"Don't worry about that," Oliver said. "That was some good shit. Is that how it is with you guys?"

"Deke's always pretty direct," said Parlee, sipping the beer Deke just poured for him. "But he's got a couple of things right. I've played this game my whole life on teams that I ran and on teams that didn't need me. There is no place on earth like being in the batter's box. It's a place we'll go anywhere to find. Same for a pitcher and his mound or a catcher like you, squatting behind the plate. Nowhere in this world can you find places like that and I don't think it matters if it's in Ashippun or Atlanta.

"But Deke's right," added Parlee, staring into the half-full glass he twirled in his fingers. "There's no magic in this game, not that I've ever seen. As much as the poets and writers and guys who haven't played the game want there to be, it just ain't there. It's a game that kicks your ass. I ain't telling you anything new. It takes the right kind of makeup in a guy to keep playing. I've played with guys three times more talented than I could ever hope to be and they give it up by the time they're twenty-five, they can't stand to have the game kick their ass. Just like Deke said, I don't care how good a guy is. If he don't want to play I don't want those fuckin' guys on my team."

"Is it the winning?" Oliver asked. "You guys win championships all the time. Is it the winning that keeps you playing?"

"Shit, I don't know," said Parlee, scanning the back bar. "Don't get me wrong, winning's great. You never get tired of it." He fixed his eyes on Oliver. "But you know what? I don't like winning more than I hate losing.

"I can't fucking stand losing," Parlee said. "It gnaws at ya forever. Think about it, you probably carry a loss around with you far longer than any win. We won the Rock last year and when it was done, when we were in the dugout afterward, it was like a let-down. Like you build it up way too much in your mind. Then when it's over, you realize a billion Chinese just don't give a shit."

Oliver chuckled and snorted as he took a gulp of beer.

"But you lose that championship game and that's all you think about all winter long," Parlee said. "It's almost like the only reason I want to win is because it's just another game I didn't lose."

Parlee realized he'd just given himself a revelation, stating something he'd never given much thought, but knowing it was true.

"So I don't think it's the winning that keeps me going."

Parlee, then had another revelation.

"I will tell you this," said Parlee, sitting up, leaning toward Oliver. "There are guys you just love to beat. Not just the young, cocky bastards who need their asses handed to them either. When Deke and Colt and I hooked on with Neosho for a few seasons, they had this guy who was one of the best hitters in the league. He'd tell ya all about it, too. Big blow-hard, pace up and down the dugout, talking about how he's hittin', how he won this batting title or that. Tell ya about the four hits he got the game before as if you weren't sittin' in the dugout watchin'."

"I've played with guys like that at every level," Oliver laughed. "They're everywhere."

"We win the title and he's beside himself," Parlee said. "Couldn't believe it. The first championship he'd won anywhere. He was just ballin' his goddamn eyes out. He didn't win the batting title that year and I thought we might have taught him something about winning. About moving runners over, being a team guy."

"I'll bet it didn't sink in," Oliver said, "never does with those guys."

"No shit. The next season he was worse than before," Parlee said. "He's stomping around, pissin' and moaning about not winning the batting title the year before and how that wasn't going to happen again. We won again despite him. But that was it.

"Colt and Deke would have punched him if we played there another year," Parlee remembered. "We went to Ashippun and we've never lost to that guy."

"The kind of guy you just want to beat because he makes it all about himself and not the game," Oliver said. "Yeah, I can see that."

"It's more about not wanting to lose to a guy like that," Parlee said. "Losing to those guys lets them validate themselves."

Oliver drew a breath, "What else is Deke right about?"

The bathroom door opened and Deke all but filled up the small door frame with his broad shoulders as he came out.

"He's right about how lucky you are to have the game chase you," Parlee said. Deke sat down at the table, leaned back in his chair, both hands running up and down his dirty ball pant thighs. "He's right about the game being what you make of it and the satisfaction you get out of it. Last Thursday I hit a triple during our game in Ashippun. Nobody saw it. But you know what? Every night since, when I go to bed I go to sleep thinking about that hit and all I can think about is how I want to do it again. Whatever magic's there, that's it. That's how the game runs through your blood like nothing else you could ever put in there.

"Lets you respect yourself," Parlee said. "Without baseball, we're just another couple of small town jerkoffs trying to get through life. We still ain't much more than that, but it's something."

Parlee looked at Deke. He was succumbing to the long weekend. Deke's eyes drooped. He let his glass stay empty.

"You gotta get me home so I can work in the morning."

"Jesus Christ," Oliver said. "I didn't even think about you guys having to work in the morning."

Deke grabbed Parlee's car keys off the table to head out to the impala.

"Great meeting ya, man," Deke said as he shook Oliver's hand.

Oliver got up to go to the bathroom. Parlee went to the pay phone to dial up Elmer Marks, the Rock River League commissioner, to get the league's Sunday scores. There was only one result he wanted since Horicon had obviously rescheduled its league game.

Ashippun lost, 3-1, and Parlee knew that wasn't good news. The Turk would be pissed, especially after finding out that Deke and Parlee could have made the game in time and didn't. He'd also have to tell Turk that Colton and Clay are through for the season.

Oliver was back at the table when Parlee sat down. Parlee was reflective, pensive. Finally he said "To be honest, I've been thinking the exact same way you have. I don't know if I'm going to keep doing it. Too much shit going on that you can't control. If I could just let the game play. . ."

Parlee's voice trailed off and they both stared at the half-full pitcher of beer. Neither made a move for it.

"That's just it," Oliver said.

"I keep going back to what an old man told me a long time ago," Parlee said. "This game don't quit you, you quit the game. It'll go on just fine without you. It's gone on just fine without Ruth and Cobb and DiMaggio and it will go on without Spahn."

"And without the Braves in Milwaukee," Oliver said.

"That's the shits right there," said Parlee as he picked up his glass, pointed it at Oliver and slugged down its remaining gulp. "I think the game will go on just fine without the likes of you and me. The game might mean something to us, but we don't mean shit to the game."

"Well," said Oliver, scanning the empty bar with searching eyes. "There's a lot of season left. We don't have to decide right now."

"Good thing," Parlee said. "There a George Webb's near here?"

"Keep going east on Blue Mound," Oliver said. "Like to go with but a bunch of us are going fishing out on the big lake tomorrow, early. Off day and then the Cubs."

They got up, sore from playing a game they each wondered is worth playing any longer. Parlee left a five dollar tip for Irma.

Outside, Parlee and Oliver shook hands and tried to read what was in the eyes of the other.

"I'll be back in," Parlee said. He fired up the Impala and drove the sleeping Deke to the local restaurant chain made famous by giving away free hamburgers during the Braves' twelve-game winning streak in '57.

CHAPTER 15

Parlee stood by himself at the far end of the dugout at Ashippun's Fireman's Park. He got himself out of the hot August sun for a moment before the start of the Platers' final game of the season.

Parlee was impatiently waiting for Wehlert to read off the lineup. The last few games, Wehlert had increasingly made a bigger deal out of revealing the lineup. He didn't go around to players taking hitting or playing catch before the game to tell them where they'd be playing that day. Instead, he regarded the lineup as a secret to be revealed just before game time.

Parlee saw things for what they were. Wehlert's handling of the lineup was the only way an insecure leader could draw some self attention from a team only he thought he controlled. So Wehlert held the team hostage until the very last minute.

Finally, Wehlert commanded the attention of the Platers and began reciting the lineup. Parlee chuckled when Wehlert read his own name at number four, even though Wehlert hadn't a hit in the cleanup slot in the past four games. By the time Parlee stopped chuckling, he at last heard his own name in the number eight hole – one notch above the American Legion kid the Turk signed up three weeks ago. That kid was still looking for his first Rock River League hit.

Parlee trotted out to right field with the feeling he was just playing out his last few innings. Tommy Kopplien was pitching – a good kid who's effort Parlee couldn't question. But the series of walks, wild pitches and the hit barrage that followed by the visiting Rubicon Red Sox gave Parlee all too much time to reflect from the outfield on a season that began to spiral downward in Plymouth and reach full-blown nose-dive status during the debacle in Horicon.

The long innings in the outfield gave Parlee too much time to think about the sadness of not finishing the season with Clay, Colton and Deke. As Koppy piled up eight walks over the first four innings,

Parlee dwelled on the bitterness he felt for the Turk after being pushed out of the field manager's role just before Horicon. Parlee didn't care that the Turk stopped pushing his way the envelopes with half the gate receipts each home game. What he couldn't take was being forced to stand by while a pompous punk kid like Wehlert drew up a lineup based only on his own ego.

The Platers were down 8-0 by the end of the fourth. The smallest Sunday crowd of the summer, maybe one hundred at best, yawned its indifference through the game. Word was that quite a few of the hardcore fans went up to Neosho to watch the Rockets battle Clyman for second place. The Ashippun Assholes could hardly harass the Red Sox, who were laying a licking on the Rock River League defending champs to secure fourth place and nail down their own berth in next week's playoffs.

Everyone seemed to be sleep walking through the game -- including Parlee when he was in the field and misplayed two fly balls. But Parlee wasn't about to give away his at-bats. Parlee walked his first time up and then, with his gum and tobacco mixture percolating just right in his mouth, he singled to left in the fourth and to right in the sixth. Each time, the kid behind him ended the inning, twice with strikeouts and once with a double play grounder to short. On the grounder, Parlee reopened the scab on his left knee with a hard slide into Rubicon second baseman Tommy Merk. Parlee and Merk had played together a couple of times on tournament teams. But Merk was a little too pissed off about Parlee's hard slide late in a lopsided game to help Parlee to his feet.

In his final at-bat in the eighth inning with two outs, no one on and down 12-0, Parlee got into one. Parlee got a high, inside fastball from the Rubicon righty and turned on the ball for all he was worth with the fat part of the bat. Parlee's bat was too much on top of the ball for a deep fly ball. Instead, the ball was a hooking line drive that headed deep into the right field corner. Parlee watched the ball's flight as he dropped the bat out of the box. He could see the right fielder misplay the ball on his first few steps, making a run straight for the foul line. But the ball carried deeper than the depth the outfielder had been positioned and when it landed fair by a foot it was well behind him. The right fielder was still running straight to the foul line when the ball landed behind him on the hard, sun-bake outfield grass and skipped into the corner of the outfield where it was held captive by the outfield snow fence.

In previous seasons the snow fence went only to the foul line. Over the last couple of years Parlee had hit similar balls that landed fair, skipped into foul territory and grounded past the fence and out of play for ground rule doubles. Several times over beers, Parlee had harped to the Turk about extending the fence into foul territory to keep balls in play. Only after Parlee had Deke bring it up did the Turk put up twenty extra feet of snow fence at each foul line.

With the ball still in play, Parlee spiked first and headed to second with his head down. Before turning second, Parlee looked over his shoulder to see the right fielder just getting to the ball. He knew he had a chance. As Parlee was sprinting to third, the third base coach, one of the kids, was holding both hands in the air to stop him there. But Parlee knew this would be the only chance the Platers would have to spoil the shutout of a Rubicon pitcher who wasn't good enough to deserve throwing a scoreless game. Parlee clipped third at full stride as hard as he had turned first. He headed home and turned to see the second baseman out on the outfield grass, pivoting with the relay throw. Parlee put his head down and began measuring where and when to start his slide when he saw the catcher beginning to squat in front of the plate just up the third baseline. As Parlee came harder, the catcher didn't get lower. Instead he leaped off both feet to try to snare a ball Parlee just then saw go at least three feet over the catcher's outstretched glove and over the short fence between the backstop and Rubicon dugout.

Parlee scored standing up and didn't even break stride to allow his teammates time to come out of the dugout. He ran straight to the dugout and down the steps, slapping whatever hands were held out as he went to the end of the bench to catch his breath. His heart pounded, but not because of the mad, four-base dash. Parlee realized his heart beat so hard simply because of the game.

An inning later, the game, and Ashippun's season, was over with the 12-1 shellacking. It ended when Wehlert swung at a two-strike pitch in the dirt with one on and two out. Parlee laughed out loud when a half-dozen of the Ashippun Assholes, who were in the stands just for the beer, began left-righting Wehlert on his way to the dugout. It was the only time Parlee could remember seeing a player flip off his home crowd. He wished Deke was there to see it.

Parlee went out to shake hands with the Sox players and wished them well in the playoffs. He told Merk he was sorry about the slide.

"No big deal, Parlee. We'll see you next year."

Merk's words stopped Parlee for a moment as he turned to go toward the dugout. Wehlert was in there, half-dressed. He hadn't come out to shake hands, still pissed from the hometown razzing he was now showing he so richly deserved.

"Son of a bitch," Parlee muttered to his self. Wehlert and the Turk deserve one another.

Parlee took the slowest walk to the dugout he could ever remember. He went down the steps on the outfield side of the dugout, away from the rest of the team. He grabbed his bat and slowly took off his spikes, then packed his duffel bag. His teammates were either too young or too wrapped in themselves to care or consider what Parlee might be thinking. Fifteen minutes after the game was over, they were all gone to the beer stand. Next season was the furthest thing from any of their minds.

Pete was the only Plater to linger at the end of the dugout.

"Let me know what you're doing next year, will ya Parlee?"

"You bet, kid."

Parlee sat by his self for the better part of a half hour, alternately staring out at the field from the dugout bench and turning the Nokona in his hands. The laughter and chatter that came from the beer stand behind the dugout seemed as far off and faint as a wavering mirage on a desert horizon.

Parlee thought about the last ball he'd hit. Something different he'd never before considered. He looked at his hands, one holding the Nokona, the other a baseball. Hands that were callused from the knob of the bat, scarred by the rough infield grit of a hundred diamonds. His eyes followed the ropy veins up his forearms. Blue protruding streams exaggerated from years of batting practice. A road map any player can read. That fleeting instant the ball contacted with bat and bat to hands, those veins carried it all to his heart. A heart pounding to be connected again and again to that point of contact.

He put the glove on his left hand and fisted it a couple of times as he scanned the ceiling of the dugout. It was of similar construction as the dugout in Plymouth.

Parlee eyed the cranny similar to the nook where he had spied Schmidty's old catcher mitt.

Parlee took the glove and grabbed a pail he turned upside down at the far end of the dugout. He stood on the pail and reached the Nokona into the space between two two-by-sixes where they rested on the cement wall.

Parlee stepped down from the pail, looked out at the diamond one last time and then his eyes went up to the glove. He had to look hard to see it hidden there in the shadows. But it was there.

Parlee grabbed his duffel bag and bat and headed up the dugout steps. He went out the gate and walked a few paces before stepping around the Dogwood tree that had found new life after the ladies from the Ashippun Fireman's Auxiliary had landscaped the tree with rocks to form a circle containing woodchips.

He got to the Impala, fired it up and left the Ashippun Trap without looking back at the beer stand or field.

CHAPTER 16

Baseball didn't take us to France. The war did that. But we all took baseball with us. Never thought I'd ever get a chance to play on such lush fields as what was those green fields of France. People always think they know just what it is they want but they usually don't. Sometimes they get lucky and get it anyway. Hell, I knew I was lucky. There I was in France, playin' baseball with a bunch of Doughboys. I was good then. There was this first sergeant there whose family owned the St. Louis Browns. He tolt me soon as we come back from over there he'd get me a tryout.

People always want ya to know about the bad things that happen to them that they don't deserve, but they seldom mention the good. Well, bein' over there playin' in France was as good as it got for me. Truth be tolt, it couldn't have gotten any better. 'Cuz we was cavalry and all we could do is get our horses slaughtered, the war got over with 'fore our company saw much action. We couldn't figure why we was there in the first place. Guess it took 'em a while to figure out wars was being fought different than before.

Our games was quite the curiosity to the local Frenchies. They'd come out and watch, not knowing what the hell was going on out on the field. A lot of 'em came. Pretty soon, we'd be playin' in front of fifty, sixty folks almost ever day. When I got the prettiest little girl I'd ever seen to smile at me, I knew I was the luckiest man in France. Married her, too, I did. Brought her back home and that Browns feller made good on his promise. That was the closest I ever came to playin' in the big city leagues. That was in '19 and I guess us Doughboys brought that flu back to the states with us. My Capucine come down with it and for six weeks I tended to her bed that smelled more like death ever day. I missed that try-out and I still miss her.

And that's all I'm gonna tell ya about that.

***

A little more than three weeks after Ashippun ended its season, the Braves hosted the Los Angeles Dodgers on a Wednesday night, their final game at Milwaukee County Stadium. The Braves had only recently fallen out of contention for the National League pennant due to an early September slump. Parlee had done his best to try to not think about baseball since his last at-bat in Ashippun.

School started just before Labor Day and his mind was filled with his teaching duties at Jefferson High and a new school year. He'd scan the Braves box scores to see Oliver was approaching a career-high twenty homers. But Parlee slowly lost interest as the Braves fell out of contention and the team's ownership looked to the next year in Atlanta with a little too much vigor for Parlee to stomach. Nowhere Parlee went, high school football games, cafes, the teacher's lounge at school, his infrequent and brief visits to Jefferson taverns, were the Braves a topic of conversation.

It was such a contrast to years not-so-recently past when September's pennant fever gripped the entire state.

By the time school was in its third week, Parlee's knee scab had healed and fallen off. He'd felt the nickel-size piece of dried blood and puss fall down along his shin as he shook the leg of his trousers while standing in front of his class one afternoon. His mouth was no longer sore from a summer's worth of Applejack and he'd been hangover free for about a month.

Still, his last at-bat lingered in his mind and put him to sleep most nights.

When school let out on September 22, 1965, Parlee went out to the parking lot at Jefferson High and got into his six-year old black Impala, gassed up for its final trip to County Stadium. The school was located one residential block deep from Highway 18 on the city's west side. Just two years old, the new high school sprawled land on the outskirts of town toward the Crawfish River where it was looked down upon with pride and envy by its predecessor, a more traditional three-story stone school building located high atop a hill three blocks to the east.

Parlee turned to go east on 18 and passed the new junior high in the old high school building as he skirted the hill just prior to crossing the downtown bridge over the Rock River, meandering its way to a meeting with the Crawfish a half-mile south. Once through downtown, Parlee looked to his right to catch a glimpse of the Fischer Field diamond where the Blue Devils play near the shadow of the Jefferson County Courthouse. He considered the possibilities and a conversation he'd had a week ago with Bower, who was still running the Blue Devils.

If he was just five years younger. . .

On the outskirts of town, 18 snaked past St. Colletta's School for the mentally handicapped, a place called home by a sister of JFK. The town had been turned upside down and vigorously shaken when the president made a visit three years ago. It was the last time the president would see his sister and the event and aftermath provided Parlee and his Jefferson High colleagues with many a quality teaching moment.

Parlee powered the Impala into the countryside, slowing only a bit about six miles out of town for Helenville. Passing Helenville on 18, one would never know it contained a baseball diamond nestled between cornfields and a woodlot on the north edge of the unincorporated burg. As he drove, Parlee glanced off to the north and considered the possibilities.

If he was ten years younger. . .

Through Dousman he passed the Sum Place Else Tavern, a frequent stop on his excursions to and from County Stadium over the seasons. He was there after the Mathews homer in game four of the '57 Series and four days later, following the Wisconsin Avenue victory parade. In '58 he'd stopped there on the way into the fifteen or so home games he'd attended. It was a good place to grab the beer fans could carry into the stadium in those days.

He'd been at the Sum Place following a Monday afternoon game in '59 when the Braves opened a best-of-three playoff series at home with the Dodgers after finishing the season tied with Los Angeles for the National League pennant. It was a rainy, cool late September day and Johnny Roseboro hit a solo homer in the sixth for a 3-2 Dodger win. The next day in Los Angeles, shortstop Johnny Logan got hurt and with Red Schoendist already out, the Dodgers overcame the 5-2 ninth-inning Braves lead to capture the pennant when the winning run scored in the twelfth inning on a play Felix Mantilla couldn't make from short.

Parlee was making his way to Waukesha when he again thought about the regret of that playoff and how the Dodgers went on to handle the White Sox in the World Series in six games. It was at that bar back in Dousman where Parlee talked for hours with locals he didn't know about the changing state of the Braves. After losing the game on Roseboro's homer, no one in the bar that night gave the Braves a chance to go out and win twice in the Los Angeles Coliseum – not with Spahn unable to start after tossing a complete game on Saturday against the Phillies in the next-to-last regular season game the Braves had to have. It took but one game for the Braves to prove them right and their hopes of making three consecutive World Series appearances were dashed with that extra-innings loss.

After that first '59 playoff game, as the Milwaukee team flew to its Los Angeles doom, the tone of the conversation that night in the Dousman tavern was about the changing attitude of Braves fans. It was a change that started after the disappointing seven game World Series loss to the Yanks in '58. Starting the next year, expectations were exceeding the cult-like love and devotion heaped without question on the team since the Braves were seemingly dropped from the dark Boston skies and into the sunshine of County Stadium in the spring of '53. In '59 not everything the Braves did was cheered the way it had been through the mid-part of the decade. Fans didn't react to a bases-loaded pop up by the home team with a "nice try!" the way they once did. No longer did the fat women with cow bells come out in droves to County Stadium. Never before had fans balked at games when rain was in the forecast. Booing of the home team, an act that in previous seasons could get a fan beaten, was becoming common place for bad play. For the first time, Parlee told his Dousman audience, Milwaukee fans were acting like baseball fans in other cities.

At the time, Parlee welcomed the change. When the Milwaukee crowd applauded pop ups or routine grounders hit by the home team in white uniforms, Parlee would ask those around him what the hell they were cheering about. He knew that the "Bushville" name heaped on the Milwaukee crowd by the pompous New York press during the '57 Series was not without some merit. And he sure as hell didn't miss those goddamn obnoxious cowbells.

It had taken a long time, six years, but by the end of the '59 season the novelty of the Braves had worn off. Right up to closing time that night following that disappointing defeat, Parlee argued with the Dousman barkeep and three of his pals, road construction workers building pieces of the new Interstate highway. They disagreed about what the change in the attitude of fans meant and how it could affect the future of the Braves in Milwaukee. Parlee said the change was good for the image of the Milwaukee hardcore baseball fan. He was certain enough support existed to sustain the Braves in Milwaukee forever. The Dousman regulars were unconvinced and insisted that any fall off of fan support was a bad omen — especially given the fact a half dozen teams had moved to greener pastures in the time since the Braves came from Boston to Milwaukee.

"You just wait," the bartender told Parlee as he poured another seven-ounce glass of Blatz from the tapper in the wall of the back bar. "I don't think Perini would ever move them but some greedy bastard might get his stinkin' mitts on 'em and take 'em someplace else."

As he navigated the string of stop and go lights through Waukesha, leading into West Allis, Parlee thought about how the Dousman guys had gotten it right. It took the sale of the club to outside interests to make the move possible. Until this year, the

Braves were still drawing as well as any club in the big leagues.

The Impala rolled into the County Stadium parking lot about an hour before game time. The lot didn't have that familiar festive feel of a ten-acre party — especially late in the season, a time when the Braves almost always remained in contention. The feel was that of a large, sullen wake. People were grilling hotdogs and pulling cases of beer from their car trunks almost as a last-chance sense of duty to pay their respects. It was far from a celebration of a baseball game and season.

Parlee parked and wandered the lot, mingling with fans who were cooking brats, hot dogs and burgers on grills. He scrounged a beer and a burger from a group of about a dozen fans who'd made the trip in from Lake Mills in two station wagons and a pickup truck carrying ice chests, two grills and three card tables.

When Parlee told the group he lived in Jefferson, a guy manning one of the grills stopped flipping dogs and closed the lid of the cooker. He was a big, round man about fifty or so with a dark mustache.

"Jefferson?" said the man as he narrowed his eyes at Parlee. "Didn't you used to play with the Blue Devils?"

"Yeah, I did. For a couple of seasons six or seven back."

"I used to help out with the Lake Mills team. You give it up?" The Lake Mills Grays are a rival of the Blue Devils in the Home Talent League. Parlee remembered playing at Campus Field in downtown Lake Mills, where the diamond nestled before concrete bleachers angled from a wooded hillside. Its fenceless outfield extended into the high school football field.

"No," said Parlee, taking a swig from a Miller High Life. "I've been playing up in the Rock. Neosho for a couple of years and then out at Ashippun."

"What's the matter? Your home town team not good enough for you? What the hell you looking for in those places?"

"Don't know," Parlee said. He realized he really didn't. "Just looking for a game, I guess."

"Shit, you sound like these bunch of carpetbaggers," a guy off to the side of the grill, biting into a brat held with both hands. The big, round man leaned forward to allow excess mustard and sour kraut to drip onto the asphalt of the parking lot. Ketchup stained the belly of his Lee denim jacket.

Parlee hadn't thought of himself as a carpetbagger but instantly knew the term fit. As Parlee pondered that notion for the first time, the group began taking turns bemoaning the loss of the Braves, grim canticles Parlee was certain they'd been reciting to one another since the move was announced.

"There's no goddamn loyalty," a man in a Braves cap said. "Not to the fans, not to the city."

"Who the hell says these new owners, Bartholomay and those assholes, have the right to pull Major League Baseball out of Milwaukee?" a younger guy with a bottle of Miller in one hand, cigar in the other. A blue hat with a gold LM sat crooked and crinkled on his head. "Who gave them that power?"

"Yeah, how come they get to decide? They don't know shit about us," concurred a chunky blonde woman about the same age who was hanging on the young man's arm. "How could the commissioner let these guys come in, buy the team and then they get to decide to move?"

The woman grabbed her boyfriend's cigar from between his fingers. She put the wet end in her mouth and drew her lungs full of smoke.

"Why didn't they put it to a vote," she talked casually as the smoke came back out her mouth, clouding her words. "What ever happened to letting the people decide?"

An older man who was closing up the tail gate door of the Chevy Biscayne wagon sidled up to Parlee as if he was going to let him in on a secret. He spoke in low tones while the circle of tailgaters consoled one another with their redundant complaints.

"I've been to every opening day here for the last thirteen years," the man said to Parlee. "Been to every home World Series game. That '59 playoff game. Three times a year I fill up the station wagon with little leaguers from Lake Mills and Johnson Creek and in we come. Raising the town's generation of Braves fans, baseball fans. Just like people do in communities all over the southern part of the state. You ever been in the bleachers when they're full of kids? Kids who go to sleep nights to dream that someday they'd be big leaguers? It's one of god's greatest creations. Now it's going to be gone because some outa towners buy the team and say so? How can that be allowed to happen?"

Parlee could see true hurt in the man's eyes.

"Yeah, I've been out in the bleachers during Little League days," Parlee said. He could still see the faces of hundreds of small boys, gazing in awe-struck wonderment from beyond the outfield fence at the site of a full and raucous stadium. Many of the bright eyes were seeing the sight for the first time. It was a sight their young minds would carry with them always. Big league ball players! Hank Aaron, right there! Scores of school buses in the parking lot beyond left field. Each kid dressed with a braggart's pride in his Little League uniform, an array of colors and sponsors from small businesses in Greendale, Hales Corners, Brookfield, Muskego, Lake Geneva, Wilmot, Elkhorn, Hartford, Beaver Dam. Each with a glove, poised to snag a Mathews homer they were certain was headed their way. They'd all dream that night in exhausted sleep of one day hitting a County Stadium homer of their own. A new Milwaukee Braves pennant monitoring those dreams from its perch on the bedroom wall.

"That might be the truest statement I've heard in a long time," Parlee said. "That is one of god's greatest creations."

"And Atlanta's the home of the goddamn devil," the mustachioed man at the grill said as he slammed the lid, a plate of hotdogs in his hand.

Parlee thanked the group for the beer, burger and conversation.

"I'd like to say I'll see ya at opening day," said Parlee, turning to the older man. "But. . ."

"Nothin' to say that ain't been said," said the old man, still speaking in hushed tones. He handed Parlee a fresh bottle of Miller for his walk into the stadium. "It's a goddamn travesty is what it is."

Parlee could tell by the size of the crowd in the parking lot there'd be plenty of room in the stadium. So he went to the Gate X ticket window and bought a lower grandstand ticket for three dollars. He went into the stadium through a turnstile, taking the ripped ticket stub from an elderly ticket taker.

"How ya holdin' up?" said Parlee as he put the stub in his shirt pocket under his coat, a safe place where he knew he wouldn't lose the memento.

"Not so good," the man said from under a cap that could be exchanged for that of a bus driver and no one would notice. The shiny black bill of the captain's-style cap underlined yellow lettered "Stadium Tickets" on blue course cloth. "I put away what I make here to take the wife south each winter. She hates the winter and we have a little trailer down by Tucson, close to the kids. Looks like I'll have to get a real job from here out or just stay down there year round. Never thought I'd see this day."

Parlee had to move along with a line forming behind. He stepped into the concourse, orienting himself, figuring he was on the third base side of home plate. Parlee steered himself to his right, taking in the pre-game sights and sounds of the concourse for the final time. Vendors scurried through the crowd hawking beer, cotton candy and red hots on their way to the tunnels that led into the stands. Their shouts echoing in the concourse turned mausoleum.

Parlee passed a wooden booth, a kiosk that sported a sign for programs. An elderly attendant in another bus driver style hat was bent behind the booth's elevated counter looking as if he was gathering his final belongings.

Parlee asked for a program. The man popped his head above the counter and looked down on Parlee.

"All sold out," he said. "Cheap bastards didn't print any after the season began. If we'd have had the crowds to run out in July, then that would have been it."

"All gone all over?" Parlee asked.

"You can check. I think they gave each of us the same amount. I only had eight. Wadn't even worth comin' in for."

Parlee continued his trek toward the first base side of the stadium, back of the Braves dugout.

He popped out of the tunnel to take in the field in time to see Mathews, not Bragan, at home plate exchanging the lineup card with Dodger Manager Walter Alston.

"Bragan's probably scardt he'd get booed off the diamond," Parlee heard a man say to his friend as the two walked the aisle behind the box seats.

Koufax was throwing for the Dodgers and Parlee wanted an up close view of the best lefty since Spahn. So he hedged his way down among the red box seats just off the foul ball screen between home plate and the Braves dugout. Parlee picked a row about eight up from the screen and squeezed past two older guys seated on the aisle to a span of about five empty seats. There were empty seats in front and in back of Parlee and he figured if the seat's rightful owners emerged, he'd have other options.

The Braves took the field to a standing ovation from a crowd Parlee thought couldn't be too much more than ten thousand. Catcher Joe Torre warmed up starter Wade Blassingame. Oliver was over at first tossing grounders to Mathews at third, Woody Woodward at short and Frank Bolling at second. In left, Billy Cowan long-tossed with Mack Jones in center. Aaron played catch in right with a ball boy stationed along the foul line.

The number of hand-made signs filtering through the crowd drew Parlee's attention. "Farewell Eddy!"; "Thanks for the Memories!"; "Been Nice knowing you!" and "Don't Forget Us!" One of the more hopeful signs spanned about 50 feet of the fence above the left field bleachers behind the half dozen or so fans in the section. "See you next year Braves!"

At least one was unrelated to the pending move. "Koufax is a Sorehead!" read a sign held by a man behind the Dodger dugout.

In time, Torre threw the ball down to Bolling at second and the Braves final game in Milwaukee was set to begin.

As Maury Wills settled into the batters box, a cheer started pulsing from the left field seating, working its way to the heart of the stadium behind home plate. Parlee scanned the stadium to see where people were turning and pointing to find a man holding a sign for all to see as he made his way through the aisle that separated the box seats from the lower grandstand section. The man continued his march toward the home plate area, rotating the sign above his head with both hands for all to see. People who saw it for the first time cheered and urged the man on, the cheers getting closer to Parlee.

At last, the man was close enough for Parlee to read the sign. Carved from corrugated cardboard in the shape of a tombstone, black, running painted lettering spelled "RIP Carpetbagger!" Parlee joined the cheering.

Parlee's attention was drawn back to the field when Wills ripped a single to left. With Jim Gilliam at the plate, Wills stole second, more on Blassingame, Parlee thought, than Torre. Gilliam singled to put runners at the corners and Wills scored on a ground out by Willie Davis.

Parlee watched intently as Koufax shut down the Braves in order in the first, striking out Cowan and Jones. A leg kick and delivery so smooth, the ball exploded from Koufax's hand toward the plate. Equally devastating was a curve ball that broke straight down through the hitting zone. Parlee knew he'd never have a chance in the box against a guy like Koufax, especially being a left-handed hitter.

But in the bottom of the second, Torre, Oliver, Mathews and Bolling each took advantage of their chances. As Torre strode to the plate to lead off the inning, Oliver took a knee with his bat on the on-deck circle. Parlee waited for the crowd buzz to quiet before he gave two quick whistles between his teeth, the second at a higher pitch than the first. Oliver, still kneeling, turned to the familiar signal to see Parlee standing about six rows up behind home plate.

Oliver touched his hat to Parlee as Torre hit a Koufax offering to center for a single. The crowd began to generate enthusiasm not seen all season as Oliver and then Mathews singled to load the bases. The bugler who'd been a part of the County Stadium scene all through the '50s, blew his familiar "Charge!"

The unexpected happened when the light-hitting Bolling turned on the first pitch from Koufax and lined a homer to left for a grand slam. The small crowd of three that was on the bases mobbed Bolling as he came to home plate after slowly rounding the bases, taking it all in.

For Parlee, it was like '57 all over again. Fans were delirious. There just wasn't as many of them. But what were there stood and cheered until Bolling came back out of the dugout to tip his hat.

It was a short night for Koufax after Mack Jones led off the third with his twenty-ninth homer of the season and Aaron followed with a sharp single. That brought Alston out of the dugout and out to the mound while the fans behind the Dodger dugout chanted "Koufax is a Sorehead" as the Dodger great left the County Stadium mound for the last time.

Right hander Howie Reed came on and got Torre to hit a grounder to shortstop for a double play. Parlee watched as Oliver walked to the plate. On the first pitch from Reed, Oliver swung and hit a high drive to left-center field. Parlee stood, thinking the ball was gone, urging the ball to go.

Leftfielder Lou Johnson turned to chase the ball to the fence. Davis ran from center to Johnson's flank. As Johnson and Davis got to the fence, the ball surprised everyone in the park, who, like Parlee, thought it to be gone. Instead, the ball hit off the very top railing of the outfield fence and shot away from the Dodger outfielders and into the no-man's land of centerfield.

The crowd let loose a mixed cheer and groan -- disappointed the ball stayed in play, excited for what could happen in the coming seconds.

Parlee looked to see Oliver on his way to second with no intention of stopping there. Parlee flashed to the ball he'd hit in Ashippun, held in play by the extended snow fence. He saw the ball in center field, no Dodger close.

"Go!" Parlee yelled with instinctive excitement. He knew Oliver had a chance.

Oliver chugged toward third and was being waved home as two Dodger infielders and Davis chased after the lonesome ball in center.

The crowd reached its feet with a gasp of excitement as if urging the thorough bred favorite to the finish line of a horse race. Oliver churned the final furlong as a desperate and aimless throw looped onto the infield to no one in particular, from no one in particular.

Oliver scored standing up and into the arms of an excited Mathews.

Parlee and the rest of the crowd clapped and whistled as Oliver made his way with heavy feet to the Braves dugout.

Parlee sat long before those around him to drink in the ironic coincidence of what he just witnessed.

With the Braves leading 6-1, the contest settled into the routine of a normal game. The Dodgers scored twice in the fourth on Jim Lefebvre's homer. Then they chased Blassingame with three runs in the fifth to tie the score at 6-6.

With Koufax out of the game, Parlee found little reason to maintain his post behind home plate. He wondered the stadium seats and concourses, grabbing a beer here, a hotdog there, taking in the sights and feel of the team wake.

A witness to an execution.

Yet all will survive and move on and that's what Parlee suddenly found himself ready to do.

In the seventh the scoreboard flashed the attendance at 12,577. As the tie game moved into the later innings, that crowd gathered around the lower rails on either side of the dugouts, eager to take its frustration, anger, sympathy and nostalgia to the field itself.

But all were held back, not by the railing, not by security guards. The game held back the crowd as it trudged past the ninth inning, into the tenth and then the eleventh. The crowd prolonged the game with its long, sad and loud farewells of Mathews, Aaron, Torre and all the Braves.

When Mathews came to the plate in the bottom of the eighth for what could have been his last Milwaukee at-bat, the crowd stopped the game with a three-minute standing ovation. Parlee watched with sadness as Mathews, visibly touched, stood outside the batters box until just the right moment to step in and quiet the crowd.

The crowd repeated itself in the tenth when Mathews returned to the plate after Oliver led the inning off with a walk. Again the game was delayed by an ovation that served the dual purpose of bidding farewell to Mathews and urging him to end the game with one mighty swing of the bat.

Mathews surprised everyone in the park when he squared to bunt and sacrificed Oliver to second. The crowd wouldn't cheer Bragan for ordering the bunt. Instead, it cheered Mathews for a smart baseball play. The reward was nullified when Sandy Alomar popped out and Denis Menke ended the inning by lining out.

Johnson's single scored Wills with the go-ahead run in the top of the eleventh. In the bottom of the inning with one out, Jones reached on an infield hit. Aaron came to the plate to yet another long ovation. But as baseball often portends, the game was unexpectedly and inappropriately ended when Aaron sent a liner to center that was snagged on the run by Davis, who threw back to first to get Jones for a double play.

Wes Parker had no sooner secured the ball at first when the initial wave of rail jumpers made their way onto the field, impatient throngs heading to home plate and the mound.

Parlee looked down on the scene from the area behind home where he had watched the early portion of the game. The bugler began a slow, mournful version of "Taps." Players and coaches made their way off the field and into the dugouts, careful to avoid the citizens swarming the diamond.

In a short time Parlee heard two quick whistles, the second a pitch higher than the first. He looked down toward the corner of the dugout to see Oliver waving him down to the field.

***

"You run pretty good for a man they call 'Beefalo'," Parlee said as he climbed the waist-high rail at the end of the Braves' dugout, landing on both feet next to Oliver.

"Hell, I was runnin' scared from second on," Oliver laughed. "A guy my size gets thrown out at third or home and they'd make me be a stewardess on the plane tomorrow all the way to San Francisco."

Parlee followed Oliver down the dugout steps, the two ignoring the bevy of unorganized activity out on the diamond. The dugout's concrete floor was strewn with the familiar remnants of a baseball game – gum wrappers, balls of tape, pools of spit tobacco juice, spilled liquids of several different shades of earthy colors. Drying chaws.

"How'd your season wind up?" Oliver asked Parlee as they settled onto the bench at the end of the dugout away from home plate. Before them on the diamond grown men were running the bases, some sliding into second and third base, even though the bags were long gone.

"It turned into a goddamn train wreck," said Parlee as he brought his tobacco pouch from his jacket pocket and pulled loose the draw string. "I always wanted a chew in a big league dugout."

"Jesus, you still have this thing?" Oliver said as he grabbed the pouch from Parlee who stuffed a chaw in his cheek. "I remember Jule Downing found this in your pants pocket that summer on the farm when she did laundry and she about had a shit fit."

"Closest I ever came to losing it," Parlee said as he churned the Applejack in his mouth. Oliver worked the pouch between his fingers.

"When was the big collision in the train wreck?" Oliver asked.

"Started going off the tracks right after Deke and I showed up here that weekend last of June," Parlee said. He leaned back and took in the view of a big league diamond from the dugout for the first time.

"Deke," Oliver said, shaking his head, "that guy's a walking riot waiting for a crowd to show up."

"Wait 'til you hear this," Parlee said, spitting juice on a spot on the dugout floor already stained with tobacco. "That week we get back and Turk, the guy who runs the team, is pissed we came here instead of going to our game that we lost up in Juneau that Sunday. Top of that, Turk's pissed our best guy got signed up there in Plymouth and another guy who went with us broke a finger. Two of the best players in the league and they're done.

"So he won't spilt the gate anymore and hands over the field manager duties to a punk who's been playing with the team for less than two seasons," Parlee said.

"Right when he probably needs you the most," Oliver said.

"That's one way to look at it," Parlee said. "Just not the Turk's way.

"So we lose the next Sunday up in Slinger, a team we always beat, and then we got to go to Horicon and win or we're out of contention," Parlee said. "We win, we're two games out with six to play. We lose, no way we win the league."

"Horicon, that's Sheridan's team?" Oliver asked. He was seated on the top of the back support, feet on the bench seat as he leaned in to listen to Parlee.

"Yeah, this is Fourth of July up there and they're making a big deal out of the game," Parlee's eyes twinkled as he thought about the scene. "We're defending champs coming in. They can all but eliminate us. Huge crowd. All of Horicon's there, we brought a shitload of people. Big pre-game for the National Anthem. They had a bunch of Boy Scouts bring out the flag across center field with all these World War II guys."

"Ooh, ooh," Oliver said, leaning in closer as Parlee spit again between his feet. "I think I know where this is going."

"You got it," said Parlee, wiping his chin. "I'm still hitting second then. Their big righty they paid for struck out Pete our lead off guy and then I swing late on a good fast ball and shoot one down the left field line for a luck double. Our fans are going nuts, Deke comes up.

"Deke can hit anyone," Parlee said. "I think he would have got Koufax tonight."

"Hey!" Oliver said.

"Sorry. Nice hit, by the way." Parlee backtracked. "Deke's a goddamn born hitter and he locked into their ringer. Kind of guy Deke eats up. This guy doesn't think anyone in our shit league can hit his fast ball. Deke sits on him, gets his fast ball and drills a humpback liner over the shortstop's head. I score without a throw and when I cross home plate I see Deke jawing at Sheridan at first. The ump's standing right there and said something and I thought it was done.

"Sheridan looks like he's walking away and you could see Deke said something else," Parlee stood and faced Oliver to embellish the story with some play acting. "All of a sudden Sheridan turns with his fist cocked, winds up and swings as hard as he can. Deke ducks at the last second and catches the full blow of Sheridan's right hand square in his big–assed batting helmet. Helmet goes flying, hits our first base coach right in the nuts. Learn later, Sheridan breaks his hand.

"Holy shit!" Oliver said.

"Gets better," said Parlee as he made a fist and cocked his arm. "Deke rights himself and squares up in front of Sheridan. Big prick had thrown his mitt down and was holding his hand, bent over."

Parlee demonstrated by bending at his waist. Then he stood and again cocked a fist.

"Deke reaches back about as far as Kenosha and swings full gas at Sheridan."

Parlee demonstrated.

"He catches Sheridan right on the side of the face," Parlee threw a downward punch. "Breaks his orbital socket, goes down in a heap."

"So he breaks his hand and his eye socket?" Oliver, amazed. "Which eye?"

"Left."

"He a left- or right-handed hitter?

"Right."

"Shit, he might never be able to hit again," Oliver said. "Lead eye. What happened to Deke?"

"He didn't know it but he was knocked out on his feet." Parlee said. "Had a concussion. Doesn't remember a fuckin' thing. We all go running out there and their guys all come running out. Closer I get, I can see Deke's loopy. I got next to him so no one would sucker punch him. Their guys are pushing our guys and our guys are pushing their guys. I didn't get the feeling their guys were very offended that their big turd was layin' face down like a piece of shit in the dirt.

"I get Deke into the dugout and he doesn't know anything," said

Parlee as he climbed up and sat on the back of the dugout bench alongside Oliver. A young, dark-skinned man came down the steps on the home plate side of the dugout, scanned the back wall and grabbed the lineup card tacked there.

Parlee looked at Oliver.

"Smart guy, there, I should of grabbed that," Parlee said, then back to Horicon. "To this day, Deke doesn't remember a thing. Can't even remember riding up there or getting the hit or swinging at Sheridan. Nothing."

"Or what he said to Sheridan, to touch it off?" Oliver dipped into Parlee's pouch for a chew of his own. "What do you suppose he said?"

"You're right," Parlee said. "Can't remember any of it. Took about an hour for the umps to sort things out, scrape Sheridan off the field. Bottom of the first, I'm trotting out to right and I go over by the first base ump. Older guy I've known for years."

"'Harley,' I says, 'did you hear any of that? Deke doesn't remember anything.'"

"'Damnest thing,' Harley says, 'I heard him plain as day. Asks Sheridan which Boy Scout had the cutest ass.'"

Oliver tilted his head back in a belly laugh.

The two laughed until they started to cramp. Parlee recreated the melee twice more. About a half-dozen fans were on their knees on the infield, scrapping dirt into jars and brown liquor sacks. The continuous circle of base runners dodged the dirt lifters.

"They had all they could do to keep the cops out of it," Parlee said as the two finally caught their breath. "League elders were pissed. Deke got suspended for the rest of the year. Might not let him play next season.

"That was it," Parlee threw up his hands and let them fall in his lap. "Lost, 4-1. We didn't win another goddamn game the rest of the year. All of July and into August. Crowds fell off. We were shitty. Didn't have Deke or the two other guys we lost in Plymouth. Turk blamed me for all of it."

"Fuck him," Oliver said.

"I told him that exact thing. Several times."

They stared out at the scene. Behind them, up in the stands, the bugler played "Taps" for the third time. Parlee could see fans with tools working over the seats along the left field line.

"Jesus," he said. "There won't be anything left of this place by the time they run everyone out.

"But I'm with you," Parlee continued. "I decided to be done. Tired of fighting everything else."

"Well, shit," Oliver said as he leaned forward to spit a stream of Applejack juice. "I was going to tell ya that I'm back with you guys."

"What?"

"Yeah, I decided to go to Atlanta," Oliver said. "Past few weeks I got thinking about what you've been trying to tell me and then Deke's pretty persuasive. But you guys are right about this game. It runs through your blood like nothing else can.

"I don't think I'll ever forget running those bases tonight," excitement rising in Oliver's voice. "I got back in the dugout and my heart was pounding. And it wasn't from the running. It was because of the game."

"Holy shit," Parlee said.

"I can't explain it," Oliver looking out at the diamond. "We've played like dogshit this last month and right out of contention. You'd think that'd make me want to quit even more. But that ain't it. It's the game, just like you said. I guess I'd forgotten. All this shit going on but the game's still there. It didn't quit me, how can I quit it? I can't. At least not while I think I can still play.

"The other thing, too, I realized," Oliver said after leaning to spit, "this game has a way of making a guy respect his self. You work hard to be a better player, a better teammate, I think it makes ya a better person. Let's ya walk around proud."

"Fuck me," Parlee whispered to himself as he looked down into his lap where he held the tobacco pouch with both hands, making a connection.

"So I've come around to thinking like you and Deke. It don't matter if the game's in Ashippun, Horicon, Melonville or where ever in hell you guys play. Or Milwaukee or Atlanta. You just gotta fuckin play as long as you can. Hell, I'm one away from a twenty homer season."

"Look at these people," Oliver swept his hand out to the orderly mob running the field. "This game does something to people. We don't always have to understand it, but we have to realize it. It's right there."

Oliver and Parlee looked out toward home plate. The cops who had tried to surround home plate had finally given way to a swarm of hands that eventually dug the plate from where it had rested like a monument for thirteen seasons. Two teenagers held the plate above their heads and moved toward the grandstand to applause, cheers and whistles from everyone left in the stadium.

The organ player, who for years, cheerily tapped out the Mexican Hat Dance and other catchy, hand-clapping vignettes, settled in for a long score of "Auld Lang Syne." Fans locked arms to form lines that swayed to the New Year's anthem that took on a melancholy tone in the morose County Stadium setting.

"Look at these people," Oliver said. "Most probably didn't play above Little League if they played at all."

Oliver pointed to a large, round man in his thirties, skipping from home plate toward first. The man's beltless denim jeans descended his large waist, exposing a good portion of the man's ass crack as he skipped past the dugout.

"Tell me you've seen that guy play in the Rock River League," Oliver laughed, followed by Parlee exploding a chuckling stream of tobacco juice toward his feet. "This game means so much to all kinds of people in a lot of different ways. Ways I'll never begin to understand. Ways I don't need to know. But I do need to know we're damn lucky to be able to play it."

As the organ wound Auld Lang Syne to its sad conclusion, Mathews and Aaron came off from the railing next to the dugout, down the steps and headed into the tunnel leading back to the clubhouse.

Parlee levered himself to his feet, stood on the bench and then jumped down to the floor of the dugout.

"I gotta see this," Parlee said as he moved to the end of the dugout and looked up the tunnel.

There were numbers 41 and 44 taking a slow, musing walk up the ramped tunnel for the last time. Together they posed a sad, solitary figure.

Parlee felt a push from behind.

"Let me in there," a photographer nudged Parlee out of the way. The man pointed the camera up the tunnel and its flash lit a sad litany for the baseball world to contemplate.

Parlee walked back toward Oliver.

"Jesus," said Parlee, fighting back a tear, unsure yet of its meaning.

"Yeah, it's pretty damn sad," Oliver said. "Most of us have been bracing for this the last couple of weeks. Did you see the other day we had eight hundred people in here? Shit, they all could have come on one bus. This has to be over with. But as bad as it's been, it didn't make today any easier. Eddie's as blue as I've ever seen him. Hank too. This town means a lot to those guys, the way the town took them in, treated them like family."

Just when Parlee sat back down, a clubhouse attendant, a gray haired man about sixty, wearing a windbreaker and Braves cap, stuck his head out of the clubhouse tunnel.

"We gotta get everyone going," he said to Oliver. And he disappeared as fast as he came.

"Shit," Oliver said. "The Packers are playing here this weekend and because we ain't coming back, they want us all packed up and out of the clubhouse. Then we got an early flight to San Francisco tomorrow."

It dawned on Oliver and Parlee that this meant the end of their post-game meetings.

"Look, man," said Parlee as they shook hands and gave one another a one-arm hug, hands still clenched together.

"I don't now what's going to happen," said Oliver, still holding onto Parlee's hand. "But I might just look back on all this when I'm through and know that guys like you and Deke saved my career."

"Shit," Parlee said as he stepped back. "When the season's done and you come back to Milwaukee, give me a call, we'll hook up."

"You know it," Oliver said. He turned and Parlee watched him walk the length of the dugout and disappear up the tunnel.

Parlee felt as though he'd made his peace with Oliver, the Braves and County Stadium. He skipped up the dugout steps without looking back down. Parlee climbed a rail and headed up the stadium aisle stairs without looking back at the diamond. He went out the concourse and into the parking lot without looking back at the stadium.

About three rows into the parking lot he passed a group of tailgaters who'd carried signs into the stadium. Parlee stopped to scan the signs. He saw the mock headstone "RIP Carpetbagger". It leaned against a brown '62 Plymouth Valiant. A skinny, drunken man in his late 20s, sat on the car's trunk hood.

"How much for the sign?" Parlee asked.

"What sign?" the man's lolling head swayed and then settled toward Parlee.

"The tombstone sign."

The man seemed to be attempting to grasp an understanding of the conversation.

"Hell, it's yours if you want it," the man said, his head bobbing on his neck. "What the hell am I gonna do with it. Not like I can use it again next year. Aha, ha, ha aha!"

"Thanks," Parlee swept up the sign and swiftly went on his way.

"Your funeral, man! Aha, ha,ha,aha!"

"Bushville," muttered Parlee as he angled the direction of the Impala. The headstone sign was fashioned of thick corrugated cardboard from a large shipping box. The lettering was thick and legible, finely outlined and then filled in with what appeared to be black shoe polish. It couldn't have been put there by the drunk, Parlee thought.

The parking lot had thinned out considerably quicker than a normal home game. Fans spent their extra time in the stadium after the extra-innings affair. Like Parlee, most got right in their cars and left, the way people do when leaving a cemetery following a burial -- scattered to the rest of their lives, the bond that brought them all here, dead and buried and gone.

Parlee steered out of the County Stadium lot for the last time and found his way back to Highway 18 heading west. It was late, going on midnight, by the time he settled onto the two-lane highway. Through Dousman he considered a stop at the Sum Place Else for yet another eulogy, but realized he was finished with it. He had a different kind of stop to make.

A rebirth?

When he got further west to Highway 67 he turned right to go north instead of continuing west to Jefferson. He went through a sleeping Oconomowoc and into a sleepy Ashippun. He motored into the empty and dark Fireman's Park. He followed the driveway around to the woodlot behind the diamond's grandstand. The Impala bounced over the park's uneven ground before coming to a rest about twenty feet behind the first base dugout.

Parlee killed the motor but left on the headlights. They lit the concrete back of the dugout, the Dogwood tree in the foreground, about ten feet in front of the Impala's chrome grill. Parlee got out of the car and walked through the open gate and onto the diamond. He could see the bump of the mound in the odd shadows cast by the Impala's headlights. The outline of the outfield snow fence lay beyond. Parlee felt his way down the dark dugout steps. The headlights did no good down there but the dugout was as familiar to Parlee as a blind man's bedroom. He kicked around for the pail to find it remained under the bench seat where he'd left it after the last game. He slid it to the end of the dugout and stepped up on it with one foot. Parlee crawled his hands up the wall, groping in the dark. He reached into the crevice between the two-by-sixes, relieved to feel the Nokona. Parlee pulled the glove out with his right hand and stepped down from the upside down pail. Once on firm ground with two feet, he cradled the glove in both hands and pressed it to his face to inhale and take in its familiar leathery smell.

He felt ashamed for what he'd almost done.

Parlee went out. He tossed the glove into the passenger's seat of the Impala and grabbed the car keys. The key chain still included the key to the padlock of a large rectangular wooden storage box along the field fence by the entrance gate. The box stored bases, rakes and a short-handled spade Parlee found following a few seconds of groping in the darkness.

Shovel in hand, Parlee dropped the lid of the box and re-clasped the padlock. He took the spade to the Dogwood and carefully dug a circle around the small tree. After about ten minutes of digging and tugging at the dirt, Parlee grabbed the tree low at its base and pulled it out of the ground. He held it up for inspection in the Impala's headlights, satisfied with its roots. He shook loose dirt from the roots as he walked to the back of the car. Parlee set down the spade from one hand and tree from the other to fumble the key into the trunk lock. He popped the trunk and placed the spade and tree into its cavernous cavity, lit by a single, small bulb.

Parlee clapped the dirt off his hands and got back into the driver's seat. He started the Impala and looked ahead at the empty hole vacated by the Dogwood. "Oh, shit. Not done yet," he said under his breath and he twisted to reach into the backseat to grab the sign.

He took the sturdy sign to the loose dirt around the hole and wedged it upright in the mound and between two softball-sized rocks. He stepped back to look at his handiwork. He cared not if the sign blew away before anyone else would see it.

"RIP Carpetbagger," he said. "That's me."

***

Parlee snaked the Impala west on a series of town roads until he came to County Highway R where he turned south. The road led him to downtown Watertown where he turned to go west on Main Street, across the Rock River, up a hill to a stop light at Highway 26. As he sat at the light in the two o'clock stillness, Parlee gazed at the enormous Catholic Church that towered over the intersection and whose steeple could be seen for miles on the approach to Watertown on Highway 26 from the south. Someone once told Parlee the church contained cornerstones made from the Blarney Stone in Ireland. He had no idea if that were true and stopped pondering the possibility when the light changed and he headed south on 26.

The highway took Parlee past the tall, circular galvanized grain bins of Johnson Creek. Round monuments of Jefferson County's corn farmers. He entered Jefferson from the north and swung left on 18 before taking a quick right to Fischer Field, the home of the Jefferson Blue Devils.

The diamond is shoe-horned into a neighborhood park that runs into the back of a grade school. The diamond's outfield snow fence is put up every spring at the close of school and taken down each August.

The diamond's backstop is no more than thirty feet from the street curb and Parlee parked along the curb and angled the Impala's headlights into the park the best he could. He got out, popped the trunk and grabbed the shovel in one hand, tree in the other. He made his way in the darkness lit only by the headlights and a street light past a small set of bleachers that fills each game Sunday with students and residents from St. Colletta's. Unfettered innocence wildly cheering their hometown Blue Devils as though they are big leaguers.

Parlee found a spot and went to work. He dug into the sod, churning dirt and grass in the spade. After about ten minutes, Parlee was satisfied the hole was deep and wide enough to take the tree. He placed the tree, and wondered if its southern roots could withstand the coming harsh winter. He thought the same about himself as he tamped the fresh dirt around the tree.

He'd think about that tomorrow after school when he'd head over to Tommy Bower's garage to borrow a watering can and bring him to the park to show him the Dogwood.

As he got into the Impala, Parlee made a wish the game wouldn't quit him quite yet.

***

Bein' a ball player is the best thing you can be. Being an ex-ball player might be as bad as it gets. Reckon a lot of things is like that. When I was playin' there was nothin' like it, even though I ain't never really played for nothin'. Game day was the best. But even the days betwixt the games were good 'cuz you'd be thinkin' 'bout that last game and that next game and what you was gonna do. Off-season when it was cold where ever I was, seemed like ever thing I did I did tryin' to get ready for the next season. I'd try to get my forearms stronger so's I could hit better. I'd try to keep my throwin' arm loose or I'd hold a ball the way I tolt ya to throw that drop ball. Couldn't wait for that next game whenever it was.

After I finally figured out I couldn't play no more I didn't know who I was no more. I didn't know what to think about. Got so I couldn't remember the feelin' of connectin' with the ball, how that feelin' would go up my arms and right into my very bein'. Didn't know why I should bother takin' care of myself. Didn't know how to even respect myself.

People like to do what they used to do. 'Specially after they stopped being able to do it.

That's why I keeps tellin' ya boy.

Play as long as ya can.

Play as long as ya can, just 'cuz of the game.

That game will take care of itself and it'll take care of you.

BLACK ROSE writing™

Made in the USA
Lexington, KY
14 April 2014